"You're beautiful."

Nolan had to clear his throat. Yeah, way to blurt it out. "I don't know if I've said that, but you are."

"I'm not sure this—" Allie wagged her fingers, presumably encompassing the two of them "—is such a good idea. I mean, I like you, Nolan, but Sean surely needs to be your priority right now."

"A parent doesn't decide never to date again, because it upsets his kid. Especially since, in the long run—" Whoa. In the long run? He wasn't *thinking* long run. Not yet. Or at least—he hadn't known he was. "I want to keep seeing you, Allie."

Her expression was startlingly vulnerable when she looked at him. "It's been an awfully long time since I had any kind of serious relationship."

"It has been for me, too." He scrubbed a hand over his chin. Decided to confess more. "I've always been a loner. You've made me...not want to be."

Dear Reader,

Every story I've ever read involving the Witness Security Program seemed to have a suspense plot. Interesting, but me, I always get thinking about the psychology of any unusual situation. I found the whole idea of giving up your identity and taking a completely new one—knowing that likely it would be forever—to be intriguing and yet disturbing. What would it be like to lose even your name? Have to give up a career and even hobbies that are distinctive enough to identify you?

For some reason, I kept thinking about the children most of all. The adults, at least, know what's happened and why. They have good reason to be traumatized, sure, but they are complete personalities, at least. But what about those children? Worse yet, what if they're pre-teens, or even teenagers, already confused, struggling for an identity?

I'm not always sure why I'm drawn to some ideas, some dilemmas, some problems, while others don't resonate for me at all. I suspect the fact that my family moved a lot when I was young has something to do with why this idea caught fire right away for me. By the time I was nine years old, I'd lived five different places, one of which was a small village outside Mexico City. Moves are always scary for kids. Strangely, the move that truly terrified me never happened.

I was seven or eight years old when my dad was offered a position as the head of the Peace Corps volunteers in the Dominican Republic. I was petrified. I have a vivid memory of lying in bed in the dark, rigid with terror. In the end, Dad turned down the job, and our subsequent move to California instead was a huge relief.

I can only guess that, for this story, I was drawing on that huge well of fear I still remember. Add a dash of the bewilderment any kid being forced to move feels...and then ask the kid to give up her name and lie for the rest of her life about who she was and is. What a recipe for growing a troubled human being! One who desperately needs to feel she belongs.

Hope you love Allie and Nolan's story as much as I did when writing it! I like to hear from readers, so contact me c/o Harlequin, 225 Duncan Mill Road, Don Mills, ON M3B 3K9, Canada.

Happy reading!

Janice Kay Johnson

Anything
for Her

JANICE KAY JOHNSON

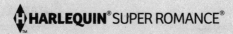

Recycling programs
for this product may
not exist in your area.

ISBN-13: 978-0-373-71836-8

ANYTHING FOR HER

Printed in U.S.A.

HARLEQUIN®
www.Harlequin.com

ABOUT THE AUTHOR

The author of more than sixty books for children and adults, Janice Kay Johnson is especially well-known for her Harlequin Superromance novels about love and family—about the way generations connect and the power our earliest experiences have on us throughout life. Her 2007 novel *Snowbound* won a RITA® Award from Romance Writers of America for Best Contemporary Series Romance. A former librarian, Janice raised two daughters in a small rural town north of Seattle, Washington. She loves to read and is an active volunteer and board member for Purrfect Pals, a no-kill cat shelter.

Books by Janice Kay Johnson

HARLEQUIN SUPERROMANCE

SIGNATURE SELECT SAGA

*The Russell Twins
**A Brother's Word

Other titles by this author available in ebook format.

CHAPTER ONE

Touch delicate, Nolan Radek slid his hands over the broad slab of granite. He'd once been told he had the gift of "stone hands," a description he'd liked. He closed his eyes, the better to feel instead of relying on sight. Silky smooth…no. The pads of his fingertips found a hint of roughness there.

Opening his eyes, he studied it, turned the sander back on and eased it over the spot, then tested again. Better. He stroked the entire slab, which would be a garden bench, and was pleased with the vinelike effect of the darker veins within a pale green base. Occasional splashes of rusty-red might be the flowers.

The client had asked for a bench that would appear part of the landscape, having the solidity of stone and yet surprising the eye when it picked the bench out from the surrounding greenery.

A diamond polishing pad added more gloss—not too much. Neither garden bench nor sculpture should have the mirror shine of a kitchen countertop, but it should be lustrous to the touch. Instinct and long practice told him when to stop.

The two massive chunks that would form the support had been left rough-hewn but for a few asymmetrical streaks of smoothed granite that highlighted texture and grain. He intended to polish only the part of the back that would come in contact with the human body. Contrasts in texture were part of nature.

Tempted to start work on that slab, Nolan reluctantly decided to wait until morning. He had a kid now, and it was time he put on dinner.

Besides, he was a little surprised that Sean hadn't come out to the workshop since he got home from school. He was usually eager to help. Nolan supposed it wasn't uncommon for foster kids to work hard to please in hopes they'd be allowed to stay.

Having removed his ear protection, Nolan ran his fingers through his hair and shook his head like a dog springing from the pond. Granite dust flew. He shed his coveralls, hanging them beside the back door, and used the utility sink to sluice off his hands and face. He checked to make sure everything was unplugged, turned off all the lights, then locked up and strode the short distance across the backyard to the farmhouse he called home.

After letting himself in the kitchen door, Nolan listened to the silence. Not that long ago, he'd been content to work alone all day, then go home to an empty house at night. No longer. But instead of calling for Sean, he went upstairs, lightly knocked on the bedroom door then pushed it open.

The boy was kneeling in front of his dresser. In a flurry of movement that seemed to hold alarm, he tried to poke something in the bottom drawer and shove it closed. His cheeks flushed.

"That your grandmother's quilt top?" Nolan asked. He was careful to sound neutral, to pretend not to notice that Sean was embarrassed to be caught looking at it. Or had he been holding it, like a toddler with his blankie?

"Great-great-grandmother," he mumbled.

"Right." Nolan sat at the foot of the twin bed. "Do you mind if I take a look at it?"

He knew that it was damn near all this boy had in the way of a legacy from his family. From the sound of it, the only person who'd ever cared at all about Sean was the grandmother who'd taken him in when he was seven or eight, after his dad died.

He didn't so much as remember his mother, didn't even have a picture of her. Apparently she'd flitted off with some other man not long after her little boy took his first step.

The way Nolan had heard it, even though Sean's grandma had been too old to raise an active boy, she had never considered consigning him to foster care. In death, she hadn't had any choice. Unfortunately, his first foster placement had been a disaster. Nolan knew trust was going to be slow in coming.

The boy shrugged with exaggerated indifference. "Sure. I guess." He pulled the drawer open again and took out the bundle of fabric, holding it up to Nolan, who checked to be sure he really had gotten his hands clean, then shook the quilt top out over the twin bed.

Like most men, he didn't know much about quilts. But for some reason he knew he'd recognize a design called Log Cabin. He guessed it was a pretty common one, once upon a time. A woman could use just about any leftover fabrics she had around and still create something nice to look at.

His mother had kept an old family quilt rolled in a pillowcase in a cedar chest, which he thought was a waste. She claimed to want to preserve it. She'd called it Grandmother's Flower Garden, he recalled. Tiny scraps of pastel fabric had been hand-pieced to make flowerlike circles. Nolan was glad Sean's wasn't that feminine looking. He had something precious to hold on to, and he could put it on his bed without embarrassment.

This quilt top was more geometric than anything, and

had only two colors: a navy blue fabric polka-dotted with white, and plain white. Chains of small white squares linked bigger squares, all against the darker background. He couldn't tell what it was meant to depict, if anything.

"I wonder why it never got finished," he said.

"Grandma said *supposedly* it was the last one her grandma made before her arthritis got real bad." There was a rhythm to the way Sean reported this bit of family wisdom; Nolan could tell that he was repeating what he'd heard, with the emphasis on the same words.

Nolan nodded, fingering the fabric. "I wonder if we could find someone to put it together. So you could use it on your bed." He thought a boy who'd lost his family might sleep better warmed by a quilt his great-great-grandmother had made with love and handed down to her descendants.

Naked hope showed on Sean's thin face. "Do you think there's someone who would?"

"I don't know," he admitted, "but I can find out. I've seen a quilt shop in town that I think mostly sells fabric. I can stop by tomorrow and ask."

"That'd be cool."

Nolan ruffled the boy's wheat-blond hair. "For now, why don't you put it away. I'll start dinner."

"Are we having spaghetti?"

"I thought just hamburgers, if that's okay. Maybe baked beans and corn."

"Sure. You make good spaghetti, though."

Nolan laughed at the broad hint. "I'll make it later in the week, when I leave myself a little more time."

Sean was carefully folding the quilt top when Nolan left to go back downstairs. As he located a can of baked beans in the back of the cupboard and took out pans, Nolan worried about what might have happened to make his foster son come home from school looking for comfort. Fourteen years old, a freshman in high school, he didn't seem to have friends. He was a good-looking kid; there wasn't anything obvious about him to draw scorn from his classmates. Living with his grandmother, he'd been in a different school district, but he'd been here for second semester last year, so he already knew some of the kids. Maybe everyone knew he lived in a foster home. Would he be looked down on?

Despite the amount of food he put away, so far Sean stayed skinny, but Nolan seemed to remember that being normal for teenage boys. Sean's feet and hands were too big for the rest of him. But, damn, there'd been a time when Nolan had hardly been able to walk without tripping over his own feet, so he kind of guessed that was normal, too.

Sean had looked pretty raggedy when he first came to Nolan, and he'd admitted his clothes had mostly been acquired from thrift stores and even, a few times, from the charity that gave clothes to the really poor kids at school. That might make a teenager feel funny, wondering if someone would recognize the shirt he was wearing as their discard.

Give it time, Nolan decided. *You're fretting like an old lady.* He'd only had the boy for a couple of months, and somehow he thought he should have been able to make everything right immediately. *Snap, snap.*

Faintly amused at himself, he put water on to boil and started husking the corn. Chances were good Sean had better social skills than he had. The kid would manage.

Feet thundered on the stairs, an encouraging sound. Sean burst into the kitchen. "I'm hungry! It's cool you buy real hamburger buns. Grandma and me always just used bread. And it gets, like, soggy."

Nolan grinned. "Glad you're happy. Homework?"

"Yeah." Sudden gloom. "It sucks."

That all sounded normal to him, as well.

The water was boiling, so he dropped in four ears of corn then flipped the burgers. Damn, but he was hungry, too.

THE BELL HANGING from the door rang. In the middle of gathering tiny stitches onto her needle, Allie didn't immediately look up. Her quilt frame was at the back of the shop, next to the large space where she taught classes, but allowed her a sight line to the front door. Some days she never had a chance to sit down or even reach for the needle, and most days there were bursts of several busy hours. But she almost always had a quilt assembled on the frame, with which she could contentedly fill the slow periods. The quilts she created herself inspired her customers, and she got excellent prices when she sold the finished work.

"I'll be right with you," she called.

Her customers were all women. Occasionally a husband would trail his wife in and hover, some patiently, some not so much, while she made her selections. Usually at this point many of the women would respond to Allie with something like, "That's okay, I need to browse for a while anyway." This time, there was no answer. Surprised, Allie finally lifted her head.

A man was making his way gingerly toward her, between the rows of bolts of fabric. For a moment she did nothing but gape at him. He didn't *belong,* even more so than most men. She couldn't decide why. He was good-sized, but not huge—maybe six feet or a little under, broad-shouldered and powerfully built, though not massive. Maybe what she was reading was *his* discomfort with being here.

He had brown, unruly hair and a plain, bony but nice face. Blunt cheekbones, a nose distinguished by a bump that suggested a long-ago break and eyes so blue Allie blinked in surprise.

She could almost sense his relief when he escaped the narrow aisles between tightly packed bolts of cotton into the clearing at the back.

She anchored the needle in the fabric. "Can I help you?"

"I hope so." He stopped at the edge of the polished wood frame and gazed at the half-finished quilt with interest. "Well, isn't that a beauty," he murmured after a minute.

"Thank you. It's a simple pattern called Lady of the Lake."

"It's the colors." He seemed to be enthralled. "And the sewing you're doing."

"Quilting," she corrected him. "This is what makes the sandwich of fabrics a quilt and not a comforter."

She was happy with this particular quilt herself. She'd used all shades of purple, from palest lavender to deep, rich plum, interspersed with a red startling enough to define the blocks.

The man lifted a big, blunt-fingered hand and said, "Would you mind if I touched it?"

"Not at all. Come around here." Part of the quilt was outside the frame.

He fingered it, seeming to savor the texture. He still held the corner of the quilt when he lifted his eyes, suddenly, to her face. They were not only vividly blue, they were penetrating. Allie had the uneasy feeling he was seeing more in her than most people did.

"Beautiful," he said again, his voice deep and even a little gravelly, as if he ought to clear his throat.

Feeling her cheeks heat, Allie wondered if he was still talking about the quilt.

Get a grip.

"Can I help you?" she asked.

"I'm looking for someone willing to do what you're doing right now. We have this part—" he touched the top "—but the thing never got finished. I guess I figured these days the sewing—the quilting," he corrected himself, "was done on a machine."

"Machine-quilting is more common than hand-quilting like I do," she agreed. "And most often, what hand-done quilts you see were made in China or somewhere else with cheap labor, and usually the stitches are big and fairly sloppy."

He nodded slowly.

"I'd have to see what you've got to tell you whether it's worth getting hand-quilted. How old is it? Was it hand-pieced? What's it look like?"

His expression was mildly befuddled. "Well, it's different than this. It's only two colors, for one thing. Dark blue and white."

She nodded encouragement.

"Little squares and big squares and…" He seemed to struggle to find the right words and finally shrugged as if giving up. "They form a pattern."

Allie laughed. "There are quilts with one big picture in the middle or a giant star, something like that. Otherwise, a pieced quilt by its very nature ends up with symmetrical blocks."

He nodded thoughtfully. "It's not new." He considered her, looking a little wary. Allie had the feeling he wasn't much of a talker and probably not given to confiding in many people, and especially not a total stranger. But after a minute his face relaxed, as if he'd made up his mind. "I've got a foster son—he's fourteen—and supposedly his great-great-grandmother made this quilt top. The story is that her arthritis had gotten so bad she couldn't finish."

Intrigued now by the quilt and not only the man, Allie

calculated. "Um…if he's right about the great-greats, it's probably at least eighty years old, then. Maybe a hundred."

"That might be."

"I'd like to see it."

"Your work is beautiful," he said simply. "I want you to do Sean's quilt."

Smiling, she shook her head. "I won't make any promises. I do take on a project like that once in a while, but it has to be something special. Interesting enough for me to want to give it a great deal of time."

"I understand," he said, and looked as if he really did. "I'll bring it to you."

"Okay." She smiled at him, let the thimble fall from her forefinger and held out her hand. "I'm Allie Wright. This is my store."

"Nolan Radek."

His large hand engulfed hers. She felt thick calluses, and saw nicks and healed wounds on the back of his fingers and hand. No banker or attorney here; these hands were well used, as hers were, though in a different way.

He didn't seem to want to let her hand go. And for some strange reason, she wasn't in any hurry, either. His grip was so warm and solid. They looked into each other's eyes, neither of them smiling anymore. She'd swear she could hear her heart beating, as if it had taken flight. Breathless, Allie knew she'd never responded to a man in this way. And she didn't even know him.

He finally released her, his reluctance palpable. He did clear his throat now. "It was good to meet you, Ms. Wright."

"Allie."

"I can come back tomorrow."

"Good. I'm here until five."

He nodded, studied her face one more time as if memorizing it, then turned and walked out. She saw his head swiveling as he went, as if he wasn't so much uncomfortable now as intrigued by the raw material that went into a quilt like the one she was working on. If he'd been a woman, she would have guessed that she'd have a new student and customer. Of course, there *were* men who quilted, even if she didn't know one, but...not Nolan Radek, she thought. Those large hands weren't made for itty-bitty snippets of fabric or a teeny tiny needle.

She wondered what he did do with them that had earned him so many wounds. And then wondered what those hands would feel like on a woman's body.

On her.

Her face hot again, she was grateful for the sound of the bell and the chatter of women's voices. Leaving the needle and thimble where they were, Allie went to wait on her customers.

USUALLY EAGER TO start work come morning, Nolan got Sean out the door and poured himself a second cup of coffee while watching out the kitchen window as the school bus stopped out front then lumbered into motion again and out of sight along the winding country road.

He sat back down at the table, amused at himself. He'd asked his foster son for permission to take the quilt top into town for the shop owner to see, but he hadn't said, *I'm aiming to be there the very second she unlocks the door.*

He and Sean hadn't talked about girls yet. At his age, the boy had to be thinking about them a whole lot, but chances were good he'd be stunned if he knew his new foster dad had developed an instant crush on a pretty woman. Nolan thought it might be interesting to see how Sean would handle him dating.

Might be interesting *to* date, Nolan reflected. It had

been a while. He'd never been very good at it. Women didn't like having to wring every word out of a man.

Of course, there was no saying Allie Wright wouldn't turn out to be married or at least committed already. Or not interested in Nolan. He didn't believe that, though. The one moment, when it seemed as if neither of them could look away from the other, had to be mutual, didn't it?

Instead of opening his workshop, he swept the entire downstairs of the farmhouse then dusted besides. Had to do it once in a while. He clock-watched the entire time, grabbing his wallet, keys and the bagged quilt top at quarter to the hour.

West Fork wasn't a big town. It had been built on a bluff looking down on a fertile river valley in the foothills of the Cascade Mountains north of Seattle. Historically, the roots were agriculture and logging. Logging was pretty well dead as an industry in these parts, and agriculture was heading that way.

A few stubborn dairy farmers still hung on, and corn, peas and strawberries were the big crops on land that was too prone to flooding to ever be buildable. Otherwise, West Fork was increasingly becoming a bedroom community for Everett and even Seattle, as new developments were springing up on the outskirts of town. The Boeing plant in Everett was only a forty-minute commute.

Chain stores had popped up out by the freeway, but downtown had kept its character. False-fronted buildings housed antiques stores as well as an old-fashioned hardware store, real estate office, weekly newspaper office, barbershop and salon. The bowling alley was a busy place. Nolan had heard the one-screen movie theater might have to close, because the conversion to digital was too expensive. But he couldn't remember when he'd noticed the quilt shop open—could've been here for a couple of years, he supposed. He was sorry he hadn't had reason to wander into it a long time ago.

A parking spot was vacant right in front of the store. The Open sign hung in the door. He imagined it was still swinging from Allie having flipped it over.

When he stepped inside, the bell on the door rang. Today, she was up front behind an old-fashioned counter with a cash register. She looked up and smiled.

"Oh, good. You came back."

"Said I would."

Something crossed her face. A shadow? "People don't always mean it."

He nodded, agreeing even though when he said something, he did mean it.

She saw the grocery bag he held clutched in his hand. "You have it with you."

Nolan only nodded again.

"Why don't you bring it in back and we can lay it out on top of the quilt I have in the frame?" She came around the end of the counter and started toward the back of the store, Nolan following.

He hadn't expected that same punch of attraction; after all, now he knew what she looked like. But there it was anyway. He hadn't said much yet partly because he was having trouble catching his breath.

Damn, she was pretty. She looked… He didn't know. Russian or Eastern European, with very dark, shiny hair and milk-pale skin. He doubted she could tan if she wanted. Perfectly sculpted cheekbones would make her beautiful even as an old lady. She wasn't tall—perhaps five foot two or three at most—with the finest bone structure he'd ever seen. She had a long neck, exposed by the way she wore her hair, up in some kind of bun on the crown of her head. Like ballerinas wore theirs, he thought.

Nolan frowned. That's what she looked like. A dancer. Graceful. Even her walk was a little different. The toes of her feet pointed out in a way that should have been duck-like but wasn't.

And then there were her eyes, a rich mossy green with glints of gold.

He was looking into those eyes right now, Nolan realized. She'd come to a stop by her quilt frame and was waiting patiently for him to do something besides gawk at her.

"Sorry," he mumbled, holding out the bag.

Her cheeks were slightly pink when she took it. Unless it was his imagination, she was careful not to brush his hand with hers.

She took the quilt top out then drew a breath of what sounded like delight. She unfolded it, studied the back then gently spread it atop her own quilt.

Nolan looked at her face, not at the quilt. He could tell she felt the way he did when he found an unusual and beautiful slab of granite, one he could do something special with.

"Burgoyne Surrounded," Allie said softly. "This is a mid-nineteenth-century pattern, supposedly based on a victory by colonial soldiers over British forces led by General Burgoyne during the Revolutionary War." She glanced up. "All of which is probably apocryphal, since the pattern actually originated so much later. It's a nice concept, though. Perfect for a boy. And how gorgeously made!" She lifted a corner and invited him to peer closely. "It was hand-pieced, and with incredibly tiny stitches. Whoever made this was an artist."

"Will you do it?"

She lifted her gaze to him. "Yes. Oh, yes. With pleasure." She hesitated. "I will have to charge you."

"I assumed you would. This is how you make your living."

"That's right. Well, primarily with the shop, but I also sell my quilts."

"Do you." He'd noticed a couple draped in the window and one large one hung on a wall.

When she told him what she typically asked, he nodded. "That's reasonable."

"This quilt is sized for a double bed," she said. "It would be possible to add a border if you want it queen-sized."

Nolan thought about it. "Seems we should leave it the way it was meant to be."

Allie smiled with approval. "I agree. Well. I'll look forward to this. I may start right away at home. I have a frame there, too. Usually I have one quilt going there, one here."

"Thank you. Sean will be excited."

The bell rang up front and he realized someone had come in. He felt something like panic. Somehow he'd thought they would have more to discuss.

"I'm in back," she called to the newcomer.

"No hurry," the woman said. "I need to pick out my fabric."

Allie folded and rolled the quilt top. "May I keep the bag?"

"Sure. Of course." He was desperate to say something attention grabbing, but his tongue felt as if it had swollen in his mouth.

"There's room for fancy quilting in these larger squares—" she touched the fabric the way he touched stone "—but my inclination is to keep it simple. Diagonal lines. Unless you wanted something different?" She lifted those green eyes to his.

"I trust you to do the right thing."

She smiled, making her more than pretty. Beautiful. He couldn't look away.

"Thank you," she said. "Oh! I'd better get your phone number, so I can let you know when I'm done."

He wanted *her* phone number. He cast a desperate look toward the new customer, who had her back turned and seemed engrossed in a row of calicos in various shades of blue.

"Allie…maybe you're married or, uh, involved with someone…."

The prettiest pink he'd ever seen infused her cheeks. "No. No, I'm not."

"Then…is there any chance you'd have dinner with me?"

Her eyes widened. "Tonight?"

He'd have liked nothing better, but he thought he'd better prepare Sean. "Maybe not tonight," he said reluctantly. "Sean—my foster son—will come home expecting me to feed him. Does it have to be a weekend, or would tomorrow night work?"

"Tomorrow night would be lovely. Of course you can't abandon your son without warning."

He half expected her to want to meet him at the restaurant, but instead she readily offered her address, which he thought was in Old Town.

"It's the carriage house," Allie said, as if reading his mind. "The owners converted it into an apartment. I was lucky to get it."

He nodded. "Six?"

"Perfect. I'll look forward to it. But now I'd better go help that poor woman."

Feeling big and clumsy, Nolan said, "Sorry. I'll, uh, get out of your way."

Allie laid her hand on his arm. Only for an instant,

lightly, but he felt the touch down to the soles of his feet. "I'm glad you came. Glad you brought Sean's quilt top. And really glad you invited me to dinner. You're definitely not in my way."

His shoulders let go of some of the tension. "Tomorrow, then."

If no one else had been in the store, he might have succumbed to temptation and kissed her. As it was, he couldn't. He only nodded and left, trying real hard to think about the Baltic brown granite countertop he was finishing for the Olsens' kitchen and not about the color of Allie's eyes.

"YOU SOUND like you've had a good week," Allie's mother commented. "Milk? Juice?"

Allie understood the segue, since Mom had the refrigerator door open. "Milk, please. Shall I drain the noodles?"

"Yes, thank you."

A minute later, they were seated at the table in the dining room in Mom's house. She was renting, too—they'd never owned a home since everything changed—but the rambler was newish and at least double the size of Allie's one-bedroom, second-story apartment. Mom seemed content with it. She always insisted she wanted to have an extra bedroom available should Allie ever need it.

Allie waited until they'd dished up the stroganoff and green beans before commenting on her week.

"Receipts have been really good," she said. "Saturday a group of ten women came in. They were from south King County, and they said they make regular expeditions from quilt shop to quilt shop looking for different fabrics. Every single one of them bought something, and two bought enough to piece big quilts. They all promised to come back."

"That's fabulous."

"And, um, I met an interesting man."

Mom looked up in surprise, her fork halfway to her mouth. "A man?"

"I think I'm insulted." Allie tried to keep her tone light. "Yes, a man. Is it that unlikely a guy would be interested in me?"

"Where on earth would you meet one?" her mother asked simply.

Allie wrinkled her nose. "Okay, I'll concede that you don't get a lot of single men in a quilt shop. As it happens, this one *did* come into the store."

Of course she had to explain. "I've already picked out fabric to back this boy's quilt. It's going to be stunning, Mom! I suspect it's even older than we first guessed. Late nineteenth century, I think."

Her mother laughed. "So the man is interesting because he brought you an intriguing quilt. I should have realized."

"Well…I'm having dinner with him, too."

Mom's eyebrows went up. "Do you know anything at all about him?"

"He's quiet and seems nice, and he has a fourteen-year-old foster son. Which suggests compassion."

"Do you even know what he does for a living?"

"Nope," Allie said cheerfully. "But I'll be able to tell you more about him after tomorrow."

Mom set down her fork. She waited until Allie's eyes met hers. "You know this always makes me nervous."

How could she help but know? And, deep inside, a small coal of resentment flared. "I'm always careful," she said, trying to hide what she felt.

"Of course you are." Her mother smiled at her. "I know it's hard. I have the same problem, meeting new people. Of course I trust you. I shouldn't have said anything."

"No, that's all right." But it wasn't. It wasn't. Allie was

twenty-eight years old. She had now spent fifteen years of her life lying to everyone she met. Lying even to herself most of the time. But she had done it, because she had to. While she understood her mother's fear, she also resented the implication that she had a big mouth. Or maybe that she was stupid.

"Well, you have a good time," Mom said. "Goodness, most dates don't lead to anything meaningful anyway! Chances are you'll find you don't have a thing in common."

That was true, of course, but Allie was struck by the fact that Mom sounded as if she *hoped* nothing came of this date. Was her focus so entirely on protecting their secret that she didn't want her daughter to fall in love and get married and have children? Because…well, was it possible to fall in love and start a life with someone while still keeping such a huge secret? Apprehension chilled her.

Later, after she'd gone home, Allie trimmed the selvage from the backing fabric of Sean's quilt, then cut equal lengths, and thought about those disturbing feelings. Why had she never noticed before that her mother always said something like that whenever Allie started dating a guy? Even when she met a girl or woman she thought might be a friend, her mother had discouraging words, although to a lesser extent. And why had she never minded so much before?

Because I think Nolan might be different. The knowledge whispered through her. *Because I felt something yesterday when he came in, and again this morning, that I've never felt before.* As if it was more than attraction. As if they'd formed an instant connection.

Allie sat at her machine and began to stitch together the lengths of navy fabric studded with tiny white stars. She shook her head. Silly, that's what she was being. Mom was right—by the time the waiter brought the check tomorrow night, she'd probably be bored to death and wonder what she'd ever seen in Nolan Radek, aside from those shockingly blue eyes.

A connection. She laughed at herself. Wow. Save the worries until she actually *did* fall in love.

CHAPTER TWO

WAS SEAN REALLY okay with this? Nolan couldn't decide. But, damn it, he was entitled, wasn't he? He hadn't signed on to become a monk, just because he'd taken in a kid.

What Sean had said was, "You probably haven't been seeing women because of me, huh? That's stupid. I mean, if you like her." He'd shrugged with elaborate unconcern.

Nolan wondered if Sean's father had dated after the boy's mother deserted them. Grandma presumably hadn't. His only real experience of adults in a relationship might have been the married couple who'd been his first foster parents. Nolan had no idea whether that couple had loved each other or not. All he did know was that they *hadn't* loved Sean, and hadn't been willing to stick to it long enough to find out whether with time they could.

This is a first date, he reminded himself. He wasn't bringing home a wife. Now, *that* might be reason to scare a boy in Sean's position.

He found Allie's carriage house with no problem. None of the old homes in West Fork were all that grand, but this was one of the fanciest, trimmed with some modest turn-of-the-century gingerbread. It appeared that the ground floor of the carriage house was now a detached garage. An outside staircase led up to the apartment. Allie came out, locked up and had started down the steps by the time he got out of his pickup.

"Sorry," he apologized. "I don't have a car. I use this for hauling."

She looked in the back, dented a few thousand times, and grinned. "No, really?"

His mouth quirked. "Guess you can tell."

Racks were installed to hold slabs of granite or marble to prevent cracks or breakage. Chunks pretty much got tossed in. The pickup had a long bed and a double set of tires in back to support the weight of a heavy load of stone.

"Is this part of the 'what do you do for a living' question?"

"Yeah, as a matter of fact it is." He opened the passenger side door and realized she wouldn't be able to swing herself up the way he did. Nolan winced.

Allie wore a skirt, but hadn't really dressed up, for which he was thankful. He'd gone as far as slacks and an open-neck sport shirt, dressy enough for any north county restaurant. She accepted his boost, but didn't seem to have any trouble with the scramble.

They agreed on Mexican food, and he backed out of her driveway. "I'm a stonemason," he said abruptly. "I work mostly with granite, sometimes marble, rarely other stones."

She stared at him. "What do you *do* with the granite and marble?"

"My bread and butter is countertops. Kitchen, bathroom." He frowned, thinking how to explain. "All custom work. People come to me when they're building or remodeling high-end houses and want something out of the ordinary." He told her about some of his other jobs: the garden bench, tabletops, even floors occasionally. "Fountains, too. And when I have time, I sculpt."

They'd reached the restaurant. Not until they were seated and had ordered did she cross her arms on the table, lean forward and fix a fascinated gaze on him. "Tell me about your sculpting."

Nolan shifted in his seat. "I'm not always good with words," he admitted after a minute.

"Maybe you'll show me your work one of these days."

"I can do that." Though he always felt uneasy showing his pieces to others. A couple of galleries carried his sculptures, but he twitched some even when the gallery owners were exclaiming over them.

"Do you do figures? Animals? Abstract shapes?"

"Yes," he said, then laughed at her pursed lips. "All of the above. I guess everything I carve has a sort of modern look. I don't do literal or detailed." He found his hands were trying to shape the air. "The stone tells me what it wants to be," he finally said, helplessly, bracing himself for rolled eyes.

But she nodded her understanding. "To some extent, I feel that way with quilts. Usually I decide to do a certain pattern, or have thought of a variation that will make my quilt different, but often the idea comes in response to a wonderful fabric that comes in and I suddenly *see* what it would do the best."

He looked at her in amazement. "That's how it is for me. It's as if something is inside that particular block of stone. I'm uncovering it more than creating."

Her nod held equal satisfaction. "Most people don't understand that, do they?"

"No."

Conversation flowed surprisingly easily after that, an experience that was rare for Nolan. Of course, he got her to do most of the talking, which helped, but she poked and prodded some answers out of him, too. They shared chips and salsa as he heard about the quilt shop, how she'd been a quilter for years until she realized her hobby was more of a vocation and decided to figure out how she could make it provide a livelihood.

"Not that small-business ownership is hugely profitable." She scrunched her nose in a way he thought was cute. "Overhead, inventory, taxes... I only have one very part-time employee, and I keep her hours down as much as I can. Do you *know* what a bite payroll taxes add?" she asked indignantly.

"Yeah," he said. "I've had employees off and on."

"Why off and on?"

"Well, it's more that I used to have employees then decided I wouldn't take on more jobs than I could do myself. I like to work alone." It was more than that, of course; what he really wanted was absolute control. He didn't like having to look over someone else's shoulder to be sure they were working to his standards. He could make more money if he had a production line of sorts going, but he did fine as it was.

Once again she surprised him with another nod. "I wouldn't want to sell quilts under my name that someone else had pieced or quilted, even if I did check them over carefully to be sure I was satisfied."

Over a burrito for him and a taco salad for her, they got around to talking about family. No surprise, first she asked about Sean. Nolan told her about his couple of encounters with the boy, and then that phone call out of the blue.

"Took a while to be approved as a foster parent. I had to jump through some hoops, which was frustrating when I knew how unhappy Sean was parked in a group home. I think the county accelerated the home visit and what have you, though. The social worker told me they never have enough foster homes for teenagers. Especially one being returned for having a snotty attitude."

"Does he?"

Nolan shrugged. "He's a kid who has had the rug yanked out from under him time and again." He told her some of Sean's history. "I'd say he's pretty damn normal, considering."

"How awful for him to get dumped again so soon after his grandmother died." She smiled at Nolan. "I knew I liked you."

So, okay, that gave him a warm, fuzzy feeling, but also embarrassed him. His motives for taking Sean in were still a little muddled, but Nolan knew one thing—it sure as hell wasn't so people would admire him.

As soon as he could, he turned the conversation back to her.

Her mother was here in town, Allie said; in fact, they'd had dinner together last night. "Mom keeps books for a couple of downtown businesses owned by the same guy— Mark Solver?"

"I know him."

"Otherwise—I don't really hear from my father."

"No siblings?"

She was silent for a moment. "A brother, but I don't even know what he's up to anymore."

"Older? Younger?"

"Older." She gave him a bright smile that seemed a little forced to him. "You?"

Apparently, she didn't want to talk about any family but her mother. He couldn't say he blamed her. God knew, he had issues with his own parents.

Parents. He didn't even like to think of them that way.

Nolan shrugged. "I grew up in Chicago. That's where my family still lives. I talk to my brother and sister regularly. Don't see any of them very often."

"The Windy City."

"That's right. Chicago was all right." He thought about

it for a minute. "Sometimes I miss it. Great food. I haven't found an Italian restaurant out here to match the ones back home. When I was ready to go into business for myself, though…I guess I wanted to get away."

No shit, he thought sardonically, and hoped this time she didn't push for an explanation.

For a moment her expression was rather searching, but to his relief she let it go. "What do your brother and sister do?" she asked. "Or your dad. Is the stonemason thing familial?"

"Nope. My brother, Jed, is an attorney, my sister, Anna, a potter."

"That's not so different," Allie pointed out gently. "You're both artists. Texture and shape matter to you."

He shrugged his agreement. He guessed there was a creative streak in their family. But it was an irony because their mother was a publicist—owned her own business— and so far as he knew neither of her parents had been of an artistic bent. And he and Anna likely didn't share a father.

As it happened, neither of them had the same father as Jed did, either.

Irritated by the tug of something like pain, he pushed the subject down deep where it belonged. He wanted to know about Allie, not talk about himself.

But she wasn't done. "How did you end up working with stone, then?"

Her question resurrected his edgy thoughts of family. He'd always wondered if his affinity for stone had been inherited. He'd never know, since he had no idea who his biological father actually was.

"I always liked rocks," he said. "I picked them up wherever I went. Seventh or eighth birthday, my parents bought me a tumbler for Christmas." He grinned. This was a good memory. "Made a god-awful racket. Everybody complained whenever I ran it. But I had a real good time with that thing. Turned out, rocks that looked plain had something pretty inside.

"Family figured I'd end up a geologist. When I was in high school, I saw an article in this insert in the *Chicago Sun-Times* about a stonemason. The guy wasn't a sculptor—that came later for me, anyway—but otherwise he did about the same kind of work I do now. I still remember a picture of this backsplash he'd done, using a dark red granite with veins of grayish-green that looked like a tree. It was really spectacular. I tracked him down and begged for a job." Nolan smiled. "I swept the workshop floor for about a year."

"I suppose you generate a lot of dust," Allie said, the corners of her mouth betraying her amusement.

"Oh, yeah. When I peel off my goggles, I look like a raccoon." He paused. "Sean begs for the chance to sweep my workshop floor."

"Because he wants to work in stone?"

He hesitated. "I don't know yet. I suspect the big power tools are the appeal for a kid his age. Plus…" He thought better of what he'd been going to say.

Turned out he didn't have to say it.

"He's trying to please you," Allie said, echoing his thought from yesterday, and he saw that her gaze had turned inward. "After my parents divorced and I realized Mom was all I had, I went through a phase like that. I was too old to let myself be clingy, but…" Her sigh sounded sad. "I suppose I tried to be as much like her as possible. If that makes sense."

It did make sense, but disturbed him, too. Had her father completely abandoned his family? Nolan reminded himself this was an old hurt for her, but it didn't feel that way to him. It spurred him to want to protect her from something he couldn't.

"How old were you?"

Her eyes focused on his. "Seventeen." She grimaced. "I should have been pulling away and instead I had this weird regression. Oh, well." She gave herself a small shake. "It's natural, I guess."

"Maybe," he said, but wasn't convinced. Regression happened to kids when they underwent trauma, from what he'd read, not your average, everyday divorce.

"Your mom into quilting?"

Allie laughed. "Heavens, no! She doesn't even sew, except for the most basic mending. It was my grandmother who originally taught me to sew. She didn't quilt, but she tatted."

"Tatted?" he echoed, mystified.

"It's another fiber art, I guess you could say. Doilies are tatted. You know, those lacy white things old ladies used to like to put on the arms of sofas. Well, Nanna made snowflakes for the Christmas tree. When she was done, she'd starch them so they were stiff." Allie's voice had become softer and softer. "They were so delicate. So beautiful."

There was an odd sort of hushed silence. Nolan pictured those snowflakes, a bit like the paper ones every school child cut out of paper but far prettier. He bet no two were alike. He hoped Allie had been able to keep some of those snowflakes for her Christmas trees, but he had a bad feeling she hadn't. There was something in her voice that told him this memory was both precious and painful.

"Your grandmother gone?" he asked.

Oh, yes. There was definitely pain in her eyes. "Gone? Yes. A long time ago." After a moment she said, "Anyway, when I was in high school, we were required to complete a volunteer project."

He nodded. Lots of high schools did that now.

"I ended up making quilts—really comforters, because they were tied rather than quilted—for preemies in the hospital. I only did a couple of tied ones, though, because when I went to the fabric store to pick out materials, a quilting class was going on. The instructor was teaching about the almost unlimited variations on a nine-patch block."

Greek to him, but he nodded. He liked to hear her talk about what she did.

"I fell in love," she said simply, then laughed. "It was like having a crush on the geekiest guy in school, the one with zits and knock-knees. I did *not* tell my friends that instead of going to the mall with them, I was dying to rush home and sew a few blocks of my Churn Dash quilt. I discovered eventually that it wasn't only an old-lady hobby, but at the time I was painfully self-conscious."

"I didn't tell the guys in high school that I liked to play with rocks, either."

They smiled at each other, and it was like the first time he'd met her eyes. She'd grabbed him and wasn't letting go. He couldn't have looked away if someone had yelled, "Fire!" The gold in her eyes seemed to intensify, like sparks. Or real gold. The lines of her face were pure and clean and elegant. He couldn't have sculpted anything more beautiful. But it wasn't only about her looks anymore; it was as if he'd cut a piece of granite, expecting beauty and finding something inside that he knew he'd never find again in this lifetime.

"I've…really had a good time tonight," she said softly, as though her thoughts had paralleled his.

"Yeah." He had to clear the roughness from his throat. "Me, too." Wait and call her tomorrow? The next day? That was probably the polite thing to do, but a sense of urgency wouldn't let him be that patient. "Can we do this again? Soon?"

This smile glowed. "Yes. I'd love to, Nolan."

"Good." He reached across the table and took her hand in his. It was only the second time he'd touched her. A tactile man, he savored a hand that was fine-boned yet strong. The skin was incredibly smooth except for the toughness he felt on a finger pad or two when she gripped him in return. He liked that she had calluses, too.

He liked everything about her.

So far, he reminded himself. People weren't always what they seemed. Probably more often than not, they weren't what they seemed. He wanted to believe she wasn't flawed beneath the surface, as occasionally happened when he started cutting and sanding a promising slab of stone. He wasn't going to be a fool, letting himself believe in her too soon.

But oh damn he wanted to kiss her.

DURING THE SHORT drive back to her apartment, Allie clasped her hands on her lap and felt the throb of her pulse. She was almost frightened by how much she wanted to know how it would feel to be held by Nolan, kissed by him, devoured by him. She'd met attractive men before, had crushes, dated fairly seriously—and now she knew how tepid her responses had been.

He certainly wasn't handsome by any objective standard. Not that he was plain, the way she'd first thought. Wrong word. His face was all angles. He made her think of the basalt outcrops along the Columbia River—not pretty, but powerful and somehow *raw.* Set in that stark backdrop, his blue eyes were even more stunning.

Sneaking peeks as they drove in near complete silence, Allie decided she liked how *solid* he was. Big, strong hands, muscles powerful enough it was easy to imagine him handling enormous chunks of stone, without giving him that thick-necked, weight-lifter look. A deep, rumbly voice and a quiet sense of humor. She liked the way he reflected before he spoke, and the unwavering way he watched her when she was talking. Nolan Radek felt… dependable.

She averted her face and grimaced. Oh, boy—nothing subtle about why she was drawn to him like a tiny metal filing to a giant magnet.

Except…she knew her feelings were more complicated than that. Lust tangled with the lure of that sense of certainty he exuded. There were those wonderful moments when they discovered they understood each other, thought alike. His face wasn't especially expressive, but his hands were—Allie doubted he even knew how often he seemed to be trying to express his thoughts with those big, blunt-fingered hands instead of his tongue. There was the way he listened to her, as if what she had to say mattered and wasn't only an interlude before the focus returned to him. If she hadn't been feeling so tense, she'd have laughed at that—Nolan would prefer the focus *never* returned to him, she suspected.

When she looked ahead again she saw that he was steering into her driveway. She'd left the light on at the top of the outside steps, but it wasn't yet needed. Nights came late here in the Pacific Northwest, even in September. She always hated the abrupt change in October, having to close the shop and come home in pitch darkness.

"Those stairs are steep," Nolan said with a frown. He was staring at them and not at her. He sounded distinctly disapproving.

"I think they're original, but they seem solid enough."

He wasn't listening. The engine turned off, he got out

and came around to open the door for her and extend a hand. Considering the distance down to the ground, Allie was glad to take it. Instead of drawing her into his arms, Nolan walked over to inspect the staircase.

"I don't like it," he finally pronounced.

"What?"

"The treads aren't a normal depth. You have small feet, so you may not notice it as much, but it makes it easier to misstep. And the railing's not solid." He shook it, and indeed there was a slight sway of which Allie had never been aware.

"I'm careful," she offered.

Still scowling at the stairs, he only grunted. "These should be replaced."

"With ones cut from stone?" she joked.

His sharp blue eyes turned back to her. "I'm serious."

"I can tell." She considered what he was saying, and had to admit she was always careful on those steps because they made her a little apprehensive. Not so much that she'd allowed her dislike of them to surface, but some part of her hadn't felt secure when she was going up or down on them. "I'll talk to the owners," she promised. "They did a beautiful job renovating the apartment. They won't want me to fall."

"All right," he said. "Let me know."

Just like that—*Let me know.* As if he felt her safety to be a responsibility. That made her feel treasured but also potentially a little uneasy. She was accustomed to taking care of herself.

"You must have done some building," she commented.

"I worked for a contractor a couple summers while I was in high school. I built my workshop from the ground up."

She nodded, unsurprised. He had that air of competence. He seemed like the kind of man who would rarely be stumped by anything mechanical, either. "Thank you for dinner, Nolan."

"Thanks for coming." *She* was now his focus, forget the staircase. He touched her cheek with his big, calloused hand. "When I asked, I was practically stammering. I thought you'd make an excuse."

"No." Breathless, Allie knew she was tilting her head slightly, seeking his fingers. "I… The minute you came into the store…"

"Good." His voice was all rumble now, a deep bass. "I want to kiss you, Allie."

She shivered at the way he said her name. "Yes," she whispered, and took a step closer to him. With one hand she clutched her purse; the other reached for his shoulder.

Now he cupped her jaw in his palm, his fingertips caressing her earlobe and tickling the small hairs behind her ear. He bent his head slowly, as if to give her time to change her mind. Or maybe he savored the anticipation instead of becoming a bundle of nerves the way she did. His gaze was utterly intent on *her*.

When his mouth brushed hers with exquisite gentleness, Allie's eyes closed. Back and forth, the pressure on her lips was first soft, then firmer. He nibbled, tugged at her lower lip. An odd sound slipped out of her, and she rose on tiptoe. Her fingers clenched his shoulder so that she could hold on. Suddenly his mouth was open and so was hers. His hand had slid around to anchor the back of her head, angling her so that he could kiss her deeply, intensely. His tongue was in her mouth, sliding against hers. She'd quit thinking, quit worrying, all sensation physical. She wanted to be closer to him, part of him. Her purse clunked to the ground so she could wind her arms around his neck, stroke the bare skin on his nape. Nothing had ever felt so good.

He groaned, muscles tightening in his shoulders. He separated their mouths. "Allie," he muttered. "Damn. I didn't mean to take this so far. God, you're beautiful."

She blinked up at him. Enough awareness returned for her to notice that the color of the sky was deepening and headlights must have just swept over them as the next-door neighbor's van turned into the driveway not more than fifty feet away. They'd have been momentarily spot-lighted. Nolan had noticed, but she hadn't.

She swallowed and sank back onto her heels. "Wow."

His fingers caressed her scalp. He didn't seem eager to take his hands off of her. "Can we do something this weekend?" He sounded urgent.

"Yes." Her own voice came out shaky. "I'd like that."

"Good," he said again, so low it felt more like the scrape of bristles on his chin than actual sound. "I'll call you."

"Please."

"Go on." He picked up her purse and wrapped her fingers around the strap, then gently turned her and nudged her toward the first step. "I'll watch to be sure you get in safely."

Which was silly, but nice. Really nice. She climbed the stairs, very aware of him at the bottom. At the top she unlocked her door, waved and told him good-night again, then went in. A minute later, she heard the deep-throated roar of his pickup engine, and he was gone.

Allie stood inside, a hand pressed over her heart. Emotions welled in her: giddy delight, disbelief, aching regret that she hadn't invited him in even though she never did that. She remembered what she'd said to her mother. *I met an interesting man.*

She laughed, tossed her purse on the sofa, rose *en pointe* and twirled, mere inches from the quilt frame that filled her tiny living room.

LIGHTS WERE ON, but Nolan's house was quiet when he let himself in. After a glance in the kitchen, he went upstairs and knocked lightly on Sean's bedroom door.

"Yeah?"

He opened the door and stepped into the opening, leaning one shoulder against the jamb. "Just wanted to let you know I'm home."

The boy shrugged. He was flat on his back on the bed, his iPod on his chest and the earbuds in. Except for clothes, the iPod was the first thing Nolan had bought for him. He had a laptop now, too, and a printer, but he wasn't spending much time on the computer, so far as Nolan could tell. Doing his homework, or so he said, but not much else.

"You get something to eat okay?"

"Sure." After a first, swift look, Sean went back to staring at the ceiling. "You like her?" he asked after a minute, sounding grudging.

"Yeah." Nolan felt his smile stretching and struggled to keep it from becoming so wide he'd look like an idiot. "I do. I think you will, too."

That earned him an incredulous flick of a glance. "What difference does it make what I think?"

Nolan's eyes narrowed at the near-sneer in the boy's voice. He'd made it clear from the beginning that he was committed to Sean—whether Sean ever became ready to talk about adoption or not, the boy was Nolan's son. It seemed Sean was having trouble believing him.

"Because I'm hoping she'll become part of my life. Of *our* life," he corrected himself, then thought, *Whoa.* He'd just met this woman. Sure, he wanted to take her to bed, but…make her part of Sean's life as well as his? Where had that come from?

"She's that hot?"

Hell, yes, she was, but he was stunned to realize his

dick wasn't the only part of him feeling exhilarated. "She looks like a dancer," he tried to explain.

The eyes cut his way again. "You mean, a stripper?"

Nolan had a feeling he was meant to be offended. Instead he laughed. "No. A ballerina. There's something... Well, you'll see."

"Does she know about me?"

"I mentioned you when I took her the quilt, remember?"

"Oh." Sean's voice was still surly. "Right."

Nolan guessed it was too soon to suggest an outing with all three of them no matter what. It was true she'd sounded sympathetic to Sean when she talked about the insecurity she'd felt after her parents' divorce, but that didn't necessarily mean she had any interest in getting to know a sullen fourteen-year-old boy. Nolan had never given any thought before to how a woman would react to him having a son, mostly because he hadn't thought much about getting serious about any woman. Now here he was, after one date, feeling damn serious. Alarmingly serious.

Too soon, he told himself again. *See how it goes. Don't risk Sean's feelings until you're a lot surer than you are yet.*

Okay, he could do that.

"You'd better hit the sack," he suggested. "Morning comes early."

Sean sneered again, but more naturally, as if he was kidding. Nolan had always been an early riser, but even he had been surprised at how early the school bus came. The elementary school started the day at what seemed a more reasonable hour, but the middle school and high school both started classes at 7:30 a.m. He assumed it had to do with the necessity to get the first round of bus routes over in time to start the second one as well as with the need to allow daylight at the end of the day for sports and the like, but he thought it was too early for kids to be at their sharpest. Sean sure as hell wasn't. Nolan all but had to propel him out the door to meet the bus at the road.

Nolan went downstairs to make sure the house was locked up and turn off lights. He paused before going back up. He heard water running in the bathroom and was hit, not for the first time, by how much his life had been changed by his decision to take in the tall, skinny boy with the greasy blond hair he'd first encountered at the grocery store, of all places.

Back in February or so, he'd been going in when a man and teenage boy were coming out, the man pushing a cart with difficulty through winter slush.

"Did you steal that?" There was an unpleasant snap in the man's voice.

"What? No!" The boy sounded shocked. "You saw me put it in the cart. I thought..."

"You thought wrong. You *ask* if you want something. Hear?"

"It's just beef jerky."

"We don't buy junk."

Watching the two walk across the parking lot, Nolan had been struck by the dislike on the man's face. How could you look at your own boy that way?

He saw them again a couple months later, in spring. The hardware store that time. He'd rounded the end of one aisle and started down the next, and there they were. They weren't talking. The kid was trailing disconsolately a good ten, fifteen feet behind the man Nolan assumed was his father. His head hung, his shoulders were slumped. His feet dragged.

There came a moment when the dad pushed the cart around the corner and Nolan and the boy were alone.

Nolan didn't understand what drove him. A solitary

man, he didn't make a habit of intruding. But he hadn't liked anything he'd seen between these two.

"You okay, son?" he asked.

The boy didn't turn around, although he did stop. He shrugged, a miserable sight if Nolan had ever seen one. His jeans were too short, Nolan noticed, exposing bony ankles in sagging socks. His hair was dirty.

Nolan laid a hand on his shoulder. "That's not an answer," he said, in his quiet way.

The boy looked at him. The sheer desperation on his face tore something open in Nolan's chest.

"He doesn't like me."

"Your father?"

The boy all but erupted in fury. "He's not my father!"

"Then who is he?"

"He's..." The shoulders sagged again. "He's my foster dad," he said dully. "I've lived with him and his wife since December, when my grandma died."

"If they took you in, they must have wanted you."

Another shrug. "They said they did."

"Sean?" the foster father called from the next aisle. There was that hateful snap again. "What are you doing?"

"I'm coming," Sean said, and started to trudge forward.

"Wait." When the boy paused, Nolan asked quietly, "Does he hit you?"

"Nah."

That was when Nolan did something even more out of character for him—he took out his wallet and removed a business card. "Sean."

The boy stopped again and looked back.

"Take this. It has my number on it. If you need someone, call me."

He took it, his fingers closing tightly on the card. He looked down at it, then up at Nolan's face. Back to the card. He didn't get it. Nolan could tell. Nolan didn't get it, either. All he knew was that he'd recognized something in the boy, a smoldering resentment and unhappiness he'd felt at about the same age. Different causes, but enough the same that he couldn't suppress the empathy he felt for a boy he didn't even know.

After a long minute, Sean had ducked his head in a sort of nod and disappeared after his foster father.

At the end of May, he'd called.

CHAPTER THREE

ALLIE'S MOTHER SMILED perfunctorily when Allie told her the date had gone great and she and Nolan were going to see each other again. Without commenting or asking more about him, she began chattering about the Friends of the Library and how someone had suggested she run for president when elections came around at the end of the year.

"Goodness, I'd never considered it," she said, "but of course I do organize the book sale, and it seems as if more and more often people are turning to me."

She sounded really pleased, Allie thought, which made her guess her mother needed more recognition than she'd been receiving. It wasn't hard to see why; her boss might appreciate her, but her job kept her tucked away in the back room. Who gave a thought to the bookkeeper, unless your paycheck was late? For so many years, Allie's and her mother's entire lives had required them to keep a low profile. It had been a long time since Allie had chafed at that, but maybe it had bothered Mom all along.

I never realized. The fact that she was surprised made her feel self-centered. When was the last time she'd wondered what made her mother happy?

"You'd do a great job," she assured her. "You ought to run."

Mom had stopped by the store just before closing and suggested dinner, surprising Allie. After all, they'd eaten together the night before last. But she'd agreed even though she really wanted to go home and work on the Burgoyne Surrounded quilt. She'd set it up in the frame but had had very little time to start on it. Sort of like high school, she thought ruefully—*I'm such a social butterfly.*

Now, if it had been Nolan calling and suggesting they get together…

She would definitely not let her mother know that she'd rather be spending this evening with him.

Allie never did quite figure out why Mom had suggested they get together so soon after the last time. She clearly wasn't interested in hearing about Nolan, and she didn't have any significant news of her own beyond the possibility of becoming president of the Friends.

Bemused, Allie escaped as soon as she could after dinner and did manage a peaceful hour of hand-quilting before getting ready for bed. She loved starting on a new—or, in this case, very old—quilt. She used a tiny needle and averaged twelve stitches to an inch despite the thickness of the three layers. It was the quilting that added stiffness and wondrous texture. Admiring the block she'd completed, she remembered the sensual way Nolan had fingered the Lady of the Lake quilt she was working on at the store.

She wished he'd called today. What if he hadn't had as good a time as she did? Men always said, "I'll call." Frequently they didn't mean it. What if she didn't see him again until he came to pick up his son's completed quilt?

Allie rolled her eyes. Oh, for Pete's sake! They'd had dinner only last night! It had been *one day,* and she was already despairing.

Laughing at herself, but still aware of a hollow feeling beneath her breastbone, she went to bed.

NOLAN TRIED TO figure out how soon he could see Allie again without upsetting Sean or making him feel abandoned. A solution occurred to him during the night on Thursday, and he called her store right after ten Friday morning.

After identifying himself, he said, "Do you slow down enough in the middle of the day to take a lunch break?"

"Yes, but I can't close the store, so I usually just snatch a bite here and there when I have a slow moment."

"Could I bring lunch by?" he asked.

There was a brief silence. "That would be nice," she said. "Can you make it one or one-thirty? I get quite a bit of business during the standard lunch hour, then things go dead afterward."

He'd be starving by then, as early as he had breakfast, but that was okay. He wanted to see her. He could grab a bite midmorning to sustain him.

He picked up deli sandwiches and cookies at the Pea Patch and walked in the door of Allie's shop at one-fifteen on the nose. His gaze arrowed in on her, back at her quilt frame, before he scanned the store and saw that they were otherwise alone.

She parked the needle and dropped a thimble on the quilt, standing before he reached her. She looked so pretty, her hair looser today than he'd seen it and her eyes somehow even greener than he remembered. She wore an elbow-length, snug-fitting, peach-colored cardigan sweater that was open over something lacy and white. Her smile tightened the strange knot in his chest.

"Nolan." Her gaze went to the bags in his hand. "Oh, I love the Pea Patch."

"I should have asked what you like," he said gruffly.

"I'm not picky."

They sat at one end of the long table that presumably was used for the classes Allie taught. He took out the sandwiches and gave her first choice, looking around at the completed quilts and quilt blocks that hung on the walls.

"I'd say I stand out as much as a bull in a china shop, but at least your wares aren't breakable."

She laughed, the gold in her eyes shimmering. "The store is rather feminine, isn't it? And I suppose your workshop is masculine to the nth degree."

"You could say that. There's nothing pretty about it."

"Except what comes out of it."

"I don't usually think of anything I make as 'pretty.'" He pretended to sound insulted. "I go for magnificent."

"Naturally." Her expression was merry, her mouth still curved. "Silly of me."

He asked if all her customers were quilters, and she told him that most were.

"I carry only one hundred percent cotton fabrics that are the right weight and texture for quilts. I debated adding other fabrics, but without having a great deal larger space I wouldn't have had enough selection to draw a wider clientele. And then I'd also have had to offer patterns, and that would have taken space, too." She spread her hands in a "what could I do" gesture. "I don't have any direct competition here in West Fork, but there's a JoAnn's Fabric not that far away, and they're huge. I can't go head-to-head, and I don't want to."

He nodded, understanding. He couldn't go head-to-head with the kind of place that turned out granite countertops for every subdivision, either, not at a competitive price.

"Mind you," she said, "JoAnn's carries quilting fabric, and I know customers sometimes go there because a chain store like that can beat my prices. They have big sales, too. My niche is the dedicated quilter. I find unusual fabrics, ones that will help create a truly distinctive quilt. Also, I can offer a level of service a larger store can't. Newer quilters need someone to lead them around and show them what works and why. And, of course, the classes are really successful for me." She grinned at him. "Plus, I have to admit I love converting women into quilters."

"I suppose quilting is a form of art for women," he said thoughtfully.

"Yes, and it always has been. There actually are men who quilt, including a few whose work is cutting edge. But fiber arts of all kinds were traditionally a woman's task, and her way of expressing herself and, probably, impressing other women. It wasn't just quilting—there's weaving, of course, hooked and braided rugs, embroidery… Think about medieval tapestries, which like most other fabric arts had a practical purpose—preserving heat in chilly stone castles."

Enjoying her enthusiasm, Nolan said, "While the men were decorating their armor."

Allie laughed. "Right."

She told him that Burgoyne Surrounded, the pattern that made up Sean's quilt top, was likely copied from a traditional pattern used in woven coverlets—one woman's art transferred to another. Nolan found the idea intriguing.

With a little urging, he got her to talk some more about the history of quilting, about how older quilts could often be dated within a decade simply by the fabrics used.

"Although it is getting a little harder," she remarked, "because these days you can buy fabric that looks like it came from the 1930s, for example. And a really well-preserved one from that era actually wouldn't look that different from a new one made from a pattern common then."

"How well preserved is an eighty- or ninety-year-old quilt likely to be?"

"Most were made for everyday use, but not all. Sometimes a particularly prized quilt or coverlet was put out once in a while for show, but otherwise kept in a cedar chest for posterity. There are some really spectacular nineteenth-century quilts in beautiful condition.

"If a woman put enough work into a particular quilt, she wasn't going to be eager to have her husband come in from the fields and sit on it to take off his muddy boots, then get under it when he hadn't had a bath in a week. Or put it on a kid's bed. Imagine how painful it would be to have put hundreds of hours into piecing and quilting, then have to subject it to a scrub board and wind and sun when it was laid out to dry." She made a face at him. "You don't have to worry about anything like that, do you? Your work is literally rock-solid. Who could abuse it?"

"Now, that's not entirely true," he protested. "A granite countertop, for example, takes some care. And even rock can be chipped, scratched and battered."

Allie and Nolan agreed that they preferred to think their creations always went to the perfect homes, where they would be treated tenderly forevermore. They both laughed, knowing how unlikely that was.

Unfortunately, a pair of women came in the door and rushed, oohing and aahing, toward a display of ocean-themed fabric that had caught Nolan's eye earlier, too.

"Dinner Saturday night?" he asked hastily, and Allie agreed with seeming pleasure before going to wait on the women. Nolan bundled up the lunch trash, murmured a quiet goodbye to her and left, aware of the women's curious gazes following him.

NOLAN SAW ALLIE twice more in the next week: for dinner on Saturday night, and when he stopped by again with lunch on Tuesday. By then he'd become increasingly aware that trying to get together with a woman, even for a purely sexual relationship, was going to be a greater challenge than it would have been before Sean.

This was partly because he could tell he was shaking his foster son's sense of security. But there were also the practicalities, starting with the fact that Nolan had to keep a sharp eye on the clock whenever he was out. Not going home at all some night was clearly out. Being really late wasn't good, either.

Sean had definitely waited up for him Saturday night. He'd mumbled again that it was "cool" Nolan was seeing a woman, but plainly he felt threatened by the loss of Nolan's undivided attention. And no wonder, when he'd come to live with him so recently and probably already figured, somewhere deep inside, that Nolan was one more person who would ditch him sooner or later.

Then there was the fact that he'd never be able to bring Allie home to his own bed, unless it was during the day while Sean was in school. Since he didn't have any friends yet, the kid never went anywhere unless he was with Nolan. Thank God Allie didn't have a roommate, Nolan thought. He had a suspicion, though, that she wasn't likely to be inviting him into her apartment anytime soon. He doubted she was casual about sex. In one way, he didn't want her to be, but…damn, he wanted her. He'd been okay with a long stretch of celibacy until he set eyes on Allie. He seemed now to be in a constant state of edgy discomfort.

Finally, in sheer desperation, he decided he had to introduce her and Sean. If they hit it off, he could spend more time with her. Whether that would forward his goal of getting her into bed, he didn't know, but, damn it, he was happy being with her, no matter what they were doing.

He'd discovered early on that Sean's background was devoid of a whole lot of the experiences he thought most kids took for granted. He'd been gradually, without making a big deal of it, trying to fill those in. He had been mildly shocked to learn that Sean had never been to the zoo.

Friday night, while they were eating dinner together, Nolan said, "I thought we'd go to the zoo Sunday."

His foster son looked at him as if he was crazy. "The what?"

"You heard me."

"Wow. Will you hold my hand to make sure I don't get lost? And, hey, you gonna buy me a stuffed monkey while we're there, too?"

"Even adults enjoy the zoo."

Sean's disbelieving stare didn't moderate.

"I thought I'd ask Allie, too," Nolan said casually.

Something ugly flashed in the boy's eyes. "If you have *her* to go with, why do I have to get dragged along?"

"Because it's fun." Pretending he hadn't noticed Sean's anger, Nolan took a second helping of green beans. "And you and I are going whether she can join us or not."

"What if I don't want to?"

"When I've suggested doing something together, have I ever bored you silly?"

"I guess not," he mumbled after a minute.

"Have faith."

Nolan grinned at the rolled eyes.

When he called Allie the next day and proposed the same expedition, there was a long silence.

"The zoo?"

"You sound like Sean."

She laughed.

"I go a couple of times a year," he said. "It's one of my favorite ways to spend a day."

"I'm ashamed to say I've only been to Woodland Park Zoo once since we moved to Washington."

"How long ago was that?"

"Ten…no, eleven years."

"Then you're past due for another visit," he said firmly. "What do you say?"

"I say that sounds like fun. And I'll look forward to meeting Sean."

"Then we're on." Pleased that she was okay with an outing that included his son, he arranged to pick her up by nine. The weather was supposed to be warm this weekend, and he'd learned that morning was best for catching glimpses of some of the more elusive animals.

Come Sunday morning, Sean didn't want to get his butt out of bed. He moaned and whined when Nolan rousted him, then grumbled all the way to her place about how crowded they'd all be in the pickup.

Nolan liked the idea of being crowded against Allie. It had occurred to him lately, though, that he should maybe think about buying a car. The time would come when he'd have to take turns driving Sean and his yet-to-be-made friends places—not possible with the pickup truck. He could choose something that might also do for Sean in a couple of years when he got his driver's license.

Once again, he didn't have to go up to Allie's door; she came out as soon as he pulled in. He got out to meet her, enjoying the sight of her coming down the stairs. She wore calf-length chinos, sandals and a T-shirt the mossy green color of her eyes. Her legs were sensational, and his groin tightened. On another level, he was glad to see that her hand slid along the railing. So she was being careful.

Sean had climbed out of the truck, too, and stood there looking as lumpish as he could manage.

"You must be Sean," Allie said with a friendly smile. "I'm so glad to meet you. When we get back later today, why don't you come upstairs and see what I'm doing with your quilt. I'd like to make sure you approve."

That stirred a little emotion on his face. "I guess," he mumbled.

Nolan held out a hand, but she said, "Why don't we take my car? I get better mileage, and it fits in parking spots for compact cars."

He didn't much like being a passenger, but agreed. Sean was relegated to being in the backseat of her Corolla, but he was probably relieved.

Mostly, Nolan and Allie carried the conversation on the drive to Seattle, but Sean wasn't rude enough to ignore direct questions. They were able to park only a couple of rows from the entrance. As they all got out and Allie locked the car, Sean looked at several families with small kids streaming across the parking lot, parents pushing strollers.

"I can't believe this," he muttered.

Nolan laid a heavy arm across his shoulders. "I wish I'd had you when you were that age. We'd have come to the zoo a lot."

That earned him a skittish look he'd seen before. Sean had trouble believing Nolan truly wanted him as a son, or that he'd give a lot to be able to go back in time and save the boy from all the uncertainties and deprivation of his life.

Huh. Maybe if he bought that car now, Sean would understand it was a kind of promise, one that said, *You* will *be staying with me.*

"Oh, this is going to be fun," Allie exclaimed enthusiastically. "Do they have snow cones here? I love snow cones."

"I think maybe they do." Nolan bumped his hip against hers. "You're easy to please."

She bumped back. "Am not. Usually the only place you can get a snow cone is the fair."

"You went?"

She gave him a humorous glance. "Are you kidding? I always enter some quilts. Both in the Evergreen State Fair and the Stanwood Fair."

"And win, I bet."

"Naturally," she said with dignity, then spoiled it with that scrunched nose. "Sometimes I get robbed, but then, there are people with no taste wherever you go."

He laughed. Sean gave her his "what *are* you" look.

Nolan paid the entrance fees and grabbed a map, steering them all toward the safari enclosure that held zebras and the stately, ungainly giraffes. Out of the corner of his eye, he saw Sean gaping as he leaned against the railing.

"There's a baby," Allie said with delight. "Sean, look!"

By the time they reached the elephants, Sean had shed his teenage cool. He was exclaiming right along with Allie, only taking occasional glances around to make sure no one in his age range was looking.

They got lucky enough to see two otters romping in the extraordinarily natural stream, shooting down over rocks like kids on a playground slide, then scrambling back up to do it again. A lioness snatched a huge fish from the water with brutal speed, making the human audience gasp. A gorilla mother cradled a young one, and when Sean crouched by the glass both stared at him with intelligent dark eyes while he stared back.

"Wow," he said after that. He sounded awed and uneasy. "They look so *human*. Not like they should be in the zoo."

Partway through, Nolan bought everyone hot dogs, sodas and, eventually, snow cones. He was having more fun watching Allie and Sean than the animals. The two of them were as entranced as any pair of five-year-olds, and not hiding it. Allie didn't leave him out, though. Every so often, she'd grab Nolan's hand and drag him forward either to make sure he saw something or just to be close to him.

He got to wondering whether *she'd* had a normal share
of satisfying childhood experiences. Maybe she possessed
the rare quality of being able to throw herself into the
moment without self-consciousness, but he kept noticing
the nearly identical expressions of astonishment and even
wonder on hers and Sean's faces. Nolan kept pondering
her reactions without arriving at a conclusion.

She sounded as though she was close to her mother.
Maybe closer than usual, even, for a woman her age. And
there *had* been a father. She'd said she was seventeen,
Nolan thought, when her parents split up. That implied a
sort of regular childhood, didn't it?

But the fact that the father had evidently walked away
without compunction bothered Nolan. And then there was
the brother, who'd also disappeared from her life.

Yeah, that was strange enough to unsettle Nolan, cou-
pled with today's childish delight. It made him realize how
little she'd really said about her background.

He had to shrug at that, though; he hadn't exactly been
chatty about his own. Their *now* was a lot more important
than what their lives had been like when they were eight
years old or ten or fourteen. There was an even more logical explanation, too, it occurred to him. Zoos tended to
be in large cities. Her family might have lived far enough
from one that they'd never gone.

Still…he was curious. And he knew himself. Curiosity
and unease had eaten at him from the first time he set eyes
on Sean and his then-foster father. Nolan hadn't felt satisfied until that phone call this spring when the gruff boy/man
voice on the other end said, "You gave me your card a while
ago and said to call you if I ever needed anything."

Mostly, Nolan wasn't that interested in people. He went
out of his way to be sure his curiosity wasn't aroused. But
once it was…he was a stubborn man.

And he liked Allie Wright. He liked her enough that it scared the shit out of him considering how little he knew about her.

AFTER A TRIP to the grocery store on Tuesday, Nolan was driving past the high school on the way home when he noticed the football team practicing. Some boys were sprinting between cones, others negotiating a row of tires lying on their sides. Half a dozen were taking turns plowing into the blocking tackle. A kicker was setting up for a field goal or extra point try.

Nolan saw that Sean, slumped in the passenger seat, was looking that way, too.

"You've got the size," Nolan commented. "Too bad you didn't try out for the team."

Sean's head snapped back around, as if he didn't want to admit he had been interested. "Doesn't matter."

"Sure it does." Nolan mulled it over. With no experience raising a kid, it hadn't occurred to him when Sean first came that they needed to be looking into things like that. Football practice had probably started in August, before school opened. "Won't be too long until basketball starts."

"I'm not that good."

"I doubt many freshmen are that good."

"I wouldn't be able to ride the bus home."

"You know I'd make time to pick you up," Nolan said mildly.

The kid's shrug was just this side of disagreeable.

"You interested at all?"

Obviously conflicted, Sean took his time answering. "Maybe."

"I could put up a hoop above the garage door. You could practice shooting."

"Really?" Something like hope shone in Sean's gray eyes. "That would be cool. If they're not too expensive."

Nolan didn't care how much basketball hoops cost. He wished he'd thought of putting one up sooner. Sean needed to get involved in some activities if he was to make friends. Sports made sense, given that he was tall for his age. He needed a physical outlet for his restlessness, too.

"The concrete pad in front of the garage is flat." When he bought the house, the driveway had been gravel, but Nolan had had it paved leading both to the garage and the workshop. He wasn't about to have a valuable slice of granite or—God forbid—a finished piece break when he hit a pothole in his truck. He nodded. "Should be ideal. We'll do it."

"Cool!" Sean declared.

Good thing, Nolan reflected, that he had an equable temperament himself. Could be the last foster parents hadn't known teenagers' emotions were all over the map, especially one who'd suffered as much loss as Sean had. Ebullience to angry sullenness could happen between one heartbeat and the next. The couple might have gone into it with good intentions but been battered by all the ups and downs.

If anything had tried Nolan's patience, it was the bureaucracy of getting approved as a foster parent. The frustrating part was that everyone knew Sean had no other even half-decent possibilities.

For Sean, Nolan hadn't had any trouble staying patient. *So far,* he reminded himself.

He glanced sidelong. "You haven't said whether you liked Allie." On Sunday, after they took her home and admired the beginnings she'd made on the quilt, Sean had been rather quiet. Nolan hadn't wanted to push it.

"She's okay," he said now. "I can see why you like her," he added, more grudgingly. "She's really little, though."

Nolan grunted agreement. Even Sean had towered over her.

The boy continued to ponder. "She moves different than most people. Like…like she's thinking about where she puts her feet or the way she turns her head. You know?"

"Yeah." Nolan hadn't thought of it that way, but there was a deliberate quality in her every movement. It made her extra graceful, but he didn't like the idea of that word: *deliberate.* As if she was posing, trying to create an effect.

The strange thing was he'd swear she didn't give a whole lot of thought to her appearance. She wore little makeup, wasn't constantly flipping the ends of her hair the way some women did, listened with gravity when he or Sean talked and didn't jump to regain center stage.

No, he decided—the graceful lines she formed with every lift of her hand, every step or tip of her head, they were just her. Beautiful.

He relaxed. *You're paranoid,* he told himself, and knew it was true. He had good reason, though. He'd grown up with a master—or should he say, a mistress?—of presenting a pretty facade to hide an uglier reality. His very own mother.

He and Allie had time to uncover each other's reality. There was no hurry.

Braking in front of the house, he hid a grin from his son. No hurry, except for the getting-her-into-bed part. His body was getting damned *im*patient.

Not getting out yet, he gazed at the garage with its peaked roof. "Yep, a hoop'll look great up there," he said. He held up one hand, palm first, and Sean slapped it in an exuberant high five.

"Yeah!"

In total accord, they hopped out and went around back to let down the tailgate and collect the groceries.

Nolan hoped he wasn't trying to buy his foster son's affection, but he didn't think so. Deep inside him was rooted the belief that parents should do their best to give their kids what they needed. Whatever else he could say about his own parents, they'd done that.

He, Jed and Anna had worn the right clothes to fit in. They'd been given bikes and even cars—albeit beaters— when the time came for each. And, yes, Dad had hung a basketball hoop above the garage. Anna hadn't been in- terested, but Jed and Nolan had enjoyed some good times with that hoop. He wanted the same for Sean.

There was nothing wrong with that, was there?

CHAPTER FOUR

FABRIC RIPPLED AS Mrs. Sellers pressed her substantial way down an aisle. Three hundred pounds if she was an ounce, she emerged triumphant at the back of Allie's store. There she stood blinking at a sight she clearly found startling.

"A new student?" She looked suspicious.

Allie's mouth twitched at the expression on Nolan's face. He sat kitty-corner from her at the table, where they'd been eating lunch. "I'm afraid I haven't converted him yet. Mrs. Sellers, this is a friend of mine, Nolan Radek. Nolan, Honoria Sellers, one of my favorite customers."

He stood and extended a hand. "Pleased to meet you."

Mrs. Sellers's now-slit-eyed gaze lowered to Nolan's large, work-roughened hand. It was a long, grudging moment before she placed her own tiny, plump hand in his for the briefest of shakes.

She then surveyed their partially eaten lunches, spread out on the table. "A friend, you say."

Allie heard the beginnings of a laugh next to her, ended when Nolan cleared his throat.

"Yes," she said hastily. "We met when Nolan brought me a marvelous late-nineteenth- or early-twentieth-century quilt top to hand-quilt." She told Mrs. Sellers the story and rhapsodized about the workmanship in the piecing. Her customer's bristles subsided as Allie talked, until her nod at Nolan was almost pleasant.

"Good for you, helping that boy remember family. I can

see why Allie likes you." Mrs. Sellers's gaze switched to Allie. "I've decided to buy the green leaf print for the backing of my quilt. You've got enough, don't you? You haven't sold any off that bolt since I was in Friday?"

"I wouldn't dare," Allie said truthfully. "I hid it away in back. Let me go grab it. And, yes, it's nearly a full bolt. There's plenty." She stood. "Excuse me," she murmured to Nolan, who nodded.

By the time she'd fetched the bolt from her small back room, taken it up front and cut the required yardage with her rotary cutter, several other women had arrived and spread out through the store. Allie rang up Mrs. Sellers's purchase and went to the back to rescue Nolan, who was being grilled by a pair of elderly women.

Instead of being greeted by an expression of desperation, she found him suppressing a grin. She felt a now-familiar squeezing sensation in her chest. For some strange reason, his smiles always took her by surprise, rearranging his face until *plain* was the last word that came to mind.

"These ladies want to know what a rude, crude man is doing, loitering around here," he explained, straight-faced.

They both giggled. "Now, you know we never said any such thing!" the elder of the two sisters protested.

He smiled at her. "I was encapsulating."

She visibly melted. So did Allie.

"Nonsense," Edith declared. "We're delighted to see Allie has found a rude, crude man." She patted his shoulder. "It's past time. She's such a lovely young woman."

Nolan's very blue eyes met Allie's. "Yes, she is."

Of course, he couldn't say anything else, could he? But she blushed anyway. "We were only having lunch and chatting, Edith." *Well, it's true,* she insisted to herself, even though she knew it wasn't true at all. They'd been… bonding. Exchanging important information. Flirting, too.

Allie turned to Nolan. "It doesn't look like I'm going to be able to finish lunch right now. I'm sorry."

"I noticed," he said. "Your sandwich and cookie will keep. I'll take the rest with me."

She liked the fact that she had yet to see him display even a hint of impatience or irritation. Her first impression of him as steady and calm had been so far confirmed. He took her work seriously, too.

She felt another funny little cramp in her chest that this time she identified as fear. Ridiculous, but undeniable. He scared her a little, maybe because he seemed too perfect. Too tempting.

She was glad to be distracted by the sisters, who pounced on several bolts of gorgeous batik fabric that lay on the large table a safe distance from the food and drinks Allie and Nolan had been sharing. She had just begun unpacking a new shipment, which, if their reaction was anything to go by, would sell well.

Edith, who had confessed to being eighty-three, and her younger sister Margaret were longtime quilters who had learned from their mother who had learned from hers. They were a rarity now; interest in the art had languished in America by the 1940s. Most women these days had to turn to classes and books instead of their own female relatives.

After Nolan had left, pecking Allie on the cheek under the curious and pleased stares of half a dozen women, she advised customers, neatly sliced fabric from bolts and rang up purchases while diverting questions about him by handing out newly printed schedules for upcoming classes. As she did all this, she pursued the thought the Brown sisters had stirred.

Most women probably took up quilting because they could make something beautiful they couldn't otherwise afford. But there was certainly another element to the astonishing revival of quilting in the past twenty years. This was one art that offered a way of reconnecting with the past.

Most patterns had a history. Some had been popular with women who'd traveled the Oregon Trail. Others had their origins in regional folk art—the Pennsylvania Dutch, or the quilts made by slaves that hinted at their African heritage. Women had named their patterns to celebrate personal and familial triumphs and tragedies, but also political events and figures.

Mostly, though, Allie suspected, in the back of her mind, every woman who quilted felt the ghostlike presence of her own ancestresses, who had sought to keep their families warm and make something beautiful, too. These days when families weren't as close as they'd once been, women felt a need to tie themselves to the past and make something for the future.

Allie could talk glibly on the subject at great length. She often did, in fact, to newly excited quilters or as an introduction to a class for beginners. She didn't exempt herself from her generalizations. But she had also never asked herself why the draw had been so powerful for her from the moment she stepped into that fabric store and saw the blocks the women in that class were sewing.

So...what about me?

Well, duh, she scoffed at herself. She was the quintessential woman with no past. Of course she wanted one, even if she had to stitch it together herself.

It might have helped if Mom and Dad hadn't abandoned so much when they fled their former life. Some of that, Allie thought, had been necessity, but not all. Mom would say she wasn't sentimental. She didn't like "old" anything. Allie had furnished her apartment from antiques stores;

her mother didn't understand why she didn't want nice new things.

As for Dad…Allie didn't know. She thought maybe he had grieved so much for what he was losing, he hadn't let himself hold on to any reminders.

Could that be true of Mom, too? Allie let herself wonder, and discovered she had no idea. Perturbed by how much she *didn't* know about her parents, she was immersed enough in her brooding not to notice how seriously a middle-aged woman was studying the Feathered Star quilt Allie had displayed on the wall until she began to ask questions.

Allie had completed it almost a year ago, and had begun to think it might not sell. The colors were darker than she usually chose—earthy and comforting, she thought, but she'd overheard a woman murmur to a friend that it was gloomy.

"I don't know how you can put so much work into a quilt and then sell it," said this woman, who'd introduced herself as Helen Richards. "It must feel like giving up your newborn baby for adoption. But if you're really willing, I want it."

The Feathered Star quilt was queen-sized and elaborately hand-quilted. The price paid, with no quibbling, was exceedingly generous.

Once Helen Richards happily left with her purchase, Allie found herself in her customary state after selling one of her quilts—torn between pleasure because her creation had found the right home, delight at the profit and grief at losing another piece of herself. She wondered if Nolan felt the same when he sold a sculpture.

When Allie finally waved goodbye to her last customer of the day and closed out the cash register, her mood was strange. Yet there was really no reason to feel such a way.

She'd been exceptionally busy today, and nearly everyone had spent money. With the sale of the quilt added in, she had no doubt she would find the receipts would be her new record. *And* she'd been able to see Nolan, even if their visit had been cut short. Lately she'd felt a little low in the morning of any day when she knew she wouldn't see him.

Maybe that was why she felt so unsettled.

We're dating. We're having fun. I think I'd like to make love with him.

That was all perfectly normal. So why did she sometimes wonder if the changes he was bringing to her life might not end up doing some damage?

I'm a mess, she admitted to herself, and identified part of her fear: Nolan wanted to know her, and how did she dare let him guess how shallow that self was?

"Have I ever had a pet?" Dumb question to induce panic, but it had. It was one of those stupid things that made her run a mental check. Taboo, or not taboo? Answer: not. "Um, yes. Not for a long time, though. Why?"

Naturally, it was Nolan who had asked in one of the phone calls she'd begun to live for. They usually came around bedtime. Sometimes they talked for an hour, sometimes only long enough to exchange brief snippets about their days, to say without words, *I was thinking about you.* He always kept his voice quiet, and she suspected he waited until Sean had disappeared into his bedroom to call. She hadn't mentioned these conversations to her mother, either.

"I want to get Sean a dog," Nolan said, sounding pleased with himself. "I thought we'd visit shelters this weekend."

"Did he *ask* for a dog?"

"No, but I've seen him stop to pet them. He and his grandmother had some kind of terrier mix. I don't know what happened to it. I hope it died before she did."

Allie knew exactly what he meant. On top of everything else, he'd feel guilty if the poor, bewildered dog had been taken to a shelter in the wake of Sean's grandma's death.

"You didn't ask?"

"The dog was mixed in with other topics. I try to let him tell me the hard things when he's ready."

She wondered if he sensed how deep her empathy for his foster son ran. She should hope not, because there was no way he'd understand it. What did a twenty-eight-year-old businesswoman have in common with any fourteen-year-old boy, never mind one with Sean's background?

Nothing, that's what.

Too much.

"I thought maybe you'd like to come," Nolan said. "You can advise us."

How a voice so low and rumbly could also be coaxing, she couldn't have said. But she found herself reluctantly smiling.

"Out of my great store of knowledge? Didn't *you* ever have a dog?"

"My mother didn't like them. She always had a Persian cat. You notice I said *she.* These were not kid-friendly pets. They made great pillows, but that's about all you could say for 'em. Dumb as a box of rocks—and I know my rocks." Amusement suffused that voice now. "Softer, though. I remember one that I was never sure could actually walk. I swear Mom would carry that damn cat to the litter box and then back again to its throne."

Curled up in her easy chair, Allie laughed at the image.

"Not exactly a growing boy's dream pet."

"A dog was bound to chase the cat, Mom insisted. *I* thought some exercise would do the cat good." Plainly, he liked making her laugh. He wasn't being entirely serious now. "That was assuming the dog ever noticed that the fluffy peach-colored mound at the end of the sofa was alive."

"So why didn't you get a dog the minute you left home?"

He was quiet for a minute. "Too busy, I guess. Ironically, I do have cats."

"No!" she gasped in mock surprise.

"Make fun of me, will you." There was the amusement again. "They showed up on my property about two years ago, a couple of scrawny half grown, half wild mongrels. Can a cat be a mongrel? Anyway, they're only distant relations to my mother's cats. I figured somebody dumped them. So I started putting food out, trapped 'em before the female threw a litter of kittens. They're still mostly outdoor cats. They let me pet them, but haven't decided whether to trust Sean yet."

"A dog might chase them," she pointed out.

Silence. "Okay, is it bad if I admit that hadn't occurred to me?"

"Very bad," she said solemnly, suppressing this laugh.

"We can be sure we get a dog that's lived with cats before. Or a puppy."

Realizing how much she wanted to be with Sean and Nolan when they picked out the dog, she had to ask. "Do you really want me to come? This sounds like something the two of you should do together, without an outsider along."

"You don't feel like an outsider," he said, and his voice had deepened further.

She had to press the heel of her hand to her breastbone to quell the sharp pang.

"I… Thank you." Allie closed her eyes and took a deep breath. "Why don't you ask Sean? My feelings won't be hurt if he'd rather go without me. Please don't press him."

"Fair enough," Nolan said after a minute. "I thought you'd enjoy it."

"I would," she admitted. "But not if I ruin the whole thing for Sean. Anyway, I really can't afford to take Saturday off."

"I checked. They're open on Sundays."

He'd checked because he wanted her to go with him. He was hinting at a whole lot more than a dating relationship, which shouldn't have stunned her but did.

"Let me know," she said, working hard at sounding cheerful and offhanded. *Nope, doesn't matter to me either way.* She ended the call as soon as she could without having him notice anything was wrong.

It's not wrong. It's good. It's great. I like *him.*

Then why this flutter of alarm?

I don't know how to do this.

And *that,* she realized, was the truth.

If she'd ever known how to be intimate with other people, she'd forgotten. She hadn't had a really close friend since middle school. Before. Being so terrified of what she might inadvertently say, she didn't dare say anything at all—which was an excellent way of appearing unfriendly to other teenagers. Or pathologically shy. Or maybe of *making* a person pathologically shy, eventually.

Am I?

Yes and no. Not in the quilt shop, but when the possibility of something closer arose…maybe. After all, she still had to think every time before she opened her mouth.

The phone rang again shortly after Nolan and she said good-night, and she snatched it up, noting belatedly that the caller was her mother, not Nolan calling right back to say, *Sean would love to have you come with us.*

Yeah, right.

"Hi, Mom. This is late for you to be calling."

"I'm not quite as stodgy as you think I am," her mother said with a laugh. "You start your day earlier than I do."

"That's true. I was actually about to head to bed. Does that make me stodgy?"

Mom laughed. "Really all I wanted was to line you up for a shopping expedition on Sunday. I was contemplating my winter wardrobe, and I decided it needs some major refurbishment."

Allie hesitated. "I...think I have plans for Sunday already. I'm sorry."

There was a tiny pause. "You *think?*"

"We haven't finalized them yet, but I did agree."

More silence. "This is the man you're seeing?"

Allie stiffened at her mother's tone. Her fingers tightened on the phone. "Nolan. Yes."

"Well. I admit I'm disappointed. Since Sunday is the only day we *can* spend together."

Which was true enough—Mom worked the standard Monday through Friday, while Allie closed her shop on Sundays and Mondays.

"Depending on where you want to go, we could make it an evening," she offered, even as she regretted the lost time on Sean's quilt.

"Oh, I had a full-blown expedition in mind. Seattle, I was thinking. And lunch, of course, my treat," her mother said persuasively. "I can't persuade you to ditch him for your mom?" The last was said humorously, as if it wasn't to be taken seriously. But Allie had no doubt that it was.

"Refurbishing your winter wardrobe isn't exactly an emergency," she pointed out. "It'll be mid-October before you so much as need a sweater."

"Well...that's true. Shall we plan for the next Sunday, then?"

"That sounds like fun," Allie said, relieved. She hadn't

liked hurting her mother's feelings. "And I'll let you know if our plans for this Sunday end up getting canceled."

"Oh, good," her mother said. "I'll look forward to it. Good night, sweetheart."

"You, too."

She could use some new clothes, too, Allie reflected, as she went to the bathroom to brush her teeth. She hadn't paid all that much attention to her own wardrobe lately, until she met Nolan. Shopping would be fun.

So would helping pick out a dog or puppy, if Sean didn't resent her addition to the expedition.

The thought gave Allie pause again. Nolan probably shouldn't have asked her. Maybe she should Just Say No, per the antidrug campaign. Let the two do something meaningful together, without her trailing along.

But oh, temptation…

SEAN MADE IT apparent pretty damn quickly that despite his mumbled agreement to Allie's inclusion today, he hadn't actually wanted her along at all. Nolan ground his teeth as he pulled into the parking lot for the Everett Animal Shelter. He was mightily tempted to say, *Trip's canceled,* and take them all home again. Except, then what? Did he drop Sean off alone at home and spend the day with Allie, the way he wanted to? Drop *her* off alone at home, and no matter how pissed he was spend the day with a kid who didn't deserve to win this standoff, if that's what it was?

To hell with it, he decided. *We're here. Maybe he'll get over his snit. Or remember he* likes *her.*

He set the emergency brake and turned off the engine. In the sudden silence, nobody moved. He watched a family hurrying in, looking eager. Close behind them came a woman and boy, maybe seven or eight, who had a dog with them on a leash. The dog's tail wagged expectantly.

The boy was crying, and Nolan realized in dismay that they weren't here to adopt—they were here to get rid of their dog, who had not a clue what his fate was to be. *God.*

"Well," he said. "I guess we should go in."

He got out, waited until Sean opened his door, then locked up. Allie slid across the bench seat after his foster son. They walked across the parking lot themselves, Sean behind Nolan and Allie, letting the distance increase.

"I'm sorry," Nolan said in a low voice. "I don't know what got into him."

"Maybe I should, I don't know, wander off and look at cats or something while you two check out the dogs."

"No," he growled. "We invited you. He's old enough to not act like a two-year-old ready to throw a temper tantrum."

"No, but..." Allie let whatever she'd been going to say trail off. She sounded undeniably unhappy, and he didn't blame her.

Opening the door and standing back for her to go ahead, Nolan then waited for his foster son. Sean slouched, dragging his feet, head hanging. Nolan was unhappily reminded of the first two times he'd encountered the boy. Maybe, it occurred to him, he'd been too hard on that first foster father. Nolan hadn't liked the way the man had talked to Sean—but teenagers were darn good at goading their parents, biological and otherwise.

By the time Sean reached Nolan, Allie had crossed the lobby and was studying a bulletin board.

"Is this something you don't want to do?" Nolan asked bluntly.

The boy flashed a look of alarm. "No! I mean, yeah. I do want a dog."

"What's the problem, then?"

"Why'd you have to bring *her?*"

"I did ask your permission."

"Yeah, like, what could I say?" he sneered.

"'No'? 'Can we go by ourselves?'"

"Like that's what you wanted to hear," Sean said in a hushed, angry voice. "You weren't *really* asking."

Was I? Nolan asked himself, and in all honesty had to admit, *Maybe I wasn't.* Damn it.

They pretty much had to go forward now.

The woman and boy with the poor, ignorant dog were talking to someone at the front desk. By the time Nolan reached it, another employee had come out to take the leash and lead the dog away. It belatedly tried to resist. The boy clutched his mother's leg and cried silently. She had begun to fill out some required form and paid no attention to the suddenly scared animal. Nolan had developed an acute dislike for her, even though he realized there were legitimate reasons to have to give up a pet. He knew he shouldn't judge so harshly without knowing her story.

Sean's distress was obvious as he watched the dog disappear in back, but when he saw that Nolan was looking, he quickly resumed the sullen mask.

Nolan explained that they were here to look at dogs and they were allowed to go in back.

Rows of sparkling clean kennels were filled with dogs of every size and shape, half of them barking. The racket was astonishing. He hoped the cats were adequately insulated from it, or they'd be even more scared.

Sean seemed to shrink, and Nolan had the thought— *yeah, a little late, huh*—that possibly he would identify too closely with the abandoned animals that had become sucked into the maw of an authority they didn't understand. He hadn't gone to an institution, thank God, but how had he felt at having strangers look him over as they tried to decide if they wanted to take him into their home? The call to Nolan had undoubtedly been his attempt to grab back some element of control. He'd have told himself *he* had chosen Nolan.

And I wanted to think we'd recognized something in each other, Nolan thought ruefully. Self-delusion.

"Maybe this wasn't the best place to start," he said. "There's a small, no-kill place in Arlington."

"No," Sean said with unexpected force. "These dogs, um, they need someone to take them home."

Oh, yeah, he was identifying, all right. Good or bad? Nolan worried, as they wandered.

Allie tried to rejoin them, but Sean snubbed her so obviously she dropped back again. Once she exclaimed in delight, as she had at the zoo, and called, "Sean! Look at this guy. No, girl."

Nolan turned. She had squatted, and was getting her hand thoroughly bathed by a scraggly creature of extremely mixed breeding. There had to be some terrier in there somewhere to explain the wiry hair. The tail was waving wildly.

"I saw it," Sean said disagreeably, and turned his back.

Nolan was *this* close to announcing there'd be no dog. But, damn it, there were so many dogs that *did* need homes. *There'll be as many next week,* he told himself, staring down at a heap of plump, brown-and-black bodies that writhed as the puppies wrestled.

Puppies were bound to get homes. Weren't they? But he saw a number of litters when he looked around. And they were all going to be big dogs, mostly Lab or shepherd mixes. Really too big for the average city dweller. Down the row he saw the family he'd spotted in the parking lot now trying out a dog on a leash. Medium-sized, maybe a corgi mix, not one of the hapless black Labs.

Nolan's mood deteriorated further. Allie became more

and more closed in, her face showing little. When he tried to drop back by her side, she flapped her hand at him and said, "He needs your attention."

"He doesn't deserve my attention," he said grimly.

"No, but…this won't help matters."

Sean glanced back, his expression hateful. Nolan ground his teeth some more and positioned himself halfway between woman and boy. They completed the circuit.

"See any that interest you?" Nolan asked.

The boy shrugged with clear insolence.

Nolan's anger might be slow to catch fire, but enough was enough. "That's it," he declared. "Time to go home."

Sean faced him, expression shocked. "*What?* But I haven't…"

"You've had all the chance you're getting. We're leaving. Now."

"That's bullshit!" His voice rose. "Why'd you suggest this at all, when all you wanted was to be with *her?*"

Nolan gripped his arm. "We're going *now.*"

Sean stumbled beside him. "I didn't *do* anything!"

Feeling as if his face had become as stonelike as a carved monolith—an Easter Island *moai,* or a grim-faced pre-Columbian warrior figurine—Nolan stalked past Allie, half dragging Sean.

"Stop," she snapped to their backs.

Nolan did, letting his hand drop from his boy's arm. He turned reluctantly.

"You shouldn't have set us all up for this," she said quietly to him. Her eyes glittered gold with something that might have been rage, or incipient tears. Or both. Then she looked at Sean. "And you. Think! Any dog you saw today might be euthanized by next week, instead of going home with you. All because you're mad at Nolan, or me." Her head was so high, she had to be stretching her neck painfully. "I'm going outside to wait. You two do what you want."

She brushed by them and pushed through the swinging door.

Nolan breathed an expletive under his breath. He'd deserved that. Sean wasn't the only one behaving very badly. And to think he'd congratulated himself not that long ago on how even-tempered he was.

"Um...some of these dogs really are going to be killed this week?" Sean's voice cracked.

Nolan hesitated. "Maybe. I don't know, but...probably. There are never enough homes."

"I guess I knew that." He hesitated. "Which ones have the worst chance?"

"Big dogs." Nolan had read enough about the problem of pet overpopulation to answer without hesitation. "Older ones."

"There aren't that many small dogs here."

"No."

The boy swallowed. "Do we have to go?"

"Sean." When their eyes met, Nolan said, "You have to choose a dog that's right for you, not only because you have some noble goal of saving it. You're a kid. You're entitled to..." He hesitated. "Take one home who will be fun. Even a puppy, if that's what you want."

Sean looked at him defiantly, his cheeks flushed. "Pedro was... He was a good dog, and he was old. I loved him."

"Your grandmother's dog."

He nodded.

"What happened to him?"

"When she died, he was put down." He shrugged jerkily. "I mean, I think it was the right thing to do. He was pretty sick. The vet said his kidneys were toast. Grandma kept saying she was going to do it, but she didn't want to. You know?"

"I know." Nolan took a chance and laid a hand on the boy's shoulder. He gave a gentle squeeze and let go. "You've been a shit today."

Sean ducked his head. "I just wanted…"

"I get it. I was insensitive." *You think?* "I'll say I'm sorry if you do the same."

"Yeah. Okay," he mumbled. "I shouldn't have… I mean, I'm sorry."

"All right. *Were* there any dogs that especially caught your eye?"

Of course there had been. Nolan kept thinking about Allie, waiting out in the hot sunlight in the parking lot. He should have given her the keys so she could at least sit in the truck. Maybe he should excuse himself… No. She knew this might take a while. She was probably hoping it would, that they didn't emerge still angry at each other, sans dog.

They didn't. Nolan inspected the three or four that had attracted Sean, and they finally came to a stop in front of the kennel that held a black Lab mix female that was supposedly five years old and, yes, cat- and kid-friendly. Her family had moved and had, for whatever unimaginable reason, been unable to take her.

Nolan thought again of the dog they'd seen being released earlier, but it was smaller and therefore probably less at risk.

The black Lab wasn't barking at the front of the kennel, like many of the other dogs. She lay curled in the back, depression in the chocolate-brown eyes that watched them. Nolan noted her release date and wondered if she'd given up.

Sean coaxed her to her feet, and talked to her until she

bumped her head against his hand and her tail gradually began to swing hopefully. They were allowed to put her on a leash and walk her outside, where she sniffed noses non-combatively with several other dogs and generally proved her good manners. She sat on command, and wrapped a long pink tongue around Sean's wrist when he patted her.

"I want her," Sean said, his glance anxious.

"I like her, too," Nolan agreed, glad to feel no hesitation. He was well aware that the responsibility was ultimately his. When—if—Sean headed off to college, the dog would be staying behind with Nolan.

They were subjected to an interview and approved. Nolan filled out the papers and paid the fee, after which they walked out.

Allie waited, sitting on a curb, her arms wrapped around her knees, her expression pensive. She turned her head, saw them and didn't move for a long moment. Her face was completely unreadable.

Nolan felt a chill of apprehension.

CHAPTER FIVE

ALLIE HAD BEEN angry and hurt enough to consider calling a cab. Or her mother. No, not that—of course she'd never give Mom ammunition against Nolan.

She'd guessed as time passed that Nolan and Sean might eventually emerge with a dog, and was relieved when they did. At least she hadn't totally ruined today's expedition.

She rose to her feet and swiped at the grit on her butt, then held out a hand to the black Lab that reached her first, straining at his—or was it her?—leash.

"Well, hello," she said softly. The dog sniffed then licked her outstretched hand. "Do you have a name?"

"According to the paperwork," Nolan said, "her name is Cassie. Sean will have to think about whether he wants to change it or not."

Allie's head jerked up, everything in her revolting not only at the concept, as if the name the dog went by was meaningless, but also at the casual way Nolan had said it. The instinct to protest was huge—*please, please, let her keep this small part of who she'd been*—but after a raging battle inside Allie averted her face and nodded. This was no time or place for her to argue. Anyway, if she did, she'd probably bring about exactly what she didn't want.

Poor Cassie.

She was a dog.

But she knows her name.

The bewilderment she'd feel, never to hear it again,

Allie understood. To wonder who or what *Tweet* was, or whatever a boy would name a dog these days.

The silence was awkward as they crossed the parking lot to the pickup, unlocked and arranged themselves inside, Cassie sitting on the floor at Sean's feet, her head resting on his knees. He clutched the leash in one hand to keep her from lying down and potentially sprawling onto Nolan's foot, and petted her with the other. She gazed up at him with eyes so hopeful, it broke Allie's heart. She had to look away.

She was churning inside anyway, from a dozen causes, so many they tangled together.

I shouldn't have come.

But I did, and I'm adult enough not to hate a sullen teenage boy because he behaved badly. Aren't I?

I am not *Allie, and I resent living my life as someone I'm not.*

Yes, but she'd been Allie almost as long now as she'd been…her first name, the one she couldn't let herself so much as *think,* because clinging to the past led to mistakes. Mistakes that could be fatal. She knew better. It wouldn't matter *that* much to Cassie the dog.

Who says? Has anyone asked her?

Nolan took his hand off the steering wheel and touched her thigh. The touch was light, reassuring—or asking for reassurance. Rigid with so many suppressed emotions, Allie couldn't give it. When he stopped at a red light, she felt his gaze, but pretended to be fascinated by…well, nothing, as the surroundings consisted of empty land with the grass now turning brown, and some industrial structures. A muddy stretch of saltwater slough curved ahead, but wasn't made more interesting by a blue heron or tugboat.

"She's being really good," Nolan said after a time.

Sean's fingers lingered on her long, silky ear. "I think she's scared."

"Nervous, probably."

Allie would have liked to pet the dog, too, who rolled her eyes Allie's way, but she didn't dare. She could hardly wait to be released from this purgatory. She should have gone shopping with Mom, she thought with longing. Only if she had…she'd have spent the whole day wishing she was with Nolan and Sean.

Stupid.

Nolan tried a couple more times to make conversation. Allie said as little as possible. At last, at last, he pulled into her driveway.

"You'll have to let me out," she said politely to Sean.

"Yeah, sure." He opened the door and said with more animation, "Come on, girl." He and Cassie bounded out, the dog immediately beginning to sniff the rhododendrons that edged the sidewalk. Allie followed them, dismayed to see that Nolan, of course, had gotten out, as well. He walked her to the foot of her stairs.

"I'm sorry," he said quietly. "This has been a lousy day for you, and it's my fault."

She took a deep breath. "After we had fun at the zoo, I understand why you thought this might work."

"That was different."

"Yes, it was."

"I'll call, okay?" Worry furrowed his forehead and deepened the blue of his eyes.

She made some noncommittal sound, unable to tell him why she was so upset. She'd get over it. Feeling so rejected was nonsensical, and her extreme upset at the idea of changing the dog's name even more so.

Cassie was investigating the yard with enthusiasm, Sean seeming happy to accompany her.

"He made a good choice," Allie said, nodding their way. Nolan's eyes tracked them. "I think so, too."

If they did change Cassie's name…I'll *call her Cassie anyway,* Allie decided defiantly. *I'll whisper it to her.*

That was assuming she ever saw Cassie—or Sean—again.

"We should get going," Nolan called to Sean, who turned the dog toward the truck.

Allie took a step back just as Nolan took one forward, likely with the intention of kissing her cheek the way he had the other day in the quilt shop, in front of all her customers. They stared at each other, the lines in his forehead even deeper.

"I'll talk to you later," she said, retreating another step, reaching behind her for the stair railing.

He nodded, and finally walked away. She was halfway up when she heard the slam of his door. Nolan being Nolan, he didn't back out until he knew she was safely at the top, her door unlocked.

His truck's powerful engine came to life; before she shut the door, a glance back saw three heads through the windshield. Cassie had been promoted to the seat. The pickup disappeared down the street.

Allie was appalled to realize that, instead of the relief she ought to feel, she was swept with desolation, as if she'd been abandoned. Which was patently ridiculous. Yes, Sean had rejected her today, but it would have been a surprise if he *hadn't,* sooner or later. Even if he'd been Nolan's biological son, at his age he'd have been likely to resent the threat to his central position in his father's life. As it was, he must feel terribly insecure. No, not feel—he *was* insecure. Not that she believed for a minute Nolan wouldn't stick by the boy. Still, his grandmother had died, and the first set of foster parents had rejected him. His mother had abandoned him. Allie couldn't remember what had happened to the dad. Had he died, too? It would be a miracle if Sean *ever* felt secure in any relationship.

With a sigh, she let go of her anger. At least, the part that was directed at him. Nolan, she thought, really shouldn't have pushed.

But the fault had been hers, too. She'd known better. Today's outing had been…too much, too soon. The implication that her relationship with Nolan was going somewhere that necessarily involved Sean had definitely been premature.

She hated the lump she felt in her throat, the yearning that filled her and the hurt. She wanted…she wanted something she didn't know if she dared reach for.

I am not Allie.

Then who am I?

NOLAN HAD A bad feeling that if he called that evening, Allie wouldn't answer. So he didn't, and then wondered if that was a mistake.

He couldn't show up with lunch tomorrow, the way he had been—her shop was closed on Mondays. Fine, then he'd drop in on her at home, he decided, liking the idea—they'd be alone! But that also made him uneasy about his plan. Except for the one time, when she'd wanted Sean to see his quilt, she hadn't invited Nolan in. She might not like it if he appeared out of the blue.

And, crap, he'd been losing a lot of work time lately, too, but right now he didn't care. He had to see her.

The next morning, after Sean shambled out to meet the school bus, Nolan looked down at the dog who sat at his side quivering with anxiety.

"Hey, girl," he said, resting his hand on her sleek head. "It's going to be you and me most every day. Except I can't let you in the workshop. Can't let you run loose yet, either, can I?" Traffic wasn't an issue on their quiet country road, but he had no idea whether she might prove to be a wanderer. For now, he and Sean had to make sure she knew this was home. Plus, they had to give the cats a chance to get used to her, and vice versa. So he strolled around the property with her for fifteen or twenty minutes, then shut her in the house and went to his workshop, followed by one mournful howl and then silence. He'd have liked to leave for Allie's, but she might enjoy sleeping in on her days off.

He had commissioned jobs waiting, but instead he went to the corner where he nearly always was working on a sculpture. This one was different from his usual, the result of an erratic inspiration. It was going to have the kind of detail he'd told Allie he didn't do.

He'd chosen a block of imported green Guatemala marble rather than his more usual granite because it was somewhat softer. He'd given thought to starting with a maquette, which in stone carver's terms was a model. But Nolan much preferred direct carving. He got bored when he, in essence, reproduced his original concept into the large chunk of stone.

His way was sometimes a mistake—the stone might end up having a flaw, or maybe he wouldn't like what he saw taking shape under his hands, or *he* made a mistake that couldn't be corrected—and resulted in him having to discard the stone, or the idea. But surprises were what kept him engaged, transforming an unpromising raw block into something that had existed only in his mind's eye.

He had started this time with a fairly detailed sketch. He wasn't an artist that way—no one would ever want to frame one of his drawings—but he was deft enough with pencil or charcoal and paper to let him see where he was going. Adjust, tinker, crumple up the paper and start over.

Satisfied, he'd begun several weeks earlier, although until recently no one else would have been able to tell *where* he was going.

He used machine tools sparingly in his carving, preferring to work with simple, handheld tools—various tempered-steel chisels, diamond tipped, for granite, a stonemason's hammer and a carpenter's rasp.

He'd roughed out the original form with a circular saw, breaking off chunks with a hammer. That form was a cylinder that reached toward what would be a point at one end were it not embedded in the flat base.

Nolan had roughed out fins at the other end. He'd drawn all over the body of the cylinder, the crude shape of his creatures, then begun trimming the stone between those lines so that the sculpted sea creatures would seem to be crawling over or attaching themselves to his cylinder—which when he was done would be a torpedo.

He concentrated today on the long tentacle of an octopus flung in a strange embrace over the casing of the torpedo, which seemed to have plunged nose-down into the seabed.

He switched between chisels, knowing which would work best, tapping with the hammer to break off bits of marble. He'd laid out an array of them; the marble was hard enough to dull tools frequently and he didn't like to stop to sharpen them until he was ready for a break.

He'd trepanned beneath the tip of the tentacle to give the illusion the suction cups hadn't quite completed the embrace. Creating those cups was possibly the most delicate part of the carving; he was pleasantly surprised by midmorning or so to realize he was satisfied with the effect. The texture left by the chisel blades remained to be smoothed away, but he'd made good progress today.

He didn't usually work for longer than a three- or four-hour stretch on his sculptures. Even though his hands were strong, fatigue could become an issue. As he'd told Allie, these weren't his bread and butter, either. More like a hobby, right now. He'd switch this afternoon to an entirely routine kitchen countertop he'd promised by Thursday.

Cassie was right inside the back door when he stepped into the house. He guessed she'd spent the past hours with her nose pressed to it. Her ecstasy now made him laugh, even though it was sad, too. How long would it take her separation anxiety to wear off? Weeks? Months? Years?

God, how long until *Sean's* wore off? Was this what, in essence, Sean did when Nolan went out with Allie?

He took the dog out for a romp, leaving the leash on the coat hook by the door. Along with food and a collar, Sean had picked out a few toys for Cassie yesterday, after they dropped off Allie.

Nolan threw the rubber ball for her over and over, hoping to wear her out. More good manners on her part—she brought it back each time and dropped it at Nolan's feet. He didn't mind a little slobber, he had to wash his hands anyway.

Tuba, the brown tabby male cat, crouched on the workshop roof and watched with slit-eyed suspicion. Juparana, the girl, was staying out of sight; she'd probably sent her brother on a reconnaissance mission.

Nolan had named both for types of granite—Uba Tuba could be a speckled brownish, like the cat's coat, and some variations of Juparana Champagne were the perfect mix of gray and peach that was, Nolan had learned, a diluted tortoiseshell coloration. Both granites were mined in Brazil, which fit since the cats were, he guessed, littermates.

Tuba vanished before Nolan decided he'd had enough.

Cassie wasn't happy about being abandoned again, but he thought that, even if she didn't know it, she'd be better off in the house than locked in the truck. At least she had water and food there.

He was dismayed when he got to Allie's to find her car not there. He drove down to her shop, parked, peered into the darkened interior and even went around to the alley and knocked, in case she was in the back room. No response.

She could be anywhere. Grocery shopping, going to the bank, visiting a friend… Sitting in his truck, Nolan tried to decide what to do next. Drive around town looking for her car? That smacked of stalking. Grab a bite to eat and then go back to her apartment?

He could do that.

One burger and serving of fries later, he returned to find Allie still hadn't come home. Leave her a note? He didn't have paper in the car, and that was stupid anyway when he could call her cell phone.

Sitting there brooding, his mood was crappy. He couldn't even pin down why he felt such urgency. Sure, she'd been annoyed yesterday, and she should be. He hadn't listened to her caution, and as a result she'd been put in an embarrassing and maybe hurtful position. But she'd understand if they had to slow it down a little, wouldn't she?

He didn't know. Nolan didn't have the slightest damn idea what had been going through her head yesterday, and he didn't like the feeling. His fingers tightened on the steering wheel, flexed. He looked down at them and deliberately loosened them.

Shit, he thought, *I'm in over my head.* He knew better than to dive headfirst like this. He couldn't begin to understand what he'd been thinking. He didn't *know* this woman, and he was already all tangled up over her. And it wasn't all because he wanted her, either. If it had been that simple, he could shrug and figure she wasn't worth the effort. There were a lot of pretty women around.

Not many so graceful, they looked as if in the next step they might become airborne. Not many intrigued by what he did, either, rather than disappointed because he didn't don suit and tie every morning. Not many with the gift of creating beauty, or of displaying delight so transparently.

"Damn it," he muttered, knowing he should go home and get his ass back to work. He'd killed an hour and a half already. He only had a few hours before Sean got home and wondered where he was.

At the sound of a car engine he turned his head and saw a white Corolla coming down the street. Relief, way out of proportion, filled his chest. He watched as the car noticeably hesitated, then turned into the driveway and Allie parked in her customary spot beside the steps.

He got out and went to meet her.

She climbed out, too, and faced him, her eyes wide and wary. "Nolan. I didn't expect to see you today."

"I wanted to talk to you."

"Is this about yesterday? I did understand why Sean acted the way he did, if that's what you meant to talk about."

"No." He frowned. "Yes. Oh, hell. I didn't like things ending the way they did."

Aggravatingly enough, he still couldn't tell what she was thinking.

"Um…you can come up if you'd like," she finally said. "Let me grab my groceries."

"I'll help." She popped her trunk, and he loaded himself down with bags, leaving her to carry only her purse and a small watermelon.

"Thank you," she said over her shoulder.

He stood aside to let her go ahead of him. "You talk to the owners about these steps?"

"Yes, they've had a man come out and take a look. He

agreed with you and they're to be replaced, although I don't know when."

At the top she unlocked her door. With a sense of anticipation—*don't even* think *about her bedroom, that's not why she invited you up*—Nolan followed her inside.

It really was a small space. She hadn't even tried to squeeze a sofa into the living area, which, come to think of it, suggested she didn't often have more than one or two people over at a time. A couple of upholstered chairs, an end table between them, and a television crowded one corner. Otherwise, the quilting frame effectively filled the room.

Beyond it was a galley-style kitchen and the tiniest dining nook he'd ever seen. He wasn't sure he could edge his bigger body around to the other side of the table—and it wasn't a large table. The merest suggestion of a hall led to two half-closed doors—bedroom and bathroom, he presumed. From the kitchen he had a glimpse into the bedroom, where a red-and-white quilt covered a bed. The headboard was lacy and white—iron, maybe? His body tightened, and he concentrated on setting the grocery bags down on the counter without breaking anything.

He ended up leaning a hip against the laminate countertop and watching Allie put away the groceries. She did that, like she did everything else, as if it were a dance. Each turn was a twirl; if she'd worn a skirt instead of jeans, it would have swirled around her legs. No missteps. Her hands were as graceful as her body. No, there was nothing deliberate about it. That was how she moved. It was catlike, he decided, while most people were giraffes or elephants. Ponderous. Nobody had ever accused *him* of grace, that was for sure.

She came to a sudden stop, a jar of olive oil in her hand. "Why are you watching me that way?"

"Because I like watching you." His voice came out rough. *Polish it,* he thought, *don't scare her.* "You looked like you were dancing."

"Dancing?" Her eyes widened with something surprising. Fear? No, it couldn't possibly be. "All I'm doing is putting away groceries."

"You must know that you move differently than most of us clods." He was careful not to move. His posture stayed relaxed. "Have you ever had dance lessons?"

"Oh...yes." She sounded breathless. "When I was little. Don't all little girls imagine themselves as ballerinas?"

"I wouldn't know."

"Didn't your sister?" Allie went on tiptoe and put away the olive oil in a cupboard above the stove. Her body formed an exquisite line. He could sculpt her.... But creative visions were shoved off-line by the sight of her creamy skin when the T-shirt rode up. His fingers tingled, craving the silky, warm sensation of enclosing her waist in his hands.

She gazed at him expectantly. He had to rewind to remember what she'd asked. His sister.

"Uh...no. Anna liked to play in the mud." He knew his face relaxed. "She finger painted—made the most god-awful messes. Anything artsy."

"Play-Doh?"

"Oh, yeah. She did have a horse-crazy phase. Not destined to go much of anywhere when you live in Chicago, but she collected these horse statues, drew horses, ran around the backyard neighing."

"A lot of girls go through that phase, too," Allie said with a laugh.

"Did you?"

"I was the exception. By that time I was way too focused on..." She came to a stop, and there was the expression he didn't understand again. "Oh, other stuff. Not that I wasn't thrilled when one of those horse-crazy girls invited me to her birthday party. We were all taken on a trail ride. The horses were fat and never bestirred themselves from a plod, but still. I'm sure we all imagined ourselves leaping fences in the Grand National."

She was too focused on...what? She didn't want to talk about whatever it was, that was obvious. Family problems? Maybe, he thought, but wasn't convinced.

"Where did you grow up?" he asked casually. "I don't think you've ever said."

She became busy stowing canned goods in a lower cupboard, giving him a nice view of her from behind, which he properly appreciated despite his agenda.

"That's because we moved a lot," she said. "Which is maybe why, when I reached adulthood, I was determined to put down roots."

"Where'd you stay the longest?"

He couldn't see her face. She was reaching into another grocery bag. "Oh...Florida, I suppose. Near Tampa. Actually a little south. I wish I could tell you I learned to surf, but I was too young."

"Did you tan?"

"Did I what?" She looked startled.

"Your skin is so white. I wondered if you *can* tan."

"Actually...no." Allie wrinkled her nose. "I burn. It's really annoying, given that I'm dark-haired and not a redhead or blonde."

"You must have gotten the coloring from one of your parents. Your mom?"

"No, she is a blonde, and tans just fine, thank you." Her voice had eased, Nolan was interested to note. She didn't mind talking about her mother.

"Your father?"

"Oh—brown-haired, sort of hazel eyes. I guess I get

that from him." She gave a one-sided shrug. "His mother was Eastern European. Romanian, I think. I guess that's where my coloring came from."

Without conscious effort, an image of Nadia Comaneci, the famous Romanian gymnast, rose before his mind's eye. During the last Olympic Games, the network had featured her, showed some snippets of her gold-medal-winning performances. Logical that mention of Romania had triggered her picture. He'd been captivated by huge, haunting dark eyes. Allie, he realized, had that same quality, shyness maybe, or something else. And then there was the grace. Arrested, he wondered: Could she have been a gymnast? But why wouldn't she say, if so?

"You're beautiful." He had to clear his throat. Yeah, way to blurt it out. "I don't know if I've said that, but you are."

"I... Thank you." In the first awkward movement he'd seen, she balled grocery bags in her hands and shoved them in a drawer. When she straightened, her eyes met his. "What did you come by to say?"

He had to think about it. "I'm not sure I came by to really say anything," he finally confessed. "I wanted to see you. Make sure you weren't too mad at me."

She crossed her arms. The pose might have looked negligent if the clasp hadn't been so tight; she seemed to be hugging herself. "I'm not mad. Just, um..."

Having second thoughts. Damn it. He'd known.

"Just?" he prodded.

"Not sure this—" she wagged her fingers, presumably encompassing the two of them "—is such a good idea. I mean, I like you, Nolan, but Sean surely needs to be your priority right now."

"To the point where I can't have friends? Date?"

"Obviously he sees me as a threat."

"Yeah, I guess he does. The thing is, I don't think it's

only due to his circumstances. If he was my biological kid, with me since he came into this world, he'd likely be manning the castle wall the same way. Kids do that. They like having undivided attention. Hell, we don't change that much as adults, maybe especially where our parents are concerned."

He could see she wanted to argue but couldn't.

"Think about it," Nolan urged. "What if your mother started to date now? Wouldn't your first impulse be defensive?"

"No! I'd be happy for her." A struggle showed on her face. "All right, I'd probably feel funny about it. Maybe... more protective of her than anything."

"Yeah?"

Her eyebrows knit. "I suppose...any time two people are used to coming first with each other, there's some... tension when that changes."

He nodded. "My point. It's something you work out. A parent doesn't decide never to date again, because it upsets his kid. Especially since, in the long run..." Whoa. In the long run? He wasn't *thinking* long run. Not yet. Or at least—he hadn't known he was.

She looked skittish, too.

"I want to keep seeing you, Allie." He felt raw; tried to sound no more than blunt. "We can take it slow where Sean is concerned. But don't write me off because I have a fourteen-year-old foster son who is running scared and can be a butt."

"I wouldn't do that." Allie's expression was startlingly vulnerable when she looked at him. "I suppose I was conflicted anyway. I'm...I suppose, shy. I don't make friends easily. It's been an awfully long time since I had any kind of serious relationship."

Or sex? Did she include sex in that?

"It has been for me, too." He scrubbed a hand over his chin. "I've always been a loner. You've made me...not want to be."

Her eyes noticeably widened, dilated. Her lips parted as they stared at each other. "Me, too," she whispered.

Nolan groaned, shoved off from the counter and took her in his arms.

CHAPTER SIX

IF NOLAN HAD kissed her any way but tenderly, Allie might have been able to resist. As it was, his arms wrapped her tight, but his lips were exquisitely gentle. Demands frightened her, but this was a "please." *Please feel the same way I do. Please don't say no.*

She did. She couldn't.

His big hands were so careful, as they moved over her back and hips, one settling on her nape, the other continuing to rove and knead, sample, tempt. Her arms circled his neck and she rose on tiptoe to fit against him better. To hang on, too. Her legs didn't feel as reliable as usual.

The kiss gradually deepened. His tongue was in her mouth, not thrusting hard but stroking. She sucked on it, and felt his big body jolt. With a groan, he half lifted her and his hips rocked against hers. Heat rocketed through her. So much, so fast.

He tore his mouth from hers. "Allie." He sounded shaken, his voice rough. "If you don't want this, tell me now."

Old fears knocked for attention, but she seemed helpless to stop herself from rubbing against him. And she *wanted* this. She wanted him.

"I'm not on birth control." Kill the mood, that would do it.

A nerve jumped in his cheek. "I've been carrying a couple of condoms since the first time I kissed you."

"I do want you." Then, "Please."

"God." Relief transformed his face before he bent his head and rested his forehead against hers. "Your bedroom."

"Yes," she whispered.

He took her hand and led her, as if she didn't know the way. She saw his gaze sweep over the room and was momentarily self-conscious. There was more of *her* in this room than anywhere else in her life. No one else had ever been in it. She'd always thought she'd have time to tuck away her few keepsakes. Panic had barely stirred when his glittering blue eyes locked onto hers again.

"Pretty," he said thickly.

Her bedroom?

"Let me pull back the quilt."

She flushed, but was grateful. Sex could be…messy.

"Hearts and Gizzards."

Nolan stopped, still gripping the covers. "What?"

Her cheeks were probably blazing now. "I… That's what the pattern is called. This is…" Why would he *care?* Oh, she was making an idiot of herself, she knew she was. "It's the first quilt I made that truly satisfied me."

She saw him look more closely.

"It's beautiful," he said, voice gruff. "Everything you make is beautiful."

"It was the quality of the piecing and quilting that…" Allie stopped. "Why am I talking about a quilt?"

He laughed and tugged her up against him. "Because you're nervous?" He seemed to think about that. "I guess I am, too. But why are you?"

"It's been a long time. And I wasn't very good at sex. Or something…" She trailed off, her humiliation growing.

"Not good at it?" He cocked his head. "You mean you didn't enjoy it?"

"It was…okay." She'd only gotten this far with a couple

of boyfriends over the years, one in college, and one a year or two after she'd graduated.

She suspected she'd gone to bed with them because of social pressure. A relationship reached a certain point, that's what you did. Only, she'd been dating as much to be normal as because she actually felt anything special for either guy. She had never really and truly *wanted* a man before, not with this heat that curled inside her, weak knees, shaky certainty.

His mouth had a wry quirk. "I can't claim to be the world's greatest lover. I've had a few girlfriends over the years, but that's all—a few. I'd like to promise you a sublime experience, but, uh, if it's all in technique, I don't know if I can."

Now she'd killed the mood. And she quite desperately didn't want him to retreat.

"I'm sort of guessing satisfaction isn't about technique," she said, still probably blushing. With her skin tone, she did that well. "Maybe it's about how you feel about someone."

"Well, it could be a combination." He swallowed. "If it's anything about what *I* feel, maybe I can promise sublime."

Allie released a huge breath. "I've never felt like this before."

He said something under his breath, fervent, almost harsh, and then was kissing her again, and it didn't matter that they'd stopped to talk about quilt patterns or previous sexual experience. Nothing mattered but touching him and being touched by him, the hard beat of his heart beneath her hand and the dizzying speed of her own pulse.

He lifted his mouth from hers long enough to peel her T-shirt over her head and make a sound of pleasure. Her hands slid under the hem of his T, finding warm, hard flesh and smooth skin until they encountered soft chest hair. Impatient, she was the one to pull back so she could divest him of his shirt. He took the opportunity to undo her bra hook and slide the straps from her shoulders.

"Beautiful," he murmured, although her self-consciousness returned. She had rather small breasts. In fact, none of her curves were all that inspiring. *Subtle* was the best that could be said about them.

Her shoulders hunched. "I'm not very…"

"You're gorgeous." His hands enclosed her breasts, and ever so gently rotated, sensitizing her nipples.

Allie closed her eyes, lost in the extraordinary sensation. There he was again, being so *careful,* and yet his tough calluses scraped her skin and sent a rush of heat arrowing between her legs. A sound escaped her, a moan or even a whimper.

Nolan said something rough and shaken, then lifted her and laid her back on the bed. She heard her sandals hit the floor. His knee came down between hers, and he bent to place his mouth where his hands had been. He kissed and licked and nuzzled before suckling her. Allie was groaning nonstop now, arching to make herself more accessible to him.

He eventually tore himself away from her breasts long enough to strip Allie of her jeans and panties. As he surveyed her, dark color streaked his cheekbones. She was stunned to see that he'd meant it when he said she was beautiful. The way he looked at her almost made her believe she was.

Suddenly she wanted to see him, too. As she reached for the button of his jeans, Allie had a flash of memory: being an almost-teenager and feeling enormously curious about the bulges—some more substantial than others—outlined so conspicuously by the leotards that the male dancers wore. Her father was modest enough that she'd never even caught a glimpse of him without clothes on.

She'd seen her brother naked, but only when they were young. She couldn't quite picture how what *he* had down there could have metamorphosed into anything that…large.

A giggle bubbled in her chest now, a little like champagne fizzing on its way down. The fact that she hadn't wanted to look closely at male genitals the other times she'd had sex should have been her first clue that something was wrong. Because she very definitely *did* want to see now.

Stripping him wasn't as easy as stripping her had been, though. The hard ridge beneath his zipper made pulling it down potentially perilous. His face contorted a couple of times while she oh-so-carefully proceeded, and he made some interesting sounds, too. Her apprehension faded when she realized the sounds expressed pleasure, not distress.

Her eyes widened at what she found when she pulled his underwear down. He lifted his hips to cooperate when Allie tugged jeans and briefs all the way off before she crawled back up to…explore.

His size was daunting. Until now, it hadn't occurred to her that their relative sizes mattered. She'd liked feeling petite, dwarfed by his powerful body. But now… Her fingers couldn't close around him, and she raised alarmed eyes to his face.

He lifted his head. "You look freaked."

"Is this going to hurt?"

"What?" He looked stunned. "No! Why would…? You're not a virgin?" Now, *he* sounded alarmed.

"No, but…I think maybe those guys weren't so big. And *I'm* not very big." Her voice wasn't, either. It was shrinking into nothingness before she finished.

Nolan's head dropped to the mattress and he gave a choked laugh. "Damn it, Allie. No one has ever said… I'm not huge, you know. You're just small."

"I know that," she said indignantly.

"We'll fit." He reared up and cupped her face, the curve of his mouth tender. "I can promise that much." He kissed her gently, nibbling at her lips.

She closed her eyes and let him wash away her fear. Not all her fears, nobody could do that, but *this* one, yes.

The next thing she knew, she was on her back, and he was kissing her passionately and stroking one calloused finger between her thighs, where she was wet and aching. She was utterly lost from that point on; she surfaced only long enough to be aware he'd torn open the package and was putting on the condom. She had to watch that, in fascination. A part of her wished he didn't have to wear one.

If we stay together, I could get a patch, or go on the pill, and he wouldn't have to.

The memories of those questions he'd asked in the kitchen, wanting to know about her mother, her father, where she'd lived, *everything,* flickered through her mind, and her heart contracted with a different fear that was more real. If this went on, she'd get more and more muddled, more unsure of what she could say and what she couldn't... and what she'd *already* said.

But he was back, touching her again, kissing her, his weight half on his elbows as he nudged between her legs and she couldn't help lifting her hips in pleasure and welcome, letting apprehension about the future go.

He eased barely in, then out, and an outraged cry slipped from her lips. He might have laughed, she wasn't sure, but the next time he pressed deeper, another inch or two, before retreating. By the time he slid home, she was begging him, had one leg hooked over his and the other foot braced on the mattress so she could lift to take him as deep as he could go.

They found a rhythm that felt both amazing and familiar. And so good. She coiled tighter and tighter as he thrust harder. His eyes held hers when she broke, spasming around him, clutching him with her entire body. His teeth gritted and he let himself go, too. He bucked against her, pulsing inside her, which seemed to prolong her pleasure.

At long last he sagged, barely catching himself on his elbows, then rolled to the side, taking her with him.

Allie cuddled close, grateful for his strong arm wrapped around her. His heart slammed under her cheek, and she felt more shaken than she could ever remember being. *I had no idea,* she thought in astonishment.

His breathing gradually slowed. She felt the moment when he lifted his head enough to kiss the top of her head.

"We fit." There was a smile in his voice.

The earlier giggles must have been trapped in there, because they popped out now. She clapped a hand over her mouth.

"Should I be insulted?" Nolan asked in mock indignation.

"No! No. I was just thinking…it *was* sublime." A rush of shyness overcame her. "At least, it was for me."

"Me, too." This time his voice was deep, slow and filled with some emotion that confounded her. "I don't think that was sex, Allie."

"What?" She separated herself from him enough to be able to see his face.

His eyes were different now, the same dark blue but more solemn, watchful. "That was making love. I don't think I've ever done it before."

Oh, dear God. A huge, painful lump caught in her throat and she stared at him. Was he saying he *loved* her?

But he didn't, the Allie who wasn't Allie protested. He couldn't. He didn't really know her. No one did. But if he *thought* he loved her…

What do I *feel?*

That was the scariest realization of all, because she had a very bad feeling she wanted him to love her. She thought he was the first and only man she'd ever met whom she could love.

But could she trust him? Was she allowed ever to trust anyone?

Her skin seemed to be cooling at shocking speed and she shivered.

Nolan sighed and tucked her back in his embrace, where she couldn't be anything but warm. He didn't say anything else.

NOLAN HADN'T GOTTEN half an hour's work done when he glimpsed movement out of the corner of his eye. He loosened his fingers to silence the saw.

Sean stopped in the open doorway, Cassie trying to shove past him. He said something Nolan couldn't hear.

He lifted the ear protectors from his head and pushed up the goggles, rubbing with his forearm at the deep creases they left.

"You're here," Sean said. Or repeated?

Nolan had the impulse to wince, and suppressed it. "Where else would I be?" he asked mildly. He'd be fine as long as he didn't start grinning. He wasn't sure he'd be able to stop, not with his body feeling so replete.

"I thought… Nothing." His face brightened. "Cassie was waiting at the door."

The dog's tail lashed happily at the sound of her name.

"I'm afraid she spent all day there. I've taken her out several times, though."

"Oh. That's cool. Did you let her off the leash?"

"Yeah, threw the ball for her. She was good."

"Cool," he said again.

Nolan waited through several twitches and the beginnings of a squirm. "You need something?"

"No, I just wanted to tell you… But it's no biggie." He started to retreat.

"I'm already stopped. Tell me."

"Oh. Well, see, there's this meeting tomorrow night. At school." He was apparently checking for parental comprehension. Nolan nodded encouragement. "It's about basketball. The coach wants to talk to parents of freshmen before they go out for the team."

"What time?"

"Seven."

"Good." He grinned. "I'm glad you decided to try out."

"You weren't planning to, I don't know, see Allie tomorrow night, were you?" Sean asked in a rush.

"No."

"Oh. I mean, it's okay if you can't…"

"I said fine. We'll talk about it over dinner." He pulled down and adjusted his goggles. "I need to get back to work now."

Sean watched him for a minute even as he donned the ear protection again and picked up the circular saw with the electroplated diamond blade, necessary to cut granite.

With a good grip on the handle, Nolan gently began, letting the blade do the cutting. When his mind tried to summon the picture of Allie sprawled on her bed, her slender, lithe body naked, he ruthlessly shut it down. This work was too dangerous to allow himself to daydream.

He kept going until later than usual, trying to make up for the midday interlude. Even so, he was far from satisfied with what he'd accomplished when he finished. Usually he'd have been frustrated, but today… Nope, no regrets. Cleaning the guts of the saw with compressed air, then running it briefly to release more debris, he was grinning foolishly and damn glad Sean wasn't here to see.

CHLOE KICKED AT the sand with her bare feet. The soles of her feet were baking, so she veered toward the incoming waves, grateful for the cool, wet, hard-packed sand left behind by swirls of foam. She didn't want to *be* here. Resentment sizzled. Her parents could have left her in New York. Nobody cared if she was here. She couldn't afford to miss two whole weeks of dance classes and rehearsals. While she was plodding along, the other girls were soaring.

And there they were, first dashing away from a wave then soaring above the beach and foamy fingers of water, bodies perfectly positioned. Jessica doing an exquisite cabriole, Rachel a *grand jeté*. They were both making harsh, cawing sounds, which seemed normal even as Chloe glowered at them. What made her maddest was that they didn't fall back to earth as they should have.

And…there was Hunter, too, the absolute hottest male dancer who was once in a while called in to demonstrate lifts to the younger girls. He was performing the *tour en l'air,* leaping straight into the air and making not only one complete turn, but two, three, four, an impossible five, and still *he* didn't come down, either, even though part of the jump was the finish in the fifth position.

Chloe refused to look at them anymore, although as she stalked away, she could still hear them calling to each other in those harsh voices, as if they'd found something disgusting to eat, like a dead fish or something. Or maybe they were laughing at her.

Madder and madder, she broke into a trot then started to run. She kicked one leg in the air and leaped into a jeté, then another and another, ending in the *grand jeté* that required her to do the splits in the air. But she couldn't defy gravity, no matter how high she leaped. It tugged her down, and she landed *hard* on the wet sand.

I hate Mom and Dad. I hate them. If all they'd wanted to do was argue about…whatever it was Mom had to decide, why had they insisted she and Jason come?

Hate them, hate them, hate them… Her rage beat like every stomp of her feet, getting harsher and harsher until *it* became the unmusical cries of the seagulls, and, disoriented, she rolled over in bed and hammered at her alarm clock.

Even once Allie had silenced it, she kept hearing the ugly sound. *Caw, caw, hate them, caw, hate them.* With a moan, she covered her face with her hands.

Dreams usually faded the moment she opened her eyes, leaving behind wisps of mood that could color her day, but not images so clear they hurt. She'd never seen Rachel or Jessica again. Or Hunter, for whom she'd nursed a thirteen-year-old's desperate crush.

She had never truly danced again, either, because that was how people were traced, she and her family had been told. To be safe, they couldn't hold the same kind of jobs, or pursue hobbies that were too unusual or that had resulted in any of them being in the public eye. Nobody had quite looked at her when the U.S. Marshal said that, although he was talking about her, and they all knew it.

Already there had been half a dozen newspaper articles about her as a rising young dancer. Even among the many talented girls in the American Ballet Theatre's Jacqueline Kennedy Onassis School program, Chloe Marr had stood out. *The Daily News* had done a big spread, the reporter having followed her through a typical week. A role in *Firebird* had resulted in a feature on television.

Her parents had explained to her that, if a young dancer of her talent and training should suddenly appear elsewhere in the country, it would draw attention. Someone would recognize her. They were very sorry, but she had to give up dance.

Only for *now,* her mother had hastened to add, although her eyes didn't want to meet Chloe's. Once the trial was over, well, it might be possible…

"But dance is my *life,*" she had cried, and begged to be left behind. She could live with the family of one of the other dancers, or Grandma. She was sure she could. "I won't go!" she had tried storming, and her father's expression had cracked to show real anguish, but Mom's was only set and white.

"You have to. If it's at all possible, later…"

But Chloe had known perfectly well that "possible" was a lie. Months or years lost in a young dancer's training and experience were gone forever, never to be regained.

As things turned out, that later never came anyway. Chloe Marr had died when the entire Marr family fled in the night. Allie hadn't even dreamed about her, not in a long time.

Dragging herself out of bed, showering until the hot water ran lukewarm, getting dressed, she felt stiff and every movement mechanical. She was unable to escape the residue of the dream, weighing her down like a hangover.

It was telling Nolan she'd lived in Florida that had done it, even though she never exactly had. But Dad's parents did, and her family had gone there so often for family vacations, it had just slipped out even though that wasn't Allie Wright's background. Allie Wright had lived in Montana and Colorado and Idaho, never staying long enough in any place to develop any sense of belonging. That's what getting flustered did to her. It made her open her mouth and say something careless and stupid. It was exactly what scared her mother. *I'm lucky,* Allie thought, *that people hardly ever ask.*

"Did you graduate from high school around here?" They asked that, or where she'd gotten her college degree. But not since she was seventeen, a senior in high school who'd had to transfer midyear, had anyone cared where she came from. Back then, the newest lies were memorized fresh, and teenagers weren't really that interested in anyone but themselves anyway. They didn't *push,* not the way Nolan had. Would keep doing.

Telling him about Florida wasn't that big a deal. Lots of people had lived there at some point in their lives, and at least she really had been there.

What had most paralyzed her was the fear that she'd run into someone who had actually lived in one of the places she was pretending she'd come from. Or that she'd get her stories tangled.

She'd been sure she would, even after her family's first move, when there had only been the one new background to memorize and recite when required. That easily, she'd been made nearly mute from panic. It only got worse after they were wrenched away again, and she had yet another new name and completely different story to recall.

Well, she'd had other issues then, too, like losing Dad and Jason and what pretense of a life they had built after giving up their *real* lives.

I am all tangled up inside, she thought miserably, picturing what happened to three delicate silver or gold chains, stored loose in a box for too long. Seemingly all by themselves, lying loose, nobody moving that box, they still somehow wound together in a confounding snarl that defied the deftest of fingers. *That's me. The three of me, intertwined and knotted. And...I don't know what would happen if I could be untangled, separated into three. There*

*is Chloe, there's Laura, there's Allie. What would hap-
pen to* me?

Wow. Split personality, anyone?

No, she knew better. She *couldn't* be separated into
three. That was her trouble, at its heart. She had spent
eleven years now trying to live as Allie alone, and she
couldn't. Not really. But recovering all of her, even privately, could be dangerous.

Her parents' voices whispered in her ear, so stern. *We're
starting all over. You can't ever forget our new names.
Never, never, never tell anyone who we used to be. Remember. Never.*

The dream, she decided, was like a crack in a dike. A
trickle had made it through. How to keep it from becoming a stream and then a flood?

The easy answer was: cut Nolan out of her life. This was
his fault. And hers, for not listening to her mother. For not
keeping to herself, the way she always had.

Allie checked the clock, and saw that she had to leave if
she was to open the store on time. *That* was safe enough.
Unless Nolan stopped by with lunch today, of course. But
surely he wouldn't, when he'd seen her yesterday and lost
so much time on his work.

Not only seen her—made love to her. *I don't think that
was sex, Allie.*

She didn't think it was, either. And she didn't want to
live without whatever it had been. Without Nolan. Because
she saw suddenly that all her efforts to piece and layer and
stitch together a past, a self, accomplished absolutely nothing if she didn't have a future. If she never married, had
children, grandchildren, great-grandchildren. What was
she staying safe *for* if not for that?

By halfway through the day, Allie had let go of most
of the strain, although a headache lingered. She'd been

indulging in melodrama, she concluded. What did it matter where she'd lived as a kid, or gone to middle school? So she'd had different names. There were cultures where people acquired different names for each phase of their life. She could think of it that way. Some of the names were secret, that's all.

Chloe was the child, the dancer, Laura the muddled teenager, Allie the adult. *They are all me; I am them.* Telling forbidden truths wouldn't make that any more so. It wasn't as if she couldn't talk about childhood experiences. The time she'd fallen from the monkey bars at school and broken her arm, Nanna's snowflakes, Lady the family beagle and, yes, her lost dream of being a ballerina. All she would have to do was…edit. *No, we never, never, never lived in Queens, and all I did was take dance lessons like many thousands of other girls my age, and did anybody care who Laura Nelson, tongue-tied, had been, except that it was Laura who had discovered quilting?* And that went to show how silly she'd been, didn't it, because that meant Laura and Allie were certainly integrated.

That calmed her, as she chatted with Libby Hutchins, an occasional customer. "Yes," she said, "we're displaying miniature quilts starting on the fifteenth. Do come see them. They're all gorgeous, and some are really extraordinary. Marybeth Winters—do you know her?—made the most astonishing basket quilt with appliqué flowers. The blocks are only three inches square. You almost have to use a magnifying glass to appreciate the detail."

Libby, who was starting a crib quilt for her first grandchild, promised to stop by.

Allie's mini-quilt shows, one a quarter, were a big draw. Customers loved having their own quilts featured.

Sometimes she chose to show quilts all using the same pattern in multiple variations, perhaps tied into a class held at the same time. Last spring, the local historical society had been delighted to have a chance to show off quilts of the 1920s from their collection, and they were talking about a turn-of-the-century display next spring.

Once the bell tinkled as Libby departed, Allie climbed back on the ladder to finish hanging one of her own quilts to replace the Feathered Star quilt just sold. She had made this one right before the Lady of the Lake that was on the frame in back. This was one of her favorite patterns, Bear's Paw, done in subtle shades of cream and rust and rose. At last she put away the ladder and stood back to admire the full effect. Oh, yes, very nice—and nicely coincidental that the fabrics for sale below it were the complementary browns shading into rusts and then peaches and pinks.

She was pleasantly surprised to realize her headache was gone. She was even able to laugh, a little, at last night's dream. Rachel and Jessica, with the ugly voices of seagulls... *Hah! Maybe I didn't like them as much as I thought I did.*

Smiling, she decided to measure out and cut the deep purple fabric she intended to use to bind the Lady of the Lake quilt, which was nearing completion. And then—oh!—she'd have the fun of creating something new. She'd had a sort of vision of what she could do with Wild Goose Chase, which wouldn't really be a chase at all....

CHAPTER SEVEN

THE MEETING SET UP by the coach to talk to prospective basketball players and their parents turned out to be a casual affair, held in the school library. The parents appeared relaxed, the boys less so. Nolan could see why from the minute they walked in.

Upwards of twenty boys had showed up, and there might be a few more whose parents couldn't make it tonight, or who would decide later to try out for the team. And these were only the freshmen or sophomores taking a first shot at the team. It didn't count the returning varsity or junior varsity players.

In other words, likely not every kid here tonight would make the team. Which resulted in the boys all eyeing each other sidelong in silent appraisal. The parents were probably all doing the same, if more subtly. Nobody wanted to think, *My boy won't make the cut.*

Nolan was amused to find himself as anxious as any other parent. He didn't have to worry, he decided; if nothing else, Sean was the tallest boy here. Given another year, he'd pass Nolan in height, and showed promise of indeed being tall enough to lead the West Fork team as forward or even center by the time he was a junior or senior. The other boys here all had that same gawky way of moving, too, so that wasn't a hindrance.

The coach was encouraging and discouraging by turn. He made clear that he expected complete dedication to the sport once the season opened. No smoking, no drinking, no drugs, no missed practices unless they were mighty sick. No fights, minimum C-average. If a boy violated any of the restrictions, he was off the team, no recourse. He looked from one face to the next to be sure every boy here was taking him seriously. Then he talked to the parents about their share of the commitment, and checked to be sure they were listening, too.

Tryouts were mid-October, practice started late in October, except for the boys who were also playing football and who had to juggle practices.

"I make a practice of urging students not to try to play both sports," he told them. "You can't give the same level of commitment or performance if you are. We allow it, though, especially at the JV level. It's one way to find your sport."

He was frank that some of the boys wouldn't make it. "All of you," he said, "will put on height or muscle or speed or just determination over the next year, so if you don't make it this year, try again."

When the meeting broke up, he went around shaking hands and talking to as many boys and their parents as possible.

"Glad to see you've decided to try out," he said, assessing Sean. "I had my eye on you and planned to talk to you these next few weeks if you didn't show up tonight."

"Really?" Sean's voice squeaked, which brought mortified color to his face.

"You look like a basketball player to me." The coach nodded and moved on.

"Because he thinks I'm going to be tall," Sean burst out, once he and Nolan were crossing the sodium-lamp-lit parking lot.

"I think it might be more than that. You're going to be a good athlete."

Sean didn't say anything else until they were closed in the pickup. "You really think so?" he asked then.

"I do." Nolan turned the key in the ignition and the engine roared to life. "Let's plan to get that hoop up this weekend."

He'd ordered one online and expected it to arrive before the end of the week. He sometimes had to remind himself to involve Sean in his everyday repairs and projects, but because he persisted he could already see an improvement in his foster son's competency and confidence.

Too bad he wasn't as enthusiastic about cooking, despite his vast appetite, Nolan thought drily.

"Are you going out this week?" Sean asked, ultra-casually.

Nolan cast him a glance. "Don't know."

They got nearly home before Sean cleared his throat. "I guess Allie is mad at me."

Nolan tried to read the tone. Shame? Repentance? Secret glee?

"I think she understood," he said noncommittally.

"Is she mad at you?" the boy asked, in a smaller voice.

Was this one definitely contrite, or hopeful?

Nolan put on the turn signal even though there was no other traffic this time of night on the country road. "I guess she was," he agreed.

"Oh."

They pulled up front of the house. Nolan locked the pickup and started for the house, Sean trailing him. Nolan stopped and waited; whenever the boy lagged behind that way, Nolan always pictured him with his last foster dad.

They walked the last few feet side by side, but Sean balked at the foot of the porch steps. "Did I wreck things?"

Nolan hesitated, picking over his possible responses before settling on one. "Did you? No. Did we? It was a close thing. But don't try to take all the responsibility, Sean. I shouldn't have invited her."

"I don't even know why I acted that way," he mumbled.

Nolan smiled and clapped him on the back. "Sure you do. But it's nothing to brood about, all right?"

"Maybe it would be okay if we did something with her this Sunday."

Nolan raised an eyebrow. Well, well. Did he mean it?

"We'll see," he temporized, unlocking the door. Cassie exploded through it in a frenzy of body-wriggling delight. "Now go on, give her some time outside before you start getting ready for bed."

The happy dog diverted him from his grumbles. Nolan was smiling as he went to the kitchen to set up the coffeemaker.

He wondered what Allie would say if he invited her someplace this Sunday in company with Sean. Good idea, or bad?

ALLIE HAD ALREADY spent an obscene amount of money by the time she and her mother took a break for lunch at the Grill in the flagship Nordstrom store. She was glad to plunk down her bags and peruse the menu.

Once they ordered, a honey lime chicken ciabatta for her and halibut with fresh market veggies for her mother, Allie took a sip of iced tea. "You haven't bought much yet."

Mom made a face. "I think it's too hot today to get excited about cold-weather clothes."

"You mean, we have to do this all over again a month from now?"

Her mother laughed. "That's such a hardship?"

No, the hardship was having had to say "no" to Nolan,

who had taken it in good part but sounded disappointed. Surprised, too. Common feminine wisdom would suggest that she needed to say no to him occasionally. Only…she missed him.

"Of course not. You probably have friends you could go with, too."

"You know you're always my first choice," her mother said comfortably.

Mom had always been Allie's, too. She'd never seen anything wrong with being best friends with her mother. In fact, she'd believed she was lucky. Only lately had she begun to wonder.

"I've been thinking," she said. "About…oh, when I was little, I guess."

Only the slight deepening of some lines on her mother's face suggested this wasn't a welcome subject. "What have you been thinking?"

"I told you I went with Nolan and Sean to pick out a dog last weekend, right? That got me to remembering Lady."

Mom's expression eased at that. "I don't know what possessed us to choose a beagle when we had such a small yard. We should have gotten a tiny dog. Or a lazy one."

"Dad used to get so mad when she disappeared."

They both laughed, remembering the way he'd fumed to hide his worry. The whole family would spread out, walking city blocks calling Lady's name. She always seemed surprised when one of them appeared so far from home.

Usually Allie's mother blocked any talk about the past. *We've eased into it, good.* "And Nanna," Allie continued. "Does it bother you that, well, you weren't there when she died?"

Now Mom's face froze. "What do you think? Of course it bothers me!" As if aware of how her voice had risen, she scanned their fellow diners, none of whom appeared to be paying any attention to them. "Why would you ask something like that?"

"Because I've forgotten so much. I wish…I wish we'd kept more, to remember people by." She wished for more than that, but knew she couldn't say so.

"Oh, things," her mother said dismissively. "You always did like to collect mementos."

"Did I?"

"Every vacation, you'd insist on hauling home shells or pebbles and piles of brochures. Do you remember pressing flowers and leaves? You told me you wanted to keep the smells." Her mouth curved reminiscently. "You were so disappointed when you discovered that dried flowers and leaves lost their scent."

The memory of eagerly pressing flowers between the pages of a fat book, then piling a dozen other equally fat books atop, came to her as if it had been yesterday. And the dry, faded result. She'd lifted the book after she opened it and inhaled deeply, but caught only the hint of the smell she sought, or it might have been the memory of it.

I do remember, Allie thought with astonishment. She'd had a huge bulletin board over her bed, crowded with photos and bits and pieces of this and that. Postcards from places they'd been, a sand dollar that *had* smelled for a long time—quite unpleasantly, but still. Worn-out dance shoes, programs from recitals and performances, Lady's collar after she had died in her sleep one night. Notes friends passed at school. A picture of Hunter surreptitiously taken and tucked beneath a brochure from a Catskill resort where the Marr family once vacationed, so that her brother didn't see it and tease her mercilessly.

It had all been left behind.

She'd tried to begin again, after that first move when she had become Laura Nelson. But making friends wasn't easy, and there was no dance, and no Lady, and no Nanna, or Grandmother and Grandfather in Florida, either. Letters and birthday cards from them were forwarded, but they had to be so careful when they wrote back. And if there had been vacations...well, she didn't remember them. Their house had been so silent, her parents maneuvering around each other in brittle silence. The tension had grown and grown until Dad moved out. Her parents' marriage, Allie had always believed, was a casualty of the decision Mom had made and Dad had opposed—the one that ended with the whole family having to go into the Witness Security Program.

"I remember that," Allie murmured now, then saw that their food was being delivered. "We had time to go to Florida," she said once the waitress left. "Why didn't we have time to pack more?"

Mom looked at her with something like anger. "How could we disappear quietly if everything we owned had to be loaded into a moving truck? You understood then."

"No." Allie met her eyes. "No, I didn't. I didn't understand anything that was happening."

"Well, *this* certainly isn't the place to talk about it." Her mother's body was rigid.

Allie hadn't tried to discuss the past in a long time, but today she felt stubborn. "You never want to talk about it."

"What good does it do? I did the right thing. We all knew it required a sacrifice on all our parts. The best we can do is move on, not dwell on what can't be changed. You know that's what I believe."

"There's a difference," Allie said quietly, "between not dwelling and pretending a huge part of our lives never happened." Not pretending—forgetting. The difference expanded in her head. How had she been so blind? "We didn't leave everything behind because we couldn't take it. You didn't *want* us to remember, did you?"

"You were teenagers, both of you. Jason was chafing to get out on his own, you were furious at having to move. Your father and I agreed that we all needed to look ahead, not behind."

"Did he agree?" Allie asked, shocking herself. "Or did you not give him any choice, either?"

Her mother's face pinched. "You're still that bitter?" she whispered.

Allie closed her eyes. What was this gaining either of them? The past *was* past. How wrong would it have been to let a murderer walk, when Mom's testimony could convict him? That's what Dad had wanted her to do, Allie knew, but despite all Allie's grief and, yes, bitterness, she'd also admired her mother for following her conscience. So now what was she trying to say? *You should have put us first, and to hell with your conscience?*

She let out a ragged breath and reached across the table for her mother's hand, which had a tremor. "No. No, I swear I'm not, Mom. Just…confused sometimes. It's scary how much I've forgotten."

Mom's anguished gaze met hers. "Oh, sweetheart. I'm so sorry."

She had to let this go. "I didn't mean to upset you. I've just been thinking more than usual, that's all."

Mom's shoulders sagged slightly with relief. She reached for her iced tea, and froze. "You haven't said anything, have you? To Nolan?"

"No!" *Never, never, never.*

"No. Of course." Her mother relaxed again. "I shouldn't have even asked."

"It's okay." Allie forced a smile. "I'm the one who is sorry. We were having such a good time."

"Don't be silly. I want you to feel free to talk to me anytime, about anything." She reached for her fork at last. "Once we've eaten, what do you say we walk over to Coldwater Creek next? And stop at any shops on the way that appeal to us."

"Sounds good," Allie lied. "I need to drop these bags off at the car first, though. Maybe we can separate and set up a rendezvous."

They agreed, and, walking the opposite direction her mother went when they left Nordstrom, Allie was glad to be alone for a few minutes. She, who was never mad at her mother, felt as sulky as Sean had last Sunday.

Because a rebellious part of her knew damn well her mother didn't really want Allie to talk to her, not when the subject was the past. What she also truly didn't want was Allie ever talking to anyone else about it—ever. And for the very first time, Allie wondered whether that was really because of potential danger, or whether there were other reasons altogether to explain why her mom still held on so tight to her daughter.

NOLAN PARKED BEHIND Allie's Corolla and sat for a moment looking up at her apartment.

Sunday had been a crappy day for him, although he'd tried to hide how he felt from Sean. The only place they went was grocery shopping. Otherwise, they played one-on-one in front of the hoop, newly hung Saturday afternoon, and romped with Cassie. He'd gone out with Allie Friday night, and made love with her, although he'd hated having to leave her so quickly. Maybe it was stupid pride that had kept him from asking when they could see each other again, but he couldn't help realizing that *he* had made all the moves. And he wanted Allie wholehearted, not reluctant. So he'd left without saying anything but good-night.

Then he'd spent Sunday feeling as jealous as if she was out with another man, and he didn't even know why.

When the phone rang last night, midevening, he'd pounced on it beneath Sean's astonished gaze. With an effort he had straightened his shoulders and gone for an air of dignity. "Hey, Allie," he'd said, and murmured to Sean that he'd take Cassie out. So at least he had some privacy when she invited him to lunch today at her place. He'd accepted instantly, and to hell with the day of work he'd be losing, like he had last Monday.

By the time he climbed the stairs Allie had the door open and was waiting for him. She wore jeans today and a skimpy T-shirt with tiny cap sleeves baring slender, pale arms. Her hair was captured in a loose braid. To him, she looked so beautiful, he immediately felt as dazed, clumsy and tongue-tied as he had when he first met her. He didn't seem to be the kind of man a woman like her would choose, he sometimes thought fearfully, but the vulnerability and loneliness he'd glimpsed in her made him suspect her looks didn't have much standing in her self-image.

As he climbed those damn steps that, short-rised as they were, tried to trip him up, Nolan reminded himself that he didn't know that Allie *had* chosen him. Maybe from her point of view all they were sharing was a brief, casual relationship. Which might be why she didn't seem all that eager to share every little bit of herself with him.

Yeah, that would make sense—except he didn't believe there was much that was casual about Allie Wright. And most especially he had trouble seeing her having casual, never mind brief, relationships.

So maybe she *wanted* to choose him, but something was stopping her. Or maybe she was merely cautious, and he was impatient, he thought with a certain wry humor. A man who carved granite, impatient for results. Now, there was a picture.

He reached the top and touched her cheek. "Hi," she said softly, and flowed into his arms. With a struggle he kept the kiss more tender than passionate, because he could smell her cooking.

She drew him into the apartment by the hand, apologizing because their days off didn't coordinate and thanking him for coming anyway.

"No, this is good. I got in a couple of hours of work this morning. And this gives us a day when I don't have to explain to Sean where I am or what I'm doing. I'll put in half a day Saturday to make up." He watched with pleasure as she bustled in the tiny kitchen. "How was the shopping trip?"

"I bought this T-shirt." She twirled once, doing something completely natural but also complicated with her leg that made the spin something out of the ordinary. "And a whole bunch of other clothes, too. I got carried away."

"I like the shirt," he admitted. The pale rose was good with her white skin, and the deep scoop of the neckline exposed the first curves of her small breasts. The front had, hmm, a picture of a bird in flight. He thought. It was kind of abstract. Nolan grinned. It looked like something he might sculpt.

"Why are you smiling?"

"Because I like you in the shirt?" Then he told her what he'd thought. "Will you come out to my place next Monday for lunch and a tour?"

"I would love lunch and a tour." She danced by where he leaned against the counter edge and gave him a kiss on his jaw as she passed. "It's a date."

Lunch was chicken tikka masala accompanied by garlic naan bread, which she'd baked herself. She sat on the far side of the table, obviously guessing he'd have a hard time squeezing himself in over there.

Even though he was mostly hungry for her, he surveyed the food with appreciation. "I usually settle for a peanut butter sandwich for lunch. If I'm feeling ambitious, I nuke a frozen pizza. You worked hard on this."

"Cooking for two is more fun than just for myself. I don't do this every day, believe me." Her smile was crooked and tantalizing. "You know I'm lucky to get a sandwich at work myself."

He got her talking a little more about her mother. At other times he'd sensed nothing but love and pride. This time, it was as if she was having to remind herself of the pride. She spoke firmly about how hard her mother worked, how dedicated she'd been to the Friends of the Library, about what good friends they were.

"You never talk about your mother," she said finally.

Now, how was it she'd known to zero in on the parent about whom he had the most complicated feelings? No, it wouldn't have helped if she'd asked about his father, because then he might have to say, *Which father? The one I thought I knew, or my real one?*

Nolan had wrestled with himself about this. He wanted to know her with an urgency he'd never felt before. She was already unsettled by his nosiness. He couldn't ask of her what he wouldn't give.

"There's a reason for that." He tore a piece of naan bread in half, then set down both pieces, hardly aware what his hands were doing. "My mother is sophisticated but also warm and friendly. She managed to juggle owning a successful business while still making time for us kids." He paused. "I thought my mother was the greatest, until I was fourteen and got hurt in shop class at school.

I cut myself real bad. I bled so much I needed a transfusion. That's when I found out my blood type didn't match either of my parents'."

Allie's mouth formed into a shocked O.

"The shit hit the fan. I'd never thought about why I didn't look like either of my parents, or much like my brother or sister, either. Jed now, he looks like our father, and you can see Mom in Anna, even though Anna's a lot taller and more angular."

"You were adopted?"

"That's what I first assumed. I couldn't believe they'd never told me. It especially stung when I thought I was the only one of the three of us who was adopted. That's when she confessed that she'd had an affair and, while I really was hers, the man I'd always believed was my father wasn't."

"Oh, Nolan," Allie whispered, her green-gold eyes soft.

"I guess you can imagine how shocked I was. Who wants to think about their parents having sex at all?" He was trying to add some humor to this, but she didn't smile and he couldn't blame her. "Your mom having sex with some man other than your father?" He shook his head. "You could pretty well hear the pieces shattering when she toppled off her pedestal."

"Did your dad know? Or was this a surprise to him, too?"

"Oh, he knew. I went storming straight to him, and he assured me he'd loved me as his own from the minute I was born. Neither of them had been sure whether I was his or the other guy's until I *was* born, and they learned my blood type. He'd forgiven Mom, he told me, and I was his son, as far as he was concerned. I don't know what they thought. That I'd be happy with the explanation? Or maybe a little ashamed and not want Jed and Anna to know? Either way, they pegged me wrong. I told my brother and sister and asked them how they knew for sure that they weren't bastards, too?"

"That's an awful word!" Allie frowned at him.

"Technically true, though." He shook his head. "I'm… mostly past it, Allie. I'm thirty-two years old. That was a long time ago."

"So…what happened? What did Jed and Anna say?"

"They demanded to know what their blood type was. When Mom and Dad stonewalled them, they both called our family doctor to find out. Jed's matched Dad's, Anna's Mom's."

Seeing her expression, he shook his head. "No, all didn't end happily. Eventually Mom admitted she didn't know for sure who Anna's father is. Yep, she'd had another affair. At least one more. I got the feeling maybe there were others—it was just she hadn't had any more children. Why she let herself get pregnant and wasn't on the pill or insisted on condoms or… Well, there's one part of the mystery.

"Dad fumbled to explain to Anna and me that he loved our mother and she loved him, and that, yes, it hurt but living without her would hurt more." Nolan shook his head. "None of us were of an age to understand at all. I'm still not sure I do. I think most of all it was the lies that I despised. The facade of a happy family and great marriage, which couldn't be less true. I've told Sean that the one thing I won't tolerate is lies." He heard how harsh and ragged his voice had become.

Allie flinched away from him, and he could only imagine what she saw on his face to scare her that way.

She swallowed. "What about your brother and sister? How did they handle it all?"

"Not much better than me. Jed's only eighteen months younger than me. I guess he was our parents' makeup baby."

Acid seemed to scour his voice this time, and he cleared his throat. "Then there was a two-year gap before Anna came along. So she was only ten when all this erupted." He half laughed, although without much humor. "At least she wasn't already messed up with hormones like I was. After the first upset, she tried to pretend none of it had happened and got pretty resentful at me when I wouldn't play along. Even as an adult, she's never demanded DNA testing.

"Jed, well, it was complicated for him, because our parents *were* his parents, and he was afraid we'd resent him having something we didn't." This smile, although tilted, felt more natural. "You notice there was a lot of resentment going around?"

"I'm not surprised." There was enough irony in her tone to raise his eyebrows, but this wasn't the moment to question it. Nope, his current priority was spilling his guts out on the table for her to take a good look at.

"I suppose we all patched things up to some extent, especially Jed and Anna. They were younger, and what were they supposed to do? I know the distance I've kept hurts Dad." Nolan grimaced. "Probably Mom, too. But I don't seem to be as forgiving as I should be."

"Did you find out who your biological father is?"

He shook his head. "Neither of them would ever say. I assume my dad knows, but every time I asked, all he'd say was '*I'm* your father.' That's eaten at me some, never knowing. Anna says the same. I suppose it's like an adopted kid must feel, except we don't even know that our fathers ever had a clue they got Mom pregnant.

"I told you she's a publicist, I think." He waited for her nod. "She goes on the road pretty regularly with clients making the round of talk shows, and doing book signings when he's an author, that kind of thing. Chances are good the men she slept with were clients. They wouldn't have been around later to see that she was pregnant and wonder.

"I got desperate enough at one point to research her clientele during the year that I was conceived, but there wasn't any one guy who looked so much like me I could say, 'It's him.'" He shrugged. "Maybe that's not even who it was. Could have been her dentist, a guy who worked in the next office building—who knows. I gave up, eventually."

"Wow." She pressed her fingertips to her lips and gazed at him in a sort of astonishment. "That was…way more than I expected, when I thought about the way your face closed whenever the subject of your parents came up."

He laughed and reached for the torn naan bread again. "It's not something I usually talk about, I admit."

"Do you…ever go home at all? For holidays, or…?"

"Yeah," he said gruffly. "Yeah, I do. My childhood wasn't bad, you see. I believe my parents both love me. I'm still undecided how I feel about them. It's always good to see Anna and Jed. Jed's married now, and has a two-year-old girl. Cute little thing." He found himself smiling. "I was thinking this Christmas I'd take Sean home to show him off. Though he's not as cute as little Lidia."

"I don't know. If you're a teenage girl, you might think differently. When he's not sulking, anyway." She thought that over. "No, that's not true. Sulky *is* sexy, when you're a thirteen- or fourteen-year-old girl."

"God," he said fervently.

She laughed at him. "He can't possibly be any sulkier than *you* were at that age, from what you say."

"No." He rubbed his hand over his jaw. "The first time I set eyes on him, I recognized all that angst. I suppose you could say I saw myself."

He'd told her the story of his first encounters with Sean and his inexplicable offer to help if the boy ever needed him. What he hadn't told her then was why he'd identified with Sean as he had.

Allie's smile was tremulous. "You're a good man, Nolan."

He should be glad to accept any admiration from her, but if there was one thing they had to have, it was honesty. "Taking in Sean may be the first good thing I've ever done for anyone," he said roughly. "I told you. I've always been a loner."

"I know what alone feels like." Her voice was so quiet he barely heard her.

"Yeah." He scraped his chair back and stood, holding out a hand. "We don't have to be alone."

"No." She abandoned what was left of her meal as gladly as he had. She felt so damn *right* in his arms. "Not with you."

He banded her with his arms, kissed her and echoed her words.

With her...not alone.

CHAPTER EIGHT

NOLAN HAD A hell of a time getting anything done in the short time he had that afternoon before the squeal of the school bus brakes announced Sean's return. Sean appeared in the workshop doorway to say, "I'm home," then left to play with Cassie.

Nolan stared after Sean. How long had it been since he'd offered to help or expressed any interest in what Nolan was making? A while, Nolan realized, which he guessed was answer to any question of the boy's original motives. As Nolan ran a polisher over an already smooth slab of Italian granite, creamy Nuovo Brocatello with beautiful gold and pinkish veins, he pondered why Sean had quit feeling the need to help.

Was he beginning to feel secure here? Huh. Maybe. Interesting, considering he'd also made such a shit of himself in an effort to compete with Allie. Maybe that, too, was a sign of his growing belief that Nolan wouldn't dump him.

Testing the stone that was to be a kitchen backsplash, Nolan shook his head in something like amusement. He guessed not all touching parental moments were suitable for greeting cards.

One good thing: Cassie might be Nolan's devoted slave all day, but the moment Sean walked in the door she made plain she was *his* dog. Probably afraid he'd disappear, she hardly took her soft brown eyes off him. If he went into the bathroom, she waited in the hall with her stare fixed on the door. After dinner the pair often disappeared into Sean's room.

Nolan had a suspicion that, despite the two new super-duper, expensive dog beds he'd purchased, one of which was downstairs, one in Sean's bedroom, Cassie actually slept stretched out beside Sean on his bed. That upstairs dog bed, he'd noticed earlier today in passing, looked remarkably pristine.

Tonight, alone downstairs, he couldn't think of any excuse to call Allie, considering the several hours they'd spent together today. He wished he was sure enough of her that he didn't have to think of one.

He had some bookwork he ought to be doing—his least favorite part of owning his own business—but he couldn't seem to settle into it. He didn't like knowing that what he felt was lonely. Loners didn't get lonely.

Until they discovered what it felt like *not* to be alone.

After wandering out to the kitchen for the third time to dump out coffee that had cooled too much to be drinkable and pour another cup that would probably go cold, too, he reached for the phone and carried it to the living room. He hadn't talked to his sister in a while.

Despite the greater age gap between them, he was closer to Anna than he was to Jed. Because of what they had in common? he wondered uncomfortably, but reminded himself that Allie was right—he and his sister had yet one more thing in common.

Not until recently had he thought of himself as an artist, but that was the direction he increasingly saw himself going. Most days, working on commissioned countertops, fountains and the like, he itched to get back to his own piece. He'd feel an almost physical tug toward that corner of the workshop. He could see a day in the future when he could command prices high enough to allow him to sculpt for a living. If that's what he wanted. If he didn't lose the pleasure in it because it had become his job.

He'd talk to Allie about it. She'd taken that route, in a way. If nothing else, she'd listen, and understand the push/pull he felt.

About to drop into his easy chair, Nolan went still. *How things change.* Once he'd have told himself a change of direction in his career was something to think about. It would never have occurred to him to talk it out, nor to have felt so comforted at the idea that he could. Allie was getting under his skin.

And the only alarm he felt at the idea was worry that his feelings for her weren't entirely reciprocated.

He was frowning when he scrolled for his sister's phone number and touched the send button.

"Nolan," she said. "I was thinking about you today."

"Were you." He sat down and with one hand unlaced his boots.

"Mmm." He heard water running momentarily. "Sorry, I was just cleaning the kitchen."

"This a bad time?" he asked.

"No, I'm putting a cup of tea in the microwave. The lazy woman's way."

"Aren't we all lazy these days?" He stacked his stockinged feet on the coffee table and wriggled his toes, enjoying the freedom from the heavy safety boots.

"You?" Anna snorted. "You never do anything the fast way if you can do it more deliberately."

Except fall in love. The thought was...maybe not as startling as it should have been.

"Apparently I wanted the quick route to fatherhood," he pointed out. "Why grow 'em yourself when you don't have to?"

His sister laughed, as he'd expected. Only then she said, "Why grow 'em at all, if you don't have to?"

He went quiet inside, oddly startled and dismayed. "You don't plan to have children?"

"Do *you?*" she said sharply. "Aside from taking in this boy?"

They'd never talked about this subject. He hadn't given it much—any—thought before, but now he discovered a yearning inside himself he hadn't suspected was there.

Because of Allie.

"Yeah." He sounded scratchy. "Yeah," he said more strongly. "I think I do."

"Why?"

He took his feet back off the coffee table, sat up and rested his elbows on his knees. "Most people do. Selfishly, there's a lot of pleasure in seeing the world anew."

Anna didn't say anything.

"Is it that you don't like kids?" he asked, feeling his way. "Or that you have trouble with the idea of having a permanent partner?"

All he could hear was her breathing, for what had to be a minute. "I don't know if I could trust anyone that much," she finally admitted. "God, Nolan. How can either of us?"

"I was telling someone today about Mom and Dad," he heard himself say. Was *this* why he'd called her? "It got me thinking. We could have been worse off, you know. Whatever you can say about them, they both love us. Dad— I'll never understand why he stuck with her, but he did. You know, what I'm choking on is how damn trustworthy he was."

She made a sound somewhere between another snort and a *Gah!*

"I can't even begin to understand their marriage."

"I used to think he might be impotent, and if she wanted sex at all she had to get it elsewhere," Anna offered.

"I used to hide my head under my pillow when their bed started squeaking. Sometimes it got lively enough, the headboard whacked the wall."

"Don't tell me that. Oh, ew." A momentary silence. "I am so glad my bedroom was at the end of the hall."

"Yeah, it mostly embarrassed me until after the uproar. Then I'd hear them in there, and I'd feel so much rage I could have lit a fire with it. Why would he *want* her, after? Why, if they were doing it regularly, did she screw other men?"

"She won't talk about it, even now. I, um, think there was someone else recently. I've gotten so I can tell. She gets more animated, and Dad watches her with so much pain in his eyes."

Nolan bent his head and pinched the bridge of his nose. "Sometimes I hate her."

Anna grunted.

"You ever think of moving out here?"

The silence suggested he'd startled her. "Is that an invitation?"

He relaxed back in his chair. "Sure, why not? You, me and Sean. Oh, and Cassie." *And Allie. Please, and Allie.*

"Who?"

He told her about the adoption, and even about the signs he thought might suggest a lessening of Sean's insecurity.

"Who was it you told about Mom and Dad?" Anna asked suddenly. "Not Sean."

"I'm…seeing a woman."

"How long?"

He thought back. "A month, maybe."

"And you're actually talking to her."

"Yep," he said, smiling at the pure suspicion and disbelief in her voice.

"How'd you meet her?"

He told his sister about Sean's quilt top and Allie's exquisite work. About how every time he went to Allie's he saw that top becoming a quilt, and wished he had better words to describe the process, or how much of herself he sensed Allie poured into her work. Even though most often the quilts were made for someone else, she had to be doing what she did for herself. As much, he supposed, as he worked for his own satisfaction, not minding too much the letting-go part.

"I've never heard you sound like this about a woman before," Anna said. "She'd better not hurt you."

"I can't be sure yet." That was hard to say; hard to admit to himself. "I think she feels something for me. Maybe a whole lot of something, but she's holding part of herself back, too."

"Then why take a chance on her?"

Wasn't she quick to say that, thought Nolan. "I think Allie needs time to work through some things. And I don't have any reason to believe I can't trust her. She has wounds that don't seem to have healed. What's going on between us is rubbing at them, I suspect." He made a huffing sound, half chuckle. "Come to think of it, she reminds me a little of you. You wouldn't be so eager to turn yourself inside out for a guy, either, no matter how much you liked him."

"I have no intention..." she began hotly, then stopped. "Maybe I shouldn't say never."

"No." He smiled, envisioning her face, not as soft and pretty as their mother's, though she had the same blue eyes and blond hair. No, Anna's face had some of the same bony structure as his did, which nobody could call pretty. She was striking, though, and her looks showed character. He bet there were always men around. He had no idea what it would take for her to open up to one. She was hotter-tempered than he was, less content inside herself.

What he'd told Allie about his sister wasn't quite right, he thought now. Anna saw more of their parents, true. But was she close to them? No. What she did, it seemed to him, was a little like willfully scraping her bare skin against a rough-textured wall until she bled, and then going back and doing it again. And again.

"Anna, you should move away." He hadn't known he was going to say that until it came out, but he knew it was right. "You need to put distance between you and Mom."

This silence stretched until it quivered with the stress, but he refused to break it.

"This Allie," she said, surprising him, "has stirred you up. Or maybe it's Sean. Usually we don't talk about much of anything and we both go away happy."

"We both go away," he agreed.

His sister gave a bark of laughter. "Okay, maybe not happy."

"I used to think contentment was the most I could hope for," he tried to explain. "I've changed my mind."

Another silence was less easy to read.

"Maybe," his sister said, "I should come out for a visit. Check out your rainy corner of the world. I suppose potters can make a living in Washington State as well as Chicago."

"I suppose," he agreed, smiling. "And it's not windy all the time here. Or sweltering hot, or bitterly cold."

"I'll give some thought to it," she told him, and they said good-night.

Nolan felt better about the conversation than he had any with her in a long time. Dropping the phone on the end table and reaching his arms high above his head in a bone-cracking stretch, he hoped she'd follow through and show up on his doorstep one of these days.

I would like Allie to meet the best part of my family.

He wondered when—if—Allie would suggest he meet her mother.

SOMEHOW ALLIE LET herself be convinced that she wanted to go waterskiing Sunday with Nolan and Sean even though her best—make that only—swimming stroke was a dog paddle and if she let herself, she'd succumb to a panic attack.

Nolan had done the granite countertops that summer for a lakefront home that had a large kitchen, enormous butler's pantry and four bathrooms. He had explained that the owner, a man named Chuck Moore, had said, "If you ever want to try waterskiing…"

October should have been too late for water sports, but days were still rising into the eighties, although weather reports claimed that would change as soon as Wednesday. So, Nolan informed Allie when he invited her, they had to seize their moment.

During the drive, Sean was guarded but polite. He grumbled a couple of times about having to leave Cassie behind, but it didn't sound as if he really meant it.

"You didn't change her name." The relief was quick and hard.

"Nah, she knows her name." They were walking down the dock toward the big white boat bobbing at the end. He looked down at his feet. "After Grandma died, I wouldn't have wanted somebody to think they could call me whatever they wanted."

"No." Her voice cracked. When she looked up, it was to find his head had turned. Their gazes held for longer than was comfortable. What had he seen?

Nolan, who'd walked ahead with the friendly man who owned the enormous house behind them and the boat, turned and grinned at them. "Ready to go splat?"

The sight of him in nothing but board shorts and sandals made Allie's mouth go dry. Of course she'd seen him naked, but that was different. In her apartment he wasn't striding around so that she couldn't help noticing what impressive muscles he had or his long strong legs. Of course, her mouth might be dry out of apprehension, too. Allie wasn't that great a swimmer. So she made a face at him. "Oh, thanks."

"You ever snow ski or snowboard? That would give you a head start."

"No."

Sean shook his head.

"It's fun," Nolan said consolingly, dropping back to throw an arm over each of their shoulders. "Really."

"Methinks the man doth speak too much," Allie muttered, and Sean gave a crack of laughter that clearly pleased Nolan.

They all rode in the boat its first sweeps around the lake. That part was fun. The fine spray of water was cooling, the sun deliciously hot, the speed and power exhilarating. The owner's son, eighteen and a freshman at the UW, was home for the weekend and had brought a friend. They took turns first behind the boat, the son demonstrating how to take off from the water, and the friend from the dock. They both insisted the dock was easier. Allie was skeptical.

The two boys elected to stay onboard with Chuck for the next round, Nolan's turn. Sean and Allie watched from the dock. As the boat gained speed and the towline stretched taut, he rose to his feet, seemingly without effort, and skied away, leaving a white wake behind him.

"He makes it look easy," Sean said finally, sounding doubtful.

Staring after him, Allie nodded. "I'm not a very good swimmer," she offered.

He turned to stare at her. "Did you tell Nolan?"

"He said with the life vest it wouldn't matter."

They both wore them. Chuck had insisted on it. Allie found the plump, bright orange vest a comfort.

"Yeah, I guess so."

"Can *you* swim?" she asked.

"Yeah. My dad made me take lessons when I was little. One summer. And then Grandma did, too." This glance at her was more stolen than direct. "How come you didn't learn?"

"I was big into dance." *No, no, no.* "And other stuff. I later found out that my mom is scared of water. I think maybe that's why she never took us, even though we used to go on vacations to..." Big mouth.

"To?"

"Lakes. The ocean. You know." She shrugged. "I did take lessons for a week or two when we were at this resort on a lake. So that's why I can at least keep myself from drowning."

"Well, good." His irony was almost adult.

They sat in silence for a long time. The boat roared by and set off on another circuit of the lake. Nolan waved, laughing as he passed.

"School okay?" Allie asked politely.

"I guess." Sean lay back on the boards of the dock, which rose and fell slightly beneath them, and stared up at the sky. "Did you graduate from high school in West Fork?"

Allie shook her head, then wasn't sure he'd seen her. "Lynnwood. You know, that high school by the Alderwood Mall?"

"Yeah, that's weird. You can go to Macy's on your lunch break."

The sun threw dazzling shards off the surface of the lake. Even with dark glasses, she kept having to blink to protect her eyes. "Nolan didn't say. Did you go to a different district last year?"

"I did second semester at the middle school here. It was, um... I didn't really make friends. It was kind of too late in the year. You know?"

"My mom and I moved two months into my senior year of high school," Allie said softly. She was watching the boat and Nolan on the far side of the lake, not much more than specks. "That was hard."

Sean sat up and shoved lank blond hair away from his face. "Wow. Your senior year?"

She nodded, feeling pleasantly sleepy from the sun on her face.

"Where'd you come from? Around here?"

"Oklahoma." The minute she said it, she wanted to grab her answer back. It was horrifyingly like dropping something precious and watching it bounce toward the edge of the dock and the depths of the lake beyond. If only she could lunge for it and save it.

"I've never met anyone who lived in Oklahoma," he said after a minute. "Is it dry and boring?"

She tried to make her laugh natural. "No, there are cities like anywhere else. I don't think it's much like the musical anymore. If it ever was."

She got a blank stare. "The musical?"

Allie laughed again, more genuinely. "*Oklahoma?* Haven't you heard of it?"

He shook his head. "Oh, God. They're coming back. You should go next. Like, ladies first. That's what Grandma always said."

This time Allie giggled. "Coward."

The boat swung in a semicircle, slowing to a stop. It had delivered Nolan, on the end of the towline, almost directly in front of the dock, where he sank gently into the water. He swam to the ladder, pulling the ski and line with him.

His hair was dark and slick like a seal's as he climbed onto the dock, and water streamed from sleek skin and plastered the board shorts to his body. *Big bulge,* Allie thought involuntarily, remembering the dancers in leotards. His grin was exultant.

"Who goes next?"

"I think Allie should," Sean declared hastily.

She stuck out her tongue at him but rose to her feet. "Fine. I'll make a fool of myself first."

As she settled herself at the edge of the dock, Nolan crouched beside her, helping her put her much smaller feet in the bindings. She gripped the handle of the towline so tightly her knuckles showed white.

"Don't look so terrified." His voice was a gentle rumble in her ear.

"You're *sure* the vest will keep me afloat?" she begged.

"Positive."

"You don't have to go if you don't want, Allie." Astonishingly, it was Sean who spoke. He'd risen to his feet and hovered over them. He sounded almost aggressive. "You shouldn't have to do it if you're scared."

She gave him a grateful look. "Thank you. But I think I want to try. As long as the vest won't fall off even if I crash really hard."

Nolan rechecked the buckles. "Sean's right." His eyes, kind as always, surveyed her face. "If you'd enjoy yourself more just watching, that's okay."

"No. I'm ready. Lean back," she told herself.

Nolan stood and lifted a hand to Chuck, behind the wheel of the cruiser. "Go for it, honey."

Allie swallowed and waited for the yank on the line.

NOLAN STOOD BESIDE his foster son, watching apprehensively as Allie took off on her first attempt at waterskiing. He had a sinking feeling that she might be an even poorer swimmer than she'd admitted to. Most people were afraid of getting yanked off their feet; all that seemed to scare her was the possibility of being stranded midlake—which happened—without the life vest.

Somehow, though, he wasn't surprised when she rose as gracefully to a standing position as if she'd skied a hundred times, and seemed to fly off, her body beautiful and slender in a simple, one-piece black bathing suit cut high on her hips and low in back. He'd seen the two college boys eyeing her until they caught his expression. *Mine*.

"Man," Sean breathed, "look at her go." He was quiet for a minute. "Now I'm going to be the only person to fall on my face."

Nolan clapped him on the back. "You're a good athlete. And don't be embarrassed if you do fall. Even experienced skiers do. Allie is having beginner's luck."

"No." The boy frowned. "It's just her."

Nolan thought so, too, but he didn't agree aloud. "You two getting along okay?"

Sean rolled his eyes. "I was nice. As ordered."

"Did I order?"

He shrugged.

"I thought you'd both enjoy this." Nolan stared after her. She'd become very small as the boat headed for the end of the huge lake. "Was I wrong?"

"No, it's okay," Sean said, to Nolan's surprise. "Can I dive in and swim while they're gone?"

"Of course you can."

He did, then erupted back out. "It's freaking *cold!*"

Nolan grinned. "I didn't mention that?"

Spitting out profanities, Sean scrambled out of the water and flung himself full-length onto the warm dock.

"That's what keeps you on your feet while you're out there." Nolan nodded toward the distant boat. "Course, you're getting sprayed, so by the time you're back here, you're already numb."

His foster son told him where to go, not very politely.

Happy in an unfamiliar way, Nolan leaned back on his elbows and kept an eye on Allie until boat and skier disappeared from sight as they curved around the southern shore of the lake.

She made two circuits, although she didn't quite have the nerve, apparently, to let loose of the handle with either hand to wave when she passed by. She was laughing, though, so Nolan was able to relax again. Drowsing in the sun, he and Sean talked little, and in slow sentence fragments.

When the boat came back around either the boy piloting it or Allie—or both—miscalculated the drop-off, leaving her sinking into the water a good twenty yards off the end of the dock. Seeing her panic, Nolan came to his feet. The vest still seemed to be securely fastened, *good*. He dived off the dock and swam quickly to her.

She looked a little less panicked when he surfaced. "I feel like a cork."

"You look like a cork. Here, I'll take that." He grabbed the ski. "Can you make it? If not, I'll take this to the dock and come back for you."

"No, I can…well, sort of." She began kicking and doing a sort of half crawl, half dog paddle that did propel her forward, if slowly.

Sean was on his feet, watching. He reached down for the ski, freeing Nolan to put his hands around Allie's waist and boost her halfway up the ladder. The boat had circled around and Nolan was able to grab the handle of the tow-line. Allie was laughing and gulping when he joined her on the dock.

"Oh, Lord! That was…"

"Fabulous?" Nolan prompted.

"Awful?" Sean asked.

"Fabulous, once I decided I wasn't going to fall down. Though at the end it got a little scary." She laughed up at Sean. "Go for it."

He gulped. "God. Do I have to?"

"No." Nolan put a hand on his shoulder. "Same thing I told Allie."

He shook his head, sat down and wedged his feet into the rubber bindings. After a deep breath, he lifted his hand. "Oh man, oh man, oh man…"

The line stretched taut, and he was off, Nolan and Allie both cheering when he remained on his feet.

Allie sat on the end of the dock where Sean had been, legs dangling. Nolan joined her. "So, what do you think?"

"I'm really glad I did it." She smiled at him, the glints of gold in her eyes more mesmerizing than the white-hot shards of sunlight bouncing off the waves. "Thank you, Nolan."

He bent his head enough to kiss her. "You're very welcome."

It took some effort for him to keep the kiss as unde-manding as he did. He felt a stirring that would become all too obvious in wet board shorts. Something he'd have to quell before Sean got back. As the kiss deepened, he decided a last-minute plunge into the ice-cold lake would do it.

He was nuzzling her neck when Allie stiffened and gasped. "Oh, no!"

"What?" He straightened and put a hand over his eyes. Across the lake, the boat had slowed and was circling back. There was no water-skier behind. "Did you see what happened?"

"Just him and then a big splash."

"I'll bet he got cocky."

She couldn't seem to tear her eyes from the scene across the lake. "You think he's all right?"

"Yeah, I think he's all right." God, he hoped so. Despite his reassuring words, he jumped to his feet to see better. Allie did the same.

"There he is. He'll have to learn to start from the water. Unless they're going to pick him up. No." It looked as though the handle of the towline had been tossed back to the figure in the water. He was left bobbing while the boat made another gentle semicircle and gained speed. "He's up…he's up… No. Shit."

"Is he okay?"

"I'm worried about his ego, not his physical well-being."

"Oh." She was all but on tiptoe as they watched another attempt begin. "Come on, Sean," she whispered. "You can do it."

The kid made it up this time and they were off around the lake.

Allie patted her chest. "I don't know if I could take having children."

Nolan laughed. "Me, I figured if I skipped all the early years, I wouldn't have anything to worry about." Anna had found the argument convincing, right?

Allie's snort sounded an awful lot like his sister's.

He didn't resume kissing her; Sean would be by any minute. Allie sat back down and tipped her face contentedly up to the sun. He did the same. "Wish he'd had a friend to bring with him," Nolan said after a minute.

"It'll happen. I mean, he's not getting in fights, and nobody is making fun of him or anything like that, right?"

Suddenly less drowsy, Nolan frowned. "I don't think so. No fights, anyway. I'd have heard from the school about that, I'm pretty sure."

"Mmm. He'll be fine, then. It takes time, that's all."

"That's right. You said you moved a lot. You must be a pro at starting over in new schools."

"We talked about it, a little," she said after a minute. "Sean and I. He said school is okay, but that he didn't make any friends last spring. We agreed that it's harder then. Everybody already belongs. It'll be different this year."

"It's October."

"I'll bet he has guys he hangs out with at school. And maybe some girls flirting with him."

The boat roared by, closer to the shore this time. Sean's grin was jubilant as he shot past.

"I'm glad we did this," Allie said, her voice utterly free of tension, as though something had loosened inside of her. She quit holding herself up on her elbows, instead lying flat on her back. Her eyes closed.

Nolan sat looking down at her, feeling a squeeze in his chest. God, she was beautiful, poetry in motion and equally graceful on those rare occasions she was still, like now. His gaze ate up the dark curve of her eyelashes against ivory cheeks, the delicate skin of her eyelids, the wing of eyebrows, the purity of her bone structure and the long arch of her neck. The suit clung to her small, perfect breasts, slim waist and supple hips. And those exquisite legs.

The funny thing was, even as he looked, hungry, awed at his own luck and totally appreciative, Nolan knew that this grip she had on him had to do with a lot more than her beauty. It was the sunrise of her smile, the way she lifted her chin in defiance. It was her patience as she worked over the quilting frame with her back so straight and her arms held just so, the unexpectedness of the fabrics she put together, the way she listened to him, the fierceness of her anger and—hell, maybe most of all—the ghosts he could see in her sometimes haunted eyes.

Vulnerability that moved him—and frightened him.

His heart beat heavy and hard in his chest. Life had been easier before he looked into her eyes and stumbled into something unexpected. On a silent, shaken laugh, he knew. Scared to death or not, he couldn't imagine going back. A world without Allie.

He made himself turn his face away and look out over the water. Another boat passed, this one towing two skiers. He watched it and them, without seeing.

CHAPTER NINE

THAT NIGHT, ALLIE FOUND herself remembering all those vacations her family had taken when she was young, nearly always to someplace on a lake or the ocean. She'd been embarrassed that she couldn't swim and had to dabble in water close to the shore. Why hadn't her father taught her? He'd often stroked far out into the water. Either he'd helped Jason, or Jason was bolder than Allie, because he'd gone in.

She could close her eyes and picture her brother climbing onto one of those floating docks well out into a lake—that one in the Catskills, she thought—his fists raised in triumph. He probably shouldn't have set out for the dock, because she didn't suppose he'd been a good swimmer. Allie wondered if either of their parents had been watching. Likely not.

Maybe neither of her parents had known how awkward she felt. She'd been only four years old when her day care had given kids the option of taking a ballet class. From that moment on, it had been all she wanted to do. The instructor had spoken to her mother, seeing something in her from the beginning—passion or skill, or perhaps both.

Doubtless assuming it would be a fleeting obsession, her parents had allowed her to take classes—and then more classes. The cost must have required sacrifices on their part. It seemed as though, once they resigned themselves to her single-mindedness, they'd never given any thought to broadening her education or experiences.

Although that might not be totally fair. It was also possible they'd tried, and she'd rejected those opportunities. She had had her eye fixed on a goal and saw very little else.

Allie had always known that their relocation had been harder for her than it would have been for most girls her age. She hadn't only had to give up friends, the familiar, her name; she'd given up a consuming passion, her identity, her dreams, her future. It felt like *everything* then. She had been lost.

Maybe the only way she could survive was to wall off that part of her life. Remembering it hurt too much. Shying away from any reminder had become habit, more subconscious than deliberate. She never watched dance programs on PBS, had never been tempted to buy tickets to Seattle's Pacific Northwest Ballet.

That week, she even noticed how she drove several blocks out of her way going home to avoid passing the local dance school and chancing to see eager girls in their leotards being dropped off in front by their moms. She hadn't known she was doing it.

This year she'd agreed to let students hang a poster advertising their recital in her front window, but other than checking to be sure it hung straight and to note the day when the event would be over and she could rip it down and crumple it in her trash, Allie had never once really let herself see it.

Did the Y offer adult swim lessons? she wondered. It wouldn't be so embarrassing if she wasn't alone. Of course, it wasn't likely there'd be that many occasions when she wished she knew how to swim better. Mostly people didn't swim in Puget Sound. It was not only salty, it was bitterly cold. And the majority of beaches were rocky rather than sandy, too. Waterskiing, if Nolan ever took her again, well, she thought maybe she'd trust the life vest better next time.

Sean had been so enthusiastic, he'd taken a second turn, as had Nolan. By the time they returned, Sean was talking animatedly with the college boys and had enthused all the way home about waterskiing. Nolan, looking amused, had declined to buy a powerboat or to sell the house and buy a lakefront one.

"Maybe Ryan will invite you again one of these weekends," he'd suggested. Ryan was Chuck's son.

"He said he would." Sean sounded flattered but doubtful.

"He and his buddy were pretty friendly."

"Yeah, they were great, but they're in *college*."

Well, yeah. Neither Nolan nor Allie argued that Ryan would want Sean as his new best friend.

"It was a good day," Nolan said with satisfaction.

Looking at his face, Allie had felt something complicated that she didn't understand. Maybe because it *was* a wonderful, perfect day—except for the fact that she wasn't the woman Nolan thought she was.

Ever since he'd told her about his mother's affairs, she kept hearing him say, with steel in his voice, *I've told Sean that the one thing I won't tolerate is lies.*

She was lying to him every time they saw each other. Not maliciously, of course; she told herself that made a difference, but she wasn't completely convinced. How would he feel if he ever learned how different her life had been from what she'd told him? Would he understand why she'd had no choice but to lie?

Allie wanted to believe Nolan would. But then she wasn't so sure when she remembered his bafflement and fury and hurt when he talked about his mother and the lie his entire life had been because his parents hadn't been honest with him.

She tried to tell herself he'd never have to find out about

her lies. Even if, well, they became more involved or even got married, it would be Allie Wright he'd wed. It was Allie Wright he loved, not Chloe Marr, who had died for all practical purposes, anyway. And certainly not Laura Nelson, the stunned girl who had almost given up talking at all in her grief over the life left behind and her worry of saying too much.

Everyone had layers of self, some of which ended up revealed, others hidden forever. In that respect, she wasn't any different than most people.

But then she thought about what Nolan had shared with her, and knew it to be a gift. A gift she couldn't reciprocate without telling him things she'd sworn, cross her heart, never to tell anyone because if she did she'd be endangering her whole family.

But if I trusted Nolan...

She saw the U.S. Marshal's face as he leaned forward, looking at each of them in turn. "Chances are good you can never go back. Sitting here now, you are not the person you were yesterday. Holding on to who that was will only hurt you, and will possibly put you at risk.

"Don't think back, don't tell anyone, become the Nelsons who are moving to Oklahoma because you, Mark—" that was her father's new name "—were laid off from automobile assembly in Detroit and the economy is so depressed there that you decided to make a completely new start somewhere else.

"You kids have it easiest. Everyone will understand that you're unhappy about the move. Teenagers never like to leave their friends. You'll be surprised how few questions people will ask.

"This is a new reality. It is not a game—it's forever. Don't look back." His gaze drilled into each of theirs. "Don't muddy the waters by sharing with anyone at all the life you had that isn't in this bible." He laid a hand on the folder that held all the information they would need about their new identities. "Do you understand?"

They'd all nodded, the way Allie remembered it, except probably none of them really did understand. Certainly, she didn't. Maybe her dad had—it could be that's why he'd walked through those days shell-shocked. He was losing a business his grandfather had founded, passed down to his son and then to him. After the Marrs disappeared the business had been sold, and eventually Dad got the money, but by then he was an insurance agent and he'd never tried again to start up his own business.

Mom, in contrast, had been completely focused on what she thought she had to do, to the point where she seemed oblivious to her family's fears. Allie had watched her with suspicion, trying to figure out what she felt. Allie had decided then that what she saw was pride. Mom had done something big and courageous. Maybe, like most people, she'd never been sure that she could be so brave. That would change a person.

Under the weight of all the memories and her guilt that she couldn't tell Nolan the truth, she almost dreaded seeing him this morning, for the promised tour of his workshop and lunch at his house.

Yesterday, with Sean along, she could suppress her tangled emotions more easily than she could alone with Nolan. It was okay when his eyes heated with desire, but what made her squirm were the other times, when she saw his kindness and patience and hope.

And she used to think of herself as serene!

Nolan's directions took her out of town. The distance between driveways grew. Horses and sometimes cattle grazed behind board or barbed-wire fences. Occasional fancy new houses somehow looked pretentious next to the gently aging farmhouses that were their neighbors. Allie would have been awfully surprised if Nolan's house had been new or fancy, and of course it wasn't.

No animals at all grazed in what must be his pastures. They grew wild, the grass waist-high and tangled. Thickets of blackberries were trying to take over. A barbed-wire fence had sagged and rusted. She could see a tall white farmhouse and at least two other roofs. At the head of the driveway stood a single mailbox next to a simple sign with the words burned into wood: The Stone Man.

Allie smiled at that, and drove up the asphalt driveway, smoother than the road. The driveway looked out of place between the neglected pastureland on one side and alder and cedar and vine maple woods on the other. It widened in front of a detached garage, she discovered, and curved to stop at double sliding doors on the long, low third building.

The basketball hoop she'd heard about hung on the peak of the garage. Nolan had even painted a free-throw line and what she thought was a three-point line on his court. She parked carefully to one side. Nolan was walking toward her from the workshop as she got out.

He kissed her. "Tour first?" he asked, lifting his head.

"Are you kidding? I can hardly wait to see your lair."

He laughed and said something she didn't hear. All her attention was on the enormous stone figure that stood outside the door, guarding the entry. Allie walked forward slowly and stopped a few feet away, surveying the stone man, for surely that's what he was.

He had to be granite, and not one of the beautiful colored ones she'd seen used as countertops. No, he made her think of the massive foundations of the old Carnegie buildings, gray and rough-hewn. He had to be eight feet tall and was, in his own way, massive. His features weren't quite clear. Although crude, as it seemed he had to be, he was also powerful. It was as if he was becoming a man, born from the rock. He had presence.

Astonished, Allie turned to Nolan and found he was watching her, his expression rueful. "This was one of my first efforts."

"Is he a self-portrait?" She didn't know what made her think that, but saw a flash of emotion on his face that told her she was right.

"You know, I wouldn't have said that, but…yeah. Maybe." One side of his mouth tilted up. "He was supposed to be advertising. He's on my business cards."

"He's stunning," she said.

"Thank you."

Nolan opened the door and Allie found herself in an entry that reminded her of a mudroom. It held a utility sink and had a row of hooks from which hung dusty coveralls, various pairs of goggles and…she wasn't quite sure.

"Ear protection," he told her, seeing where she was looking. "Cutting stone, especially when I'm not using water, is damn noisy."

He led her into the workshop itself, a fascinating space nothing like she'd pictured. For one thing, even though it was scrupulously neat, it seemed as if a pale dust had colored most surfaces. Much of the back wall was glass, and enormous skylights ensured even on a gray day, like today, the room was bright. The amount of large and somewhat mysterious equipment surprised her, too. Somehow she'd imagined him with a chisel in hand, although she knew that was naive.

He showed her saws mounted on rails and explained that only diamonds were hard enough to cut granite. He had polishers and cutters, some that he used dry, some that sprayed water on the granite as he worked, then ran into a couple of floor drains. An enormous workbench ran the width of the space, drawers and racks holding tools, drill bits, saws, sandpaper and all kinds of odd things, including jars of some white powder that Nolan told her was used to rub stone by hand.

"I go through saws and bits like you wouldn't believe. I can sharpen the blades a few times, but I don't like to stop when I'm working, so I have backups. And I have to replace them constantly."

She turned slowly in place. The other side of the workroom was where he kept his unworked stone. He'd designed and built bins for every size and shape. Mostly she saw slabs, presumably intended for countertops, floors and the like. But there were chunks, too, sized from a square foot to ones taller than her, all raw. The colors were dull and uninteresting. She couldn't imagine how he saw the potential in each piece.

He only laughed when she said that. "Practice. Sometimes I'm disappointed when I start cutting. Sometimes I'm astounded. You have to understand, there are quarries around the world that produce certain granite or marble of known quality. I handpick the stone I buy."

He had other stones besides granite, too, although fewer pieces—marble, limestone, sandstone and alabaster.

He showed her some countertops that were ready for delivery and she watched the way he slid his fingers over the surfaces. She had trouble looking away from his hands. She knew what they felt like on her body.

Nolan tipped his head then and saw her looking at him. His eyes narrowed and the blue seemed to darken. She'd have sworn a good deal of the air in the room had been sucked out, maybe by one of those compressors he'd showed her.

"Your sculptures." Her voice came out a little high. "Will you show me what you're working on?"

He seemed to bank some of that fire. With a nod, he took her to the far corner of the room. An astonishing finished piece stood beside the huge double doors. As she gaped at it, Nolan stood back.

"Red travertine," he said. When she looked at him, he nodded at the work. "The stone."

"Oh."

It was something of the same concept as the stone man, but very different in execution. A woman seemed to be rising from what had to be the curl of a wave. Her arms were at her sides, but her torso was clearly outlined and both lithe and feminine. Her head was tipped back, as if she gazed at the heavens. Her face was detailed enough to express exultation, but far from precisely detailed. The entire piece was about movement and emotion.

"You're an artist." Allie felt like an idiot. Even though he'd said he didn't carve realistic pieces, she'd still imagined this was a hobby for him. That whatever he did would be pretty. But this was so much more than that, she was stunned.

Discomfort showed on his face. "I may be getting there."

"Getting there?" Then she saw what had to be his work in progress.

"This one isn't done." He sounded awkward.

Allie ignored him. The style of this piece was dramatically different. For one thing, clearly the details were going to be very fine indeed. The stone was a dark green, dull where it hadn't been polished, gleaming richly where it had been.

"It's, er, a torpedo, nose-down in the ocean floor." Nolan was standing behind her as she reached out to touch a sea star, exquisite and real, textured like ones she'd seen in tide pools. And the arm of an octopus reached up to embrace the torpedo, the surface of it glossy and...

"Oh! Look at the suction cups." Delighted, Allie touched them, then studied barnacles and a crudely formed crab scuttling up the barrel of the torpedo. There were lumps he had yet to carve into whatever creatures they would be. "The sea is making the torpedo its own," she said in awe.

He cleared his throat. "Yes."

Allie turned to face him. "Why on earth do you waste your time on countertops?"

"To pay the bills. And because that's where I started. Who I thought I was. A stonemason."

"But that's not who you are anymore, is it?"

He moved his shoulders as if to relieve tension. "I don't know. I haven't decided yet."

She shook her head. "You do know." Then found she was still shaking her head in a kind of daze. "I thought we did the same kind of thing, only the materials were different. But I was wrong. There are artists who work with fabric, but I'm not one. I'm only a quilt maker. You're an artist," she said again.

"You are, in your own way."

"No. I can't seem to move past the traditional patterns. True artists use fabric in new ways. At most, I reinterpret, see ways a block can be turned on its head to be new, or how color can transform the traditional. That's different. Remind me to show you pictures of some art quilts."

Of course, he argued. They were still arguing when he took her back to the house and as he made a simple Alfredo sauce for noodles and took a salad from the refrigerator.

He talked about techniques, and she did the same, explaining what appliqué was while admitting she rarely did it.

"It's finicky work. And that sounds silly, when the quilting stitches themselves are so tiny, but…it's different, and I don't enjoy it the same way. I'm actually making a combination pieced-and-appliqué quilt right now, though, only a wall-hanging size." It could be a crib quilt, she'd thought, and knew that was what she'd really had in mind. She'd wanted it to be magical and treasured someday by a child. Maybe by her own. "I'll have to show it to you."

"Tell me about it." He sounded as though he really wanted to know.

"The blocks at the bottom are the pieced ones. They're rocking horses. With each row of blocks, the horses become more fluid. Eventually they leap free of their rockers. By the top, they're running with manes and tails flying. I thought about giving the very last one, in the corner, wings," she said a little shyly.

"It sounds beautiful. I do want to see it." He took a swallow of his milk, his eyes never leaving her face. "Can you sell this one?"

Allie made a face at him. "I don't know. I haven't decided. Most of my quilts *are* for sale, you know."

"As most of my work is."

"Have you kept any of your sculptures, besides the stone man?"

"A couple of small pieces. I'll show you."

He did show her, and then he showed her his bedroom, which was plain to the point of being ascetic. White walls, oak floors, an enormous oak dresser, bed, table to hold a digital clock and lamp, and a single, upholstered chair. A door to a largely empty closet stood open. She shook her head.

"You need an interior designer."

He nuzzled her neck. "I need you."

The deep rumble of his voice sent shivers through her.

"I need you, too." She wrapped her arms around him with sudden desperation. "Please, Nolan."

"God, you're beautiful," he said as he stripped her and laid her on his bed. "I couldn't begin to make anything as beautiful as you."

"I'm not."

He growled his displeasure and kissed her breast, then suckled it. She thought she heard him mumble something about "damn college kids" but by then she was past having the ability to ask a coherent question.

She pushed him down on the bed and straddled him, smoothing her hands over his chest and shoulders. "My stone man."

He groaned. "Take me inside you, Allie. Now."

She teased him for a few more minutes, the sense of power new to her, then sank down on him. She closed her eyes and let her head fall back. A whimper slipped out of her.

"You look like my mermaid," he said rawly. He stroked her with his hands as if he had shaped her.

"Is that what she is?"

He grunted—agreement or pleasure, she couldn't tell. Was the sea the mermaid's lover? Maybe she hadn't been rising out of it, but rather above it, over it, capturing it.

Allie's body seemed to be singing with delight in each stroke. Nolan's hands kept her from faltering. Gripping her hips, he moved her faster and faster, his hips lunging up to meet her. She cried out when the hot, sweet pleasure leaped free, making her arch with the exquisite tension. He ground her down on him and pulsed deep inside her.

"Beautiful," he said hoarsely, and she collapsed on him, burying her face in the crook of his neck.

As the tide washed out, she felt more sadness than anything. How could something so perfect be built on lies? How could she not tell him?

How could she betray her mother? Because that's what she'd be doing, wasn't it?

In counterpoint to his heartbeat in her ear were the words *never, never, never.*

THE FOLLOWING WEEK became a terrible tumble of doubts. *I am being melodramatic,* Allie kept telling herself, knowing it was true. And yet. And yet. Under the weight of so much confusion, Allie grew quieter and quieter that week and into the next. Nolan watched her with worry in his eyes, but didn't insist on knowing what she was thinking.

Her mother did.

"Are you getting sick?" she asked, after watching Allie pick at dinner.

"I nibbled while I was cooking," Allie lied. The truth was, she hadn't had much appetite. Food didn't seem to fill her hollow places, so she'd quit trying. She'd become alarmed enough just yesterday to buy a home pregnancy test, even though she and Nolan had been careful, because there could be a prosaic reason for her lack of appetite. Thank goodness, it came up negative.

"You always quit eating when you get edgy about something," her mother said, her eyes sharp. "I used to worry you were anorexic."

"What?" Allie stared.

"Don't you remember? Whenever you were nervous about an upcoming competition or recital or anything at all, we could barely get you to sit down to a meal. The worse, though, was after we moved—" Her mouth clamped shut, but finally she continued, "The first time. You didn't have any weight to lose, but you managed anyway. And it wasn't as if you were shooting up in height."

No, she'd quit growing by the time she was about twelve years old. And been intensely grateful—many more inches would have ended her dream of becoming a prima ballerina.

"I took you to the doctor, but he didn't think you were focused on either food or weight or your appearance at all. He suggested counseling."

"I never went to counseling." She knew that much.

Her mother hesitated. "At the time, we were nervous about putting you in a room with a stranger where you were supposed to talk about yourself. There was too much you *couldn't* say."

Something stubborn rose in her. "You mean, that I wasn't allowed to say."

"*All* of our lives depended on you sticking to the details of our new lives."

"So what happened?"

"You didn't get any skinnier, so I decided you were simply made to be slight. But after you discovered quilting, you started looking healthier."

Until they'd moved again. Allie did remember that miserable year, until she graduated from high school. She'd become gaunt. One of her primary emotions leaving for college and dorm life had been relief at escaping her mother's fussing.

"So what is it this time?" Mom asked. "Does it have to do with the man you're seeing?"

"Nolan."

"Nolan," she said impatiently. "Or is it all those questions you had the day we went shopping?"

"I suppose...a little of everything."

"I don't understand any of this. Why on earth are you wanting to dwell on something that happened so long ago?"

How could she say to her mother, *Because I feel like I'm falling apart? Because I am not a whole person?*

No, her mother of all people would never understand. And yet, she was the only person Allie *could* talk to.

No, the only person she was *allowed* to talk to. Not quite the same thing.

An insidious thought crept into her mind. Who was telling her she was allowed or not allowed? Once upon a time, it had been the U.S. Marshals Service along with her parents. Now, it was only Mom and the inner, scared voice that said *never, never, never.*

But I'm all grown up now. Can't I decide what I can say, and who I can say it to?

She could still put her mother in danger. If, after fifteen years, anyone was still looking for her. Or cared. Or even remembered the secretary who'd heard something she wasn't supposed to and who had gone into hiding and then testified at the trial, sending a mob assassin to prison.

Fifteen years ago.

I'll have to think about this, she decided, half-afraid of the strange feeling swelling inside her that might have been liberation, or maybe courage of a completely different kind than her mother's.

"I think I might be falling in love," Allie said in a rush. "Doesn't that always set you to asking yourself questions?"

"Allie, you can't tell him anything." Alarm had quickened on her mother's face. "Don't you remember what we were taught? *This* is who we are. If he doesn't love who you are now, he's not worth having."

Part of Allie conceded that was true.

"What if we ever go to one of those places I'm supposed to have lived and he wants to see the house I grew up in? Or my high school, or…?"

"You find reasons not to go," Mom said fiercely. "If you

absolutely have to for some reason, you pick out a house and say, that was the one."

"And what if he insists on knocking on the door and the people say, 'What are you talking about? We inherited this house from my grandparents. You can't have lived here.'"

"Then you apologize and tell them all you must have been confused, and my goodness the town has changed so much you're all turned around."

"Lie," she said flatly.

"Allie, the chances of any of that happening are so remote, I don't even know why we're talking about it. We've lived in this area for almost eleven years now. You can show this Nolan where you graduated from high school and where we lived before we moved to West Fork."

"Sooner or later, he'll ask where Dad lives. And Jason."

"Montana. Or maybe either or both of them have moved. You don't know. You don't want to see them. *That's* what you tell him."

"I do!" She jumped to her feet, shocked to feel tears running down her cheeks. "I do want to see them! I miss Daddy, I miss Jason, and I will not lie about that!"

She could see that her mother's mouth had fallen open in bewilderment and what might have been fear.

Allie swiped angrily at her tears. "I'm sorry—I'm overreacting. I know I am, but I'm not very good company right now. I think I'd like to be alone."

"Allie…" Mom sounded as if she had a lump in her throat. "I didn't know…."

"Please, Mom. Not right now."

"You won't do anything foolish?"

If she had let herself laugh, it would have been an awful sound. "Kill myself? Or do you mean tell Nolan who I really am?"

Her mother's eyes got even wider. "I never thought—"

"No, it isn't my state of mind you're worried about, is it? It's my big mouth."

Allie's bitterness polluted the air. She could taste it and could tell her mother did, too.

"You know I love you." Mom sounded helpless.

Damn it, that made Allie start crying again. She *hated* to cry.

"I love you, too." Part of her wanted to fall into her mother's arms and beg her forgiveness. The other part... well, the other part didn't know *what* she wanted. "And I promise I won't tell him anything without talking to you about it first," she made herself say.

Allie couldn't stand to see that lingering fear. She could only imagine her mother's horror if she admitted that she'd already made mistakes and told both Nolan and Sean things she shouldn't have.

Her mother nodded. "I'll leave you alone as you wish, if you're sure you don't want me to help you clear the table or clean the kitchen."

Allie was able to laugh, a little. "You know my kitchen doesn't have room for both of us anyway."

Mom left after kissing her hesitantly on her probably wet and splotchy cheek. Allie stood at the top and watched her descend the outside stairs carefully.

I have to get past this, she thought. If she couldn't pull herself together and feel comfortable following the script, maybe she should quit seeing Nolan.

The thought was so bleak, she put it out of her mind immediately. She had a feeling that backing away wouldn't accomplish anything but make her miserably unhappy anyway.

I am Humpty Dumpty and I've already taken the tumble. Shutting Nolan out of her life would not put her back together again. Maybe nothing would.

CHAPTER TEN

"HOW IS IT YOU'VE lived in the Northwest for this many years and never skied?" Nolan asked.

They were at his place on Sunday afternoon, sitting on the back porch steps watching Sean shoot baskets. Every time he dribbled the ball, Cassie bounded at it, barking. He was laughing, pretending she was an opponent on the court, maneuvering past her to put the ball up.

"Lots of reasons. Neither of my parents skied." She shrugged. "It's ridiculously expensive. Besides, I don't like to be cold."

"Wimp." He nudged her gently with his shoulder. Allie bumped back.

The forecast had called for rain, so Nolan hadn't come up with any new activity to suggest, as he'd undoubtedly have done if he'd known the promised rain would hold off. He'd suggested she come and hang out instead. He'd also suggested she invite her mom for dinner.

What he was doing was being pushy. Not that it was unreasonable of him to wonder why she hadn't yet introduced him to her mother. It was now November and they'd been dating seriously for almost two months. She didn't know herself why she hadn't.

So she'd gulped, and done it. Mom was to arrive between five-thirty and six. Allie *liked* her mother. She didn't understand why she was dreading the combination of Mom and Nolan.

"Do people in Chicago ski?" she asked.

Nolan laughed. "Well, not nearby. I've only tried the sport a few times, I have to admit. But I thought it was fun."

"Please tell me it's not one of those things you think Sean and I have to experience at least once in our lives."

He laid an arm around her shoulders. "Well, sure it is. Do you really want to live your whole life without skiing or snowboarding?"

"Falling facedown in the very cold snow? Over and over? Breaking my leg?"

Nolan made a rude sound. "Not a chance. I've never seen anybody with better balance than you have. You'll be a natural." He seemed to ponder. "Why didn't you stick to dance?"

She overcame a momentary blank. "It wasn't possible after one of our moves."

He removed his arm and looked at her, something alarmingly intense in his eyes. Curiosity. She recognized it. Of course he'd heard how stiff she sounded. She was a horrible liar, the absolute worst person to have been put in a position where she had to tell so many of them.

"No dance school?"

"Not…at the level I was dancing." That was true, at least.

"That's a shame," he said thoughtfully.

Sean let loose with a shot from the three-point line and crowed with delight when it sank through the net. "Yeah! Did you see that?"

Nolan gave him a thumbs-up and Allie applauded. Cassie barked and they all laughed.

"You were right that he needed a dog," Allie said.

"Hmm." He leaned a shoulder against a porch upright. "What did you say your dog's name was?"

Oh, he'd slid that in casually, but the very fact that he'd asked made her mouth go dry. He suspected she'd been lying to him. He had to.

"Lady. She was a beagle."

"Are beagles ladylike?"

"Probably not. Mom and I were talking about her just the other day. Lady liked to wander. She was a poor choice when we lived…" No, no, no, not in the city. "In town."

"What did your dad do, that you guys had to move so often?"

Allie braved herself to meet his sharp blue eyes. "Why do you care so much about my childhood?"

"I want to know you." He paused, lines on his forehead deepening, his expression somehow somber.

"Tell me I'm wrong, Allie. Tell me you don't have scars deep inside."

Breathless, she stared back, unable to say a word.

"Sometimes I think you don't want to remember."

She wrenched her gaze from his and watched Sean, without seeing his and Cassie's antics. "Is that so unusual? You sound like you practice avoidance where your parents are concerned."

"I can't deny it. But I do go home for Christmas, and I told you about them."

"Yes." Dear God, how was she supposed to deflect him? "It was different for me," she said finally. "Neither of your parents abandoned you."

"My biological father did."

"If he knew you existed."

"That's true." He hadn't once looked away from her face. "Why won't you talk about it, Allie? What happened, that you never see or hear from your father? Did he hurt you? Abuse you?"

"No!" Shocked, she turned her head and met his eyes again. "Of course not! I loved him."

"Then why?"

"I do hear from him. He writes sometimes. It's just… things with him and my mom…" Hearing how weak that sounded, Allie winced. And braced herself. Nolan would never let her get by with it.

"And your brother?" Trust him to twist the inquisition in a way she hadn't expected.

"He sided with Dad." Her throat wanted to close. "I felt like I had to choose, okay?" Felt like? She *had* had to choose. Eenie, meenie, minie, mo, which parent do you cut out of your life? "It was the worst thing I've ever had to do."

"God, Allie." Suddenly he tugged her across the top step so that he could wrap both arms around her. "I'm sorry. So sorry. That stinks. What were they thinking?" The anger in his voice both warmed her and scared her.

"Don't say anything to Mom," she said desperately. "Please don't, Nolan."

He was silent for a long time. He'd laid his cheek on top of her head and was rubbing it back and forth. "No," he said finally, gruffly. "Of course I won't. I have no right to jump in. I know I don't."

"No." Her sharp tone contradicted the way she was burrowing into his embrace. Or was it the other way around? "You don't."

Nolan didn't say anything, and she had to suspect she'd hurt his feelings. Hers would have been hurt, if he'd said anything like that.

"Did you choose your mother because you needed her?" he asked, shocking her with his perceptiveness. "Or because she needed you?"

She wrenched herself away. Her stare must be wild. "Why won't you let this go?"

Now his expression was implacable. "I told you. Because I want to know you. Don't you want to know me?" he asked, his voice softening.

Yes. No. Her heart was hammering so hard she was almost dizzy. They stared at each other in a standoff she was terrified she wouldn't win.

"Hey," Sean said from the foot of the steps. "What's going on?" His gaze moved from one of them to the other.

"We're arguing," Nolan said easily. "So what, did you finally concede to Cassie?"

Sean cackled. "Yeah, if only she could shoot."

The dog stood beside him, tail going so hard her butt swung from side to side. She was panting, her tongue hanging out.

"You've got a hell of a shot," Nolan told him. "Your coach pleased?"

"Yeah, he said he'd planned to put me at center, but he's changed his mind and decided I'll play forward. Except I'm not so good at defense yet."

Nolan shrugged. "You'll get it." His smile grew into a grin. "It'll help when you quit tripping over those big feet of yours."

If she hadn't been so tangled up inside, Allie would have giggled at the way Nolan's foster son scowled at his feet, as if he hadn't figured them out yet.

"I went up two sizes this year."

"You've passed me by," Nolan said.

Allie estimated Sean was wearing a twelve at least, and his feet looked even more monstrous in the kind of athletic shoes that would have made her feet look big. She could only imagine them if he left them untied the way boys did.

"Do you think they'll stop now?" Sean sounded plaintive.

"Maybe. Probably not."

"Dad wasn't that huge."

"What about your mom's side of the family?"

There was a noticeable pause. "I think she was tall. Like, almost as tall as he was."

"There you go, then," Nolan said with an easy smile. "Heredity in action. Boys aren't usually done growing yet at your age."

He frowned at them. "What about girls?"

"Mostly girls are, I think," Allie told him apologetically. "Not all. I had a friend who was teeny tiny because she didn't reach puberty until she was almost sixteen. So she grew after that. But I was done by the time I was twelve."

"Well." He looked at her kindly. "You kind of got stuck."

Allie stuck out her tongue at him, and he laughed.

"What were you guys arguing about?"

"None of your business," Nolan said bluntly. He groaned. "I suppose I should start dinner."

Please, Allie thought. Maybe he'd quit asking her questions. "Yes, you should. Since you insisted on making this a big deal by inviting my mother."

Sean twirled the ball on a fingertip. "Is she, like, not that nice or something?"

"What?"

"Well…" The ball fell into his hands and he looked uneasy at her tone. "'Cause you didn't want us to meet her."

"Of course she's nice! I didn't *not* want you to meet her…." She floundered. "It was just…"

They both waited politely.

"Meeting the family is kind of…" Nolan's eyes narrowed, unnerving her. "It's not something you do when you're first dating someone, that's all."

"But he wanted you to meet me right away." Sean evidently saw something on Nolan's face and gulped. "Um, I guess you kind of had to, when we live together and stuff."

She swiveled to look right at Nolan. "I'm sorry. I didn't know I was hurting your feelings."

His expression softened. "No. I was impatient, that's all. I'm not usually," he added ruefully.

Allie only nodded. Her hands, she discovered, were clasped together so tightly she wasn't sure she could pry them apart.

I should have told Mom I've slipped a few times. So she doesn't contradict me.

Too late. And, heaven help her, Nolan was sure to grill her mother.

"Do you want to shoot some baskets?" Sean asked Allie.

Heaving himself to his feet, Nolan glanced at her with amusement. "Do you think you can throw the ball up that high?"

"I could get the stepladder," Sean chimed in.

"Is that a challenge?" Allie stood and dusted off her behind. "How hard can it be to put a stupid ball through a ring?"

They both laughed.

"And to think, I was going to offer to help with dinner." She grinned at Sean. "You're on."

She strolled down the steps, snatched the ball from the fourteen-year-old's hands and carried it to the free-throw line. Now, if only she hadn't lost her knack.

Nolan, she was aware, had grabbed Cassie by the collar and pushed her into the house, then lingered on the porch himself, still amused. Sean sauntered toward her with a shit-eating grin on his face. Allie dribbled the ball a couple of times to get in the zone, letting it come back up to smack her hands. Then she lifted it, jumped and let the ball slip off her fingertips. It made a perfect arc, dropping through the net with a swish. No backboard.

Sean gaped.

Nolan let out a hearty laugh and went inside.

Allie retrieved the ball, dribbled away from the garage, turned and shot. *Swish.*

"You conned me."

"No," she said. "If I'd suggested putting some money on whether I could make a free throw, *then* I'd have been conning you."

"You *can't* have played basketball."

"Because I'm a girl?" She shot right over his head. *Swish.*

His mouth dropped open again. He closed it with a snap. "Because you're short," he said indignantly.

Allie relented enough to smile at him. "No, I didn't play varsity or anything, because I am too short. But we had to play in PE, and for some reason I always had a really good shot." She shrugged. "I'm good at bat, too."

His eyes grew calculating. "You wanna play horse?"

"What do I win if I beat you?"

"You don't have a lawn I could mow."

"I could teach you to cut out fabric. Saturdays are busy in the store. A little extra help would be great."

The appalled expression on his face made her day.

"No way I'm going to be seen in a *fabric* store!"

"Well, then?"

"Five bucks."

"Five bucks it is."

She won the first game. Grimly determined, Sean shot from farther and farther out during the second game, eventually beyond her reach. "Horse!" he declared triumphantly.

"No fair," she said. "Play-off, and you can't use your height advantage that way."

"Fine. You start." He bounced the ball to her.

They were midgame when she heard a car in the driveway. Sean had been dribbling in preparation for a tricky side-court shot when he heard it, too, and stopped with the ball in his hands.

Her mother parked behind Allie's Toyota and got out to survey them in mild surprise. "You're playing basketball?"

"Yes, and kicking Sean's butt." She grinned at him. "Sean, this is my mother, Cheryl Wright. Mom, Sean Kearney." Thank goodness she remembered his last name.

Her mother walked to them, her hand out. "It's a pleasure, Sean. I've heard a lot about you."

"Yeah, um, hi." He looked down at his hand as if checking to be sure it was there, then shook. The screen door banged, and he turned in relief. "There's Nolan."

"I see," Mom murmured.

Allie felt really strange watching these two people size each other up. Mom was her usual stylish self, her dark blond hair cut in a wavy cap, her makeup perfect but not overdone. She wore slacks, an open-weave, elbow-length sweater over a camisole and flat shoes—nothing that should have stood out, but it struck Allie suddenly how attractive her mother was.

Petite, like Allie—the dancer's body had definitely come from her mom. Why hadn't she remarried? She'd have only been—Allie had to think—forty-five when they left Dad and Jason behind and moved to Washington. Did she feel so betrayed by Dad's abandonment she wasn't interested in trusting a man again?

Like mother, like daughter?

Allie swiveled her gaze to Nolan, who, in his usual jeans and athletic shoes and T-shirt, long-sleeved in def-

erence to the changing weather, stood at the top of the
steps, smiling at her mother. Allie realized again that he
wasn't handsome, exactly. Mom wouldn't think so, anyway. At the moment Allie was very much reminded of his
stone man statue. This was a strong man. His dark hair
was ruffled, the sleeves of his shirt were pushed up to reveal muscular forearms, and the blue of his eyes seemed
more vivid than ever.

"I'm glad you could come, Mrs. Wright." He sounded
warm, as if they were old friends. "Why don't you come
on in? Unless you want to watch the tiebreaker game."

"Cheryl, please," Mom said. "Tiebreaker, is it?"

Sean snorted. "I'm going easy on her."

Allie tilted her head. "You wish."

Laughing, Mom started up the steps. "I'd be glad to
help you instead of refereeing, Nolan."

Allie was aghast to see her mother disappear into the
house with Nolan. Alone. What would they talk about?

"Maybe we should quit," she said to Sean.

"Not a chance." He shot the ball from where he was
standing, and danced in place when it dropped through
the hoop. "Match that!"

Her heart was pounding. She was such an idiot. If only
she'd confessed to her mother about telling Sean they'd
moved here from Oklahoma. That was her only really big
screwup. The others were nothing, easily explained. *We
moved a lot.* That's all she had to say.

I can't run after them. Sean wouldn't understand. Nolan
would wonder. *I am such an idiot.*

She was too rattled. Her shot bounced off the rim.

"R," Sean declared, snatching the ball midbounce. "Try
this one." He stood with his back to the hoop, jumped and
shot as he spun. *"Yes!"*

Allie missed that one, too, and mumbled a profanity under her breath.

"S. One more chance."

She matched his next shot, although she'd already realized her quickest way to join Nolan and her mother was to lose. Still, she didn't want to be obvious, and she did have her pride.

Sean dropped a shot in from near the free-throw line, making her suspicious he was going easy on her. Her answering shot banged off the backboard, rolled around the rim...and fell off.

"Crap," she declared.

"You did good for a girl."

She blew a raspberry at him. "I did good for someone who hasn't touched a basketball in years."

His smugness suffered a jolt. "Really?"

"Really." Allie started for the house. "I thought I might have lost it, but I guess not. Maybe it's like riding a bike."

"Huh. Maybe."

Cassie was waiting right inside the screen door, her delight obvious at their approach.

"She's really bonded with you, hasn't she?"

"Yeah, she likes Nolan, too, but she sticks with me when I'm home," he said with satisfaction.

"Maybe she had a boy in her last home." Allie opened the door and the dog flew out as if she'd been separated from Sean for days, weeks, eons.

Laughing, he crouched and ran his hands over her while she slopped kisses on his face.

"I'm really glad you chose her," Allie said softly.

Sean looked up at her, his expression earnest. "I never told you I was sorry for that day."

"It's okay. I understood."

"I don't know why I was so mad." He gave an awkward

shrug as he rose to his feet. "Now if we were doing something like that, I'd like it if you came."

Her face wanted to crumple and her vision momentarily blurred. She swallowed. "That's nice. Thank you," she said with reasonable composure.

The rumble of Nolan's voice came from the depths of the house, followed by her mother's laugh. What had Nolan said? When Allie reached the kitchen, she saw Mom putting together a salad while Nolan lifted a casserole dish out of the oven.

"Hey, you're just in time," he said. "Who won?"

Allie rolled her eyes. "Who do you think?"

"She's good, though," Sean said behind her. He grinned at her. "For a girl."

She lunged toward him and he dodged. "Say that one more time and you're dead meat," she threatened.

Allie's mother chuckled. "She's always been athletic."

"Did she tell you about going waterskiing?" Nolan asked. He'd carried the casserole dish to the dining room and was returning. "She got on her feet the first try. Sean did, too. They were both sure they were going to take a header."

"I did," Sean reminded them. "Out in the middle of the lake."

Allie and he went to wash their hands and came back to find the food already on the table and Nolan and her mother waiting for them.

The casserole was something with chicken, broccoli and a curry sauce, accompanied by salad and a flaxseed bread Allie recognized as coming from the bakery a block down from her store.

After murmurs of pleasure over the food, conversation stayed general, Mom rather deftly avoiding any discussion of their family history. Nolan talked about Chicago and

Mom said she'd never been there. He did say, "Allie mentioned you lived in Florida at one time."

Her glance at Allie was razor-sharp. "Oh, briefly. We moved a lot. Allie's father got restless. There's hardly anyplace we haven't lived." She laughed. "Except Chicago. What brought you out to the Northwest?"

"We came out here on a family vacation once, when I was eleven or twelve. We had a cabin on Orcas Island. I guess that sold me on Washington. When I was ready to strike out on my own, this was the first place that came to mind."

He didn't say, *This is as far away as I could get from my parents without moving to Alaska or Hawaii,* but of course Allie hadn't expected him to.

Mom asked Sean a few questions, to which he mumbled replies. He blushed when he told her about joining the basketball team and that he kind of liked biology and thought he might be some kind of scientist, although he also liked computers.

Sean went to get the dessert, which Allie gathered was also from the bakery. That was the moment when Nolan struck.

"I don't think Allie mentioned where the two of you were before moving out here," he said, pushing from the table. "Coffee?" He began gathering their dirty dinner plates.

"Thanks, I'd love a cup." Mom smiled. "Montana. Missoula was our last stop. More urban than you'd think."

Dumbstruck, Allie stole a glance toward the kitchen. Sean was still out of sight and—*please God*—earshot.

Nolan returned her smile. "I've never been there. I guess we're even." His gaze switched to Allie. "Coffee for you, too?"

"Please," she said. "Why don't I help clear the table?"

"Nah, let's finish eating first. I figured I'd grab a few dirty dishes since I'm going that way."

Dessert was a lemon-filled cake. Allie didn't taste a bite. Her anxiety had assumed hideous proportions. The fact that the conversation didn't again touch on events before she and her mother had moved to Washington State didn't allow her to relax an iota. She was totally consumed by her efforts to remember everything she'd ever told Nolan and which ones she wasn't supposed to have said.

And Sean. God. What if he'd heard her mom? Allie could picture his puzzled gaze turning to her. "I thought you said…"

It was enough to make her shudder.

"You okay?" Nolan asked.

"Me? Of course I am. Why wouldn't I be?" Belatedly she realized how defensive she sounded. Her lying skills were deteriorating, not improving. Wouldn't you think practice would make perfect?

His eyes were speculative. "Thought you might be chilly."

"No." She struggled for a smile. "I'm fine. This is an old house. Maybe a ghost strolled by."

He flashed a grin. "Interestingly enough, the previous homeowner did die here. Heart attack, I understand. His body wasn't found for a couple of days, when the newspapers had started piling up in the box out on the road. Apparently he didn't get enough mail to alert the postal worker, but the *Times* delivery guy decided to drive up to the house and make sure the old guy was okay."

Sean was staring at Nolan. "He died *here?* Like… where?"

"I didn't ask." Nolan chuckled. "You should see the look on your face."

"That's horrible!"

"No, that's the cycle of life." Nolan's tone was remarkably gentle, reminding Allie that Sean's father and grandmother had died, the grandmother not that long ago. "The broker said the guy was ninety-three. Good, long life. I'm sure his choice would have been to die at home. He won't be haunting us. If any part of him is hanging around, he's probably glad to see the place come to life again." Nolan gave a crooked grin. "He's probably wondering why the hell I haven't gotten somebody out to mow the pasture before the blackberries take over once and for all."

Sean's expression changed. "Hey, we could get a horse."

Now Nolan outright laughed. "Not this week. No boat, no horse."

"It'd make a great Christmas present."

"You ever shoveled manure?"

"No."

"You ever ridden?"

"A couple of times."

"Hmm." Nolan sat back and quirked an eyebrow at Allie. "What about you?"

"Never."

"And you lived in Montana? Tut tut." His smile transformed his bony, not-quite-handsome face. "Horseback riding sounds like something we'd all enjoy."

Allie buried her face in her hands. The rest of them laughed.

Mom, her offer to help clean up thwarted, left after some more leisurely conversation. Allie had never in her life been gladder to say goodbye to anyone.

"We'll do this again," Nolan said to her just before she got in her car.

Over my dead body was Allie's first thought, followed by the realization there was no way to avoid it if she was to keep seeing Nolan.

"I'm dragging," she said, smiling weakly. "Somehow, every time I get together with the two of you I end up going home with new muscle groups aching. I think I'd better take off, too."

Sean smirked. "You can have a rematch."

"Darn right I'm going to have a rematch." She managed an evil grin. "You're not bad...for a kid."

Their byplay got her safely in the car. When Nolan braced a hand on the open door and asked in a low voice if she had time for him tomorrow, all she could do was nod. "Of course I do. You cooked tonight. I'll make lunch."

He circled the door, bent down and kissed her lightly. "Tomorrow," he murmured while nuzzling her ear.

Panic beat hard at her while she drove away.

NOLAN SHOVED HIS hands in his jeans pockets and watched the taillights of Allie's car flare as she braked at the end of the driveway before turning out onto the road. Something had been really off tonight. She'd been quieter than usual. He'd had to scrape food off both her dinner plate and her dessert plate. In fact, unless he was imagining things, she was losing weight. She'd gotten so slight, he imagined her floating away like a puff of dandelion.

He frowned. She wasn't that bad off, or she wouldn't have been able to play a rousing three games of horse with Sean. But his instinct told him something was eating at her.

"That was weird," Sean said.

Nolan started. He hadn't realized Sean still stood there in the pool of porch light. "What's weird?" he asked, turning.

"What her mother said." His foster son was still staring into the dark where Allie's car had disappeared. "You know. About Montana."

Nolan's attention snapped into focus. "Why is that weird?"

Sean finally looked at him. "Well, because Allie said they lived in Oklahoma before they came here. She said that's where she went to high school before Lynnwood."

What the hell? "They moved a lot. You're sure she said she was in high school there?"

"Positive." Sean sounded indignant. "I said wasn't it dusty, and she laughed at me and said there were cities like anywhere else, that it wasn't like *Oklahoma!* I didn't know what she was talking about, so she told me about the musical. I looked it up online. They did it in Seattle at the Fifth Avenue Theatre not that long ago."

"Yeah, I remember the reviews." Nolan shook his head in disbelief. "Why the hell...?"

"I don't know." The teenager was quiet for a moment. "She wouldn't lie to me, would she?"

"I can't imagine why she would." But somebody was lying, that was for damned sure. And if he had to guess... Allie had been tense from the moment her mother got there. Her smiles looked forced.

But why, why would she lie about something like that? Why prop it up with the talk about the musical? Why tell Sean at all where she'd gone to high school?

He felt sick and tried to tell himself there was an explanation. His gut told him she wasn't going to want to offer one, though, and that if she did, it would probably be a lie, too. Anyone else that evasive about their background, he'd think they were hiding something ugly. A crime.

God. He felt as if he'd taken a blow to his chest. What if she and her mother had had to move suddenly Allie's senior year of high school not because of the parents' divorce, but because *Allie* desperately needed a fresh start? What if the father had cut her off for a good reason?

CHAPTER ELEVEN

NOLAN CALLED NOT long after Allie had gotten up in the morning and apologized because he had to cancel on her today. He had an emergency rush on a job, he told her; he'd be holding up the contractor until he produced the countertops.

Allie didn't have any reason to doubt that he was telling her the truth, but he sounded more reserved than usual. Maybe somebody was with him, she tried to convince herself, but didn't believe it. Could Mom have said things while they were alone together that contradicted what she had told him?

She hadn't slept well last night. She grimaced at the thought. Okay, she had hardly slept *at all* last night. How could she go on like this?

I have to tell him.

But she'd promised to talk to her mother first. She'd do that. It was lucky he *had* canceled today. She would go to Mom's tonight and argue for the right to open their lives to Nolan. At least now Mom had met him. She'd know how solid and trustworthy he was.

Anxiety continued to ride her all day, though. She did some errands because she had to fill her time somehow, then settled down to try to piece her new quilt. But after stitching a row of tiny triangles on her machine, snipping the thread and turning to her ironing board to press out the seams and cut them apart, she stared in shock at the blue fabric—which was supposed to be background, not rocking horse. She obviously hadn't been thinking at all when she'd been cutting or sewing.

"Wow." She picked up the bundle of sewn squares and dropped it in the trash. Either she had to start over, or do something else. "I vote for something else," she told her quiet apartment.

She'd quilt instead. Her hands knew what to do. With only diagonal lines, working on Sean's quilt would take no mental function whatsoever.

As always, she was soothed by the act of quilting. The tiny stitches, the precision, the rocking motion, the way each completed block filled some emptiness in her, too, calmed her. She continued until her back ached, her fingers started to cramp and, despite the leather thimble, she'd punctured her fingertip a few too many times.

Midafternoon she made herself have a bowl of soup, all she could stomach. Despite the mist that wasn't quite rain, she went for a run later. By the time she showered and dried her hair, she only had another hour to kill before her mother should be home from work.

Maybe she should call in advance, but she didn't want to. She needed to catch her mother unprepared.

When she rang the bell and her mother opened the door, Allie saw that she'd accomplished more than she had expected. Mom looked more than surprised.

"Allie? Is something wrong?"

"I wanted to talk to you. Is now okay?"

"I was putting dinner on, but…of course it is. Come in. Have you eaten?"

"I'm not hungry."

She followed her mother to the kitchen, where she turned off a burner then faced Allie.

"What is it?"

"You know I'm not a very good liar."

Fear. Oh, yes, her mother was afraid. "What are you telling me?" she whispered.

"I've said things to Nolan and Sean that I shouldn't." The burning in her chest had to be heartburn. "I'm so muddled now, I don't even remember what I've said."

"Did I contradict you?" Mom pressed her fingers to her lips.

"Yes." Allie shook her head. "No. That's not the point. Mom, I have to tell him everything."

Her mother's eyes dilated with shock. "You can't! You know you can't."

"I love him." Allie crossed her arms, all but hugging herself. "I can't keep lying like this. I can't."

Her mother shuddered. "I don't understand what's happening to you. You *know* the risks. We've all known from the beginning that we have to live the lives we've been given. It's foolish and dangerous to try to reclaim any part of what we left behind.

"You've spent your entire adult life as Allie Wright. That *is* who you are! There is absolutely no reason Nolan ever has to know that a long time ago you had a different name."

"Two different names."

"Two," Mom agreed. Her voice was gaining strength. *She's regaining her confidence she can wear me down,* Allie realized. "You're the same person inside, sweetheart. That's who he loves. If he does."

Allie stared at her. "You think he doesn't? Is that what you're saying?"

"Of course not! How would I know? Has he told you he loves you? Has he asked you to marry him? Is that what set this off?"

"No, he hasn't asked. But what if he does, Mom? Am I

really going to marry a man who believes all kinds of un-truths about me? How could I raise children to be honest if I'm a big fat liar?"

"You're getting hysterical." Mom stepped forward to put an arm around her.

Allie lurched back. "What is it you think Nolan will do? Put in a call to the Moretti family and ask whether it's true that Joanna Marr used to work for them, only she testified in court against one of their enforcers, and, oh, by the way, she lives in Washington State now under the name Cheryl Wright?"

"Why don't we walk outside and be sure the neigh-bors can hear," her mother said furiously. "Is that what you want?"

"No!" Allie yelled. "What I want is to tell the truth to one man. I want him to know me. Why is that too much to ask?"

Her mother stared at her without saying anything for a long time. She seemed to have aged ten years in the past ten minutes. "You're the one person in the world I've al-ways been able to depend on," she said finally, her be-wilderment obvious. "I never dreamed..." She broke off.

Allie's sinuses felt hot. Her mother saw this as a be-trayal. Was it? Something hurt in her couldn't let go, though. "Did you assume I'd never marry? That you'd never have to worry about me wanting to...to trust some-one else this much?"

"How can you say that?" Mom's voice was constricted, wounded. "Of course I wanted you to have a full life! What I didn't expect was that you'd believe you had to risk our lives to prove to a man that you loved him."

"That's not it."

"Then what is it? Make me understand."

They finally sat down in the living room. Allie tried to

explain her confusion. "As Allie Wright, I'm not whole. Because I *am* Chloe, too, and even Laura. Don't you see? You were an adult when all this happened. The different names were only labels for you. You *were* whole. I never had the chance."

Mom didn't get it, she could tell. What Allie didn't know was why. Was she so fixated on her fear that the boogeyman would come after them, she couldn't see how unlikely it was? Or was she completely unable to see that her daughter was very different from her?

Allie sat looking at her mother and had an unsettling moment. They'd always been so close, depending on each other. She'd have sworn they knew each other. What she should be asking herself now was whether Mom had ever really known her. But instead she thought, *Do I really know* her?

For the first time in forever, she remembered watching her mother during that long-ago week in Florida, when her parents had argued in bursts, cutting off each time they realized one of their kids had come within hearing distance. Even outside of her own fear and disbelief at what they were arguing about, she'd been perplexed because Mom seemed different. And…she never went back to being the same Mom she'd been before.

Dad had been angry, frustrated, then ultimately stunned. She, though, had had an air of suppressed excitement. She seemed to carry herself taller, to fill more space. In fact, all the changes they underwent made Dad smaller and Mom larger. Had she liked that? Allie asked herself now. Was it possible her mother had been unhappy before, unsatisfied with who she was or with her life, and was secretly thrilled to grab at an entirely new self—a heroine? Or was it only the pride Allie had believed it to be?

Dear God, Allie thought, *I hope that was it.*

Could her parents' marriage have been in trouble already, before her mother stayed late at work that day and overheard the conversation that shattered their lives? It struck Allie now that her father had never talked to her and her brother, not apart from their mother, about what was going to happen to all of them. He was there, sometimes, but stayed quiet, letting his wife take the lead and explain. He'd never talk about it later, either. What did he think about how Mom changed?

Maybe I never really knew either of them.

Maybe her mother had never shared the disorientation the rest of them felt, or even the grief.

It was weird how memories could cascade. Suddenly she remembered how when they were at Nanna's she'd often hear sharp voices from the kitchen. Nanna had loved traditions, but Mom thought they were ridiculous. Allie discovered now that she'd captured a picture of Nanna's expression as she watched her daughter. It had been so very sad.

Mom, Allie remembered, hadn't liked Nanna's tatted snowflakes at all and had put them on the Christmas tree after a snapped "Oh, I suppose her feelings would be hurt if we didn't."

Allie had grieved when they left, knowing she'd never again see this grandmother, whom she loved so much. But Mom hadn't actually liked her own mother that much.

Not more than a minute had passed. Allie's mother watched her with distress and a lot of other emotions Allie couldn't read at all. Not that long ago, she would have been blithely certain she knew what her mother thought and felt. *But I was wrong. So wrong,* she thought, dazed.

Or...maybe I'm wrong now.

How was she supposed to know?

This was her mother, she reminded herself. Her one certainty. The only person whose love she knew was unshakable. That much was true, even if a whole lot else she'd always believed wasn't.

Maybe *she* hadn't explained herself very well.

"Mom, you met Nolan. Does he seem like someone who'd be untrustworthy?"

"That's not the point. It's not that he'd deliberately set out to give away what you told him. But you know how easily it could happen. He lives with a teenager. Sean could overhear a few words and tell his friends. Or put it up on Facebook. Or one of them might. The world isn't as small as it used to be."

That was true, of course. *And I already told Sean something I shouldn't.*

A something that wasn't very important, because it was about Laura Nelson, not Chloe Marr. And, although the U.S. Marshals had worried that someone might be close to uncovering their identity, that hadn't really happened. Obviously, Dad and Jason were fine. They still lived openly in Tulsa, and no one had stuck a gun to Dad's head and demanded to know where his wife had gone. Hastily relocating Mom and Allie might not have been necessary at all.

Mom, she thought, feeling sick, had almost seemed excited again. As if the fact that she might be in danger made her feel important.

Horrified at herself, Allie wanted to take back her speculation. She knew her mother better than that! She'd been devastated when Jason decided to stay behind, too. She had held Allie and cried. "What would I ever do without you?" she'd whispered.

What if I said now, "Mom, do you ever think maybe you're not that important? Do you really think anybody still searches the internet for clues to where you are? After fifteen years?"

But she knew she couldn't say any of that.

"Mom, I think this is something I need to do," she said instead, voice quivering.

Her mother's face spasmed. "And I'm begging you not to. I think I deserve enough of your loyalty to ask that much."

Allie felt herself go numb inside. However much her foundations had shifted, she did love her mother. The realization that she couldn't choose Nolan over Mom would leave her desolate if she let it.

She stood up. "All right. You win. I'll try—" Her throat closed up. She absolutely could not finish. Could not say, *I'll try to believe he and I can be happy with me lying to him constantly.* Could not say, *I'll try to believe I can be a complete person despite the fact that the first seventeen years of my life have been severed from me.*

Could not say, *I'll try to keep loving you as much as I always have, even though I think you just manipulated me and guilted me and never really tried to understand how I feel.*

"I need to go home." She started for the door, only then remembering she'd set down her purse in the kitchen and diverted that way. "I'm sorry."

"I wish you'd stay for dinner." Sounding unhappy, Mom followed her. "I know you're not eating enough. And I can tell you don't understand."

"I think you're wrong." Thank God, there was her purse. Allie grabbed it and kept going. "But I do understand why you're scared, Mom, and I guess I have to respect that. And I really, really don't want to talk any more about it tonight, okay?" She fumbled to get the front door open.

"All right. But…could we have lunch one day this week?"

Allie risked a look back and saw only her mother. Her best friend.

"Of course we can," she said, gently even though she felt...not much at all.

Their good-nights weren't all that different from usual. Driving home, Allie tried to convince herself that nothing really had changed, and that her mother was right. Nolan could love her without ever knowing her secrets.

SOMEHOW SHE WASN'T at all surprised when the bell above the door tinkled at precisely 1:15 the next afternoon and, when she turned from where she'd been replacing a bolt of fabric on the rack, she saw that it was Nolan who had walked into her otherwise empty store, a couple of bags of food in his hands.

"You finished your job?" she asked.

"Yeah. I missed you yesterday."

"I missed you, too." Her voice sounded weird. A little scratchy.

He didn't say anything for a minute, but he looked into her eyes with unnerving intensity. "Did you?" he said finally.

She willed herself not to overreact. She might be imagining the undertones here. "I got a lot of work done on Sean's quilt. I might have it ready for him in as soon as a couple of weeks."

"Seriously?"

"You doubt me?" Allie was proud of her mock offended stance.

He should have smiled and said *of course I don't.* Instead, there was an odd little silence, during which his very blue eyes contemplated her. "I brought lunch," he said at last, abruptly.

Okay, she wasn't imagining anything. There was definitely something wrong. Would he tell her what it was? Allie couldn't even guess.

"I especially appreciate it today," she told him lightly. "I forgot to bring anything."

He followed when she went to the back. "You're losing weight, aren't you?"

"Maybe a little. I always tend to be skinny."

"Not skinny." He frowned. "Delicate."

"That's a more flattering word." She took a chance, rose on tiptoe and kissed his cheek. "I'm glad you're here."

"Yeah." He set down the bags and tugged her against him for a more thorough kiss. "I'm glad I am, too."

He distributed today's lunch, take-out bowls of split pea soup and sourdough rolls that smelled as if they were right out of the oven, then asked if she'd done anything special yesterday.

Confronted my mother. "Nope. Like I said, mostly quilted."

He pried the top off his bowl. "You may have gotten your coloring from your dad, but I could see your mom in you."

"Yes. I got my size from her for sure."

"More than that."

"I suppose so." She hesitated. "Do you look like your mother?"

"No." He cleared his throat. "Not at all."

"I'm sorry."

Nolan frowned and didn't respond. He appeared to be concentrating on buttering his roll.

"Sean told me something," he said finally.

Allie slowly lifted her gaze to his. "What?" she croaked.

"That you said you moved here from Oklahoma." Pause. "Not Montana."

She was nearly paralyzed, unable to think. She was

already tangled in this lie. How did she get out? "That's true," she said. "Mom was… She always says that. We, um, did live in Montana. Before. But, well, Dad and Jason are still in Oklahoma, and she doesn't like to think about it, and so…she leaves out the time we spent in Oklahoma." Oh, God, that was weak. Would he buy it?

The relentlessness she saw in his eyes said plainly that he didn't. "Where in Oklahoma?" he asked. "My sister dated a guy from somewhere near Oklahoma City. Choctaw, I think."

"We were just outside Tulsa. A suburb."

"Oh? Which one?"

Of course he wasn't letting up at all. The steel in his voice told her any more evasions would be the end.

Neither Dad nor Jason were in the same town where she'd graduated from high school, though they'd stayed in the area. It wouldn't matter if she told Nolan; there was nothing to find there anymore.

"Fairfield. Nothing distinctive about it, not even the name." She summoned a smile. "I learned later there are Fairfields all over the country. And, like I told Sean, it wasn't cowboy country."

"Fairfield." He nodded, his gaze momentarily distant as if he was filing the name away for future reference. Then it refocused like a laser. "What happened that made your mother so bitter?"

"I'm…not altogether sure. I think—" *Daddy, I'm so sorry!* "—that he might have had an affair. But somehow their split involved Jason. I think he lied to cover for my father. He wouldn't tell me." She was talking too fast, she knew she was, but he'd never have believed a simple "I don't know."

"Your…loyalty to her is commendable. But do you think it's fair that she expects you to cut your father and brother out of your life because that's what she decided to do?" The words sounded sympathetic, but his expression didn't match. It could only be described as calculating.

"I was always closer to her," Allie said simply. "There was no choice for me. And my brother and I reacted differently to everything." That was true. "He got angry and rebellious as a teenager." Also true, so true. She had admired him for his willingness to rage aloud, something she'd been too stunned and confused to do. "He quit talking to me. Accused me of being a little Goody Two-shoes, going along with whatever Mom said."

Until this moment, she hadn't understood how right he was. That *was* what she'd always done. And she'd done it again last night—let her mother make a decision that should have been hers alone.

Except…maybe not. It was her mother a New York mob family had promised to kill, not Allie. That was something she couldn't forget.

Nolan's expression softened, as much as his angular face would allow. "He hurt you."

She lifted one shoulder in an almost-apologetic shrug. "Not that much. By then I was so mad at him I didn't care as much as I probably should have what he thought of me." Her mouth twisted. "My family was a mess. It's been peaceful, having only Mom and me."

"I guess you and I have that in common, don't we?" His eyes were warm again, not calculating at all. "We've run away from family."

"Yes, except in my case I trailed along behind my mother. You had the courage to do it yourself."

Me, I've never done anything but trail along behind my mother, not since they yanked me away from my life. And that, Allie supposed, summed it all up: dance *was* her life, and once she lost it, she'd never regained any sense of place or identity or meaning.

Except for quilting. Her head turned, and she took in the shop. The rainbow of colors, the glossy wood floors and creamy walls and the beautiful quilts hung, some for display, some for sale. The board that listed classes, the row of sewing machines in back, the long table and her quilt frame.

Yes, she did have a purpose and identity now. *I am a quilt maker.* But the finding of that identity had been slow. She hadn't even fully understood until now how important it had been for her to find something that fulfilled her.

"Not courage," Nolan denied. "I was tired of family pressure and tension, that's all."

"Do you have pictures of them?"

He looked surprised. "You mean in my wallet? Maybe old ones. Not my mother and father." He shifted on his seat to pull out his wallet. After a minute of thumbing through it, he removed a tattered photo. "Man, that's from a long time ago. Prom," he added unnecessarily, and kept digging through a miscellany of worn receipts, business cards and who knew what.

Allie took the photo, feeling a funny cramp in her stomach at the thought that maybe he was showing her a picture of himself and his date at prom. But no. The boy in the picture definitely wasn't Nolan. Looking closely at the girl, Allie thought she could see a resemblance to Nolan. Her bone structure was too strong for her to be called pretty. Yes, the cheekbones did have something in common with his. She had strawberry-blond hair, though, and a scattering of freckles across her nose. She was tall and skinny. Her expression suggested she wasn't comfortable in the typical too-feminine prom dress and awkward heels, with her pale red hair up in some complicated do decorated with flowers.

"Anna?" Allie assumed.

He'd found another photo. He handed it over and took the one from her hand. He laughed softly, looking at his sister. "Yeah. She grumbled all afternoon getting ready. I kept saying, 'You don't have to go,' and she'd snap, 'Yes, I do and you know why.'"

"Why?"

"There was this bitch at school who headed the popular clique and loved nothing better than belittling everyone else. I think it got so she was Anna's personal nemesis. She predicted—loudly—that no one would ask Anna to prom. By that time Anna was asserting her calling as an artist partly by wearing sacky jeans or even overalls stained by clay or glazes all the time. Clunky boots. Flannel shirts." Nolan smiled, remembering.

"My little sister. Mouthy, abrasive, didn't take any shit from anyone. Now, she wouldn't let some stuck-up airhead get to her, but she was a teenager, after all. She had some guys who were buddies, and bullied one of them into taking her to prom. I think they stayed all of a couple of hours, breathed a sigh of relief and went home." He set down the photo. "Anna's…well, not a beauty, but closer now. The men like her, anyhow. She's always got one around."

Lifting the other picture, Allie recognized it as a senior photo. Nolan's brother appeared terribly young and yet didn't have that unfinished look either his sister or Nolan did. He was conventionally handsome, his brown hair lying smooth, his smile for the camera confident and unshadowed.

"He really doesn't look like you," she said, handing it back. "Or Anna, does he?"

"No. Jed takes after our…his father. Anna and I…who

knows? Except her coloring comes from Mom. Her eyes, too, I guess."

"You don't think you might have the same father? It seems as if you have the same bone structure."

"I doubt it." But he studied the photo again for a moment before carefully tucking both back into his wallet and restoring it to his hip pocket.

She might have argued had his tone not been so final. Because he knew something about one or the other of their fathers? Because he didn't *want* to know? Or because he hated the idea that his mother might keep going back to the same man even more than he hated the idea of serial affairs?

"Do you have a picture of your brother?" he asked. Which she supposed was a natural question.

"I...actually do," she admitted. "His prom picture. What an awful moment for all of us to be frozen in time."

She went to get it from her purse, locked behind the counter. There wasn't any reason she shouldn't show it to Nolan, was there? She couldn't think of one. She also kept a picture of her father in her wallet and couldn't think of any reason not to show Nolan that one, too.

He took them from her with such care, it was obvious he thought she was giving him a gift in sharing them with him. That made her ashamed. He hadn't hesitated to take out the pictures of his sister and brother, while having to pry every nugget of information about her family from her.

He studied both photos for a long time, as if fascinated. "You do look more like your mother," he said at last. "Except for the coloring. Both you and your brother—Jason?—got that from your dad."

The bell over the door rang and she turned her head to see that a couple of women had come in. They weren't regulars. She stood and called, "Hi, I'll be right with you."

Nolan returned the pictures to her with what she thought was reluctance. "I'd better get back to work, and let you do the same."

"Thank you for bringing lunch," she said.

"I wanted to see you." He glanced toward the women, who had their backs turned, and kissed Allie. "I'll call," he said roughly.

She tried to smile. "Please."

"Allie, I wish I thought…" He shook his head. "Never mind. This isn't the time." He nodded toward the customers. "I'll clean up. Go on."

She did, but was very aware when he left a minute later without saying anything else to her. The panic that felt like a small bird trapped in her chest was with her every time she saw him lately, and every time he left and she had to wonder if she'd given away anything new this time.

Fairfield. She had admitted to that, but couldn't see how it mattered. Although Mom wouldn't be happy.

Quite suddenly she had a headache. Her stomach felt queasy, too, and she began to regret the soup.

I don't know if I can keep doing this.

But she'd continue to feel as if she was being torn in two as long as she and Nolan were together.

She saw her mother's face. Heard her say, *You're the one person in the world I've always been able to depend on.*

And then Nolan, implacable, asking, *Where in Oklahoma?*

Allie had to close her eyes against the pain that stabbed her temple.

CHAPTER TWELVE

So NOW HE knew where she'd gone to high school, Nolan thought on the drive home. Assuming she'd told the truth. He'd seen the alarm in her eyes when he pressed for specifics. Would he find there even was a town of Fairfield near Tulsa? And, goddamn it, what was he going to do if there wasn't?

Or, for that matter, if there was. Fly there next weekend and show her picture around town? From what she'd said, she had moved away over ten years ago, and she might not have lived there that long. She kept repeating that her family had moved a lot.

He wondered if there was a way he could track Allie's brother. Wright was a common enough last name, but hadn't Allie mentioned that the guy was still in the Tulsa area? If so, that would be a place to start.

Nolan made himself go back to work when he got home, but brooded all afternoon. He had to lay off when it was time to pick Sean up after basketball practice. Seeing him walking out of the gym with a cluster of other boys, laughing and talking, stopping once to half wrestle with one of them, that was a bright spot in Nolan's day. Sean had started getting phone calls at home over the past week or two. And he was talking about teammates in the casual way that suggested they were becoming friends.

"Eric says he skis, but Coach doesn't like it 'cause he's sure he'll break a leg and be out midseason. But, man, I'd really like to learn. He says I could ride up with his family…" Or, "Aidan's got a twin sister. Did I tell you that? He's kind of *doofus* looking, but she's sort of hot. I mean, you know." His hands shaped a pair of stupendous breasts. "He said she wanted to know who I was."

Today, he hopped in the truck, fastened the seat belt and planted his feet on the dashboard. "So, I made this *awesome* pass to Jared and then went for the key. He totally faked out Dylan, spun like he was going to shoot and then zapped the ball to me. I laid it up so sweet." He pumped his fist. "After practice Coach said he thinks we're going to have a *fabulous* season."

Nolan grinned at him. "That's great. All that time you've been putting in on the hoop at home is paying off, isn't it?"

"Yeah." He grinned. "I'm going to kick Allie's butt the next time we play, too."

"She was pretty amazing for someone who probably hadn't shot a basket in years."

Sean grunted his agreement. "It's like…her body is totally *centered*. You know? There's the way she moves, and she has this sense of where she is in relation to everything else. I bet she could have done something like gymnastics."

"I've had the same thought. She did say she took dance lessons when she was a kid."

Sean started grumbling about a paper he had due, and Nolan was just as glad not to talk about Allie anymore. He was too troubled by his thoughts. He knew she was lying to him, damn it! He only wished he could tell which things that came out of her mouth were lies, and which were truth.

That evening after dinner he went online and verified that, indeed, Tulsa had a suburb named Fairfield. And she was right, there were a lot of other towns named Fairfield around the country, starting with one in California.

So now what? he asked himself. Call the high school and ask for verification that Allie Wright had indeed attended? What excuse could he give? Did schools give out that kind of information?

He frowned. Why wouldn't they?

Try.

Come morning, he stood there with the phone in his hand, and conducted a serious argument with himself. How would he feel, if he found out Allie was doing a background check on him because she doubted what he'd told her about himself? Trust was part of a relationship, wasn't it?

But I know she's lying.

Did that excuse him? He wasn't sure. Was he exhibiting signs of major paranoia? Probably.

But he hated lies with a passion. And he faced the fact that he had to know, one way or another. Please God, may she never find out he'd made this call, he thought, dialing the number for information.

A couple of minutes later, he was talking to a school secretary at Fairfield High School. He claimed to be a potential employer wanting to verify attendance and graduation.

"That shouldn't be a problem," the woman said cheerily.

He heard a keyboard clicking, some mumbles.

"I'm sorry," the secretary finally told him. "I'm unable to find any student named Allie Wright. I tried Allison and some other variations. What years do you believe she attended?"

He told her. More tapping.

The answer was "no." There had been students with a last name of Wright, of course. Perhaps Allie was a middle name or nickname? He said he'd find out and ended the call.

He swore aloud, resisting the urge to throw the phone. Now what? Call her on her lie? But what if Allie *was* her middle name? Did he admit what he'd done?

"Goddamn it," he growled.

His doubt hung heavy on him all day, disrupting his concentration. He got careless and broke a saw blade, the piece flying away barely missing his arm. He swore some more and managed to pay more attention until the time came to pick up Sean again after practice.

He'd vowed not to say anything to Sean about his fear that Allie was lying to him. "I don't seem to have it together today," he admitted, once Sean got in and slammed the door. "You okay with stopping for a pizza on the way home?"

"Is Scarlett Johansson hot?" the teenager said.

Nolan had to blink. Well, yeah. He'd take that as a yes.

At his favorite pizza parlor, they ordered, then settled at their table with glasses of soda. He wasn't much of a drinker; he had an occasional beer at home, but he wanted to be sure he set a no-drinking-and-driving example for a kid Sean's age.

"So, did you ever ask Allie about the Oklahoma thing?" Sean surprised him by asking.

"Yeah. She says her mother is the one who wants to pretend they never lived there." He should stop there, he knew he should. "But I could tell Allie was uneasy about the whole thing. Wish I knew why."

"You can look, you know."

Nolan stared at him. "What do you mean?"

"Well, lots of high schools have their yearbooks online now." He shrugged. "I mean, you guys were in high school a long time ago. Maybe those old yearbooks aren't up, but you could check."

"Allie is only twenty-eight," Nolan said mildly.

Sean looked at him as if he was an idiot. "That's ten *years* ago."

"You're making me feel like an old man. I don't like it."

The kid laughed at him. "You're getting, like, middle-aged, you know. That's almost old."

"Thank you." He shook his head. "They just called our number. My arthritis is acting up. You go get the pizza."

Sean thought that was pretty funny. He was chortling when he slid out of the booth and headed toward the front.

"Yearbooks are really online?" Nolan asked him, when he returned with two plates and an extra-large pizza with everything on it. "Where anyone can look at them? I didn't photograph well." Or should he have said, *I* don't *photograph well?*

Sean surveyed him with a critical eye while still managing to take a bite and chew enthusiastically at the same time. "Yeah," he finally decided, "that's probably because your face isn't really *together*. You know? It's kind of bony, and your hair is always sticking out, and…"

Nolan held up a hand to silence him. "If you keep going, my ego may never recover."

Sean shrugged. "Allie likes you, so what difference does it make what you look like?"

"That's true." Of course, that was assuming Allie wasn't conning him big-time.

But…why would she be? What did she have to gain from pretending to like him? From making up a background that would satisfy him?

None of it made any sense. His original questions had been casual; he didn't care where she'd grown up or gone to high school. He'd never have given her answers a second thought if she hadn't been so obviously evasive, and if then she hadn't lied.

Or her mother lied, he reminded himself.

"I can help you find her yearbook online if you want," Sean offered. "If you don't think you can."

"It's probably not beyond my abilities," Nolan said drily. "If I fail, you can be my backup."

"Maybe she looked dorky in high school. She might have had zits all over her face, or dyed her hair blond or had a whole bunch of piercings."

Nolan finally did laugh. "In which case, I won't recognize her."

Sean pondered for another minute. "I bet Allie never had zits."

"I bet not, too."

When they got home, Nolan did not rush straight to his computer. He would be happiest if Sean didn't know how serious he was about this search. The kid kept popping out of his room to ask questions for his research paper and then to tell Nolan this cool thing that had happened today and that sucky one. At long last, he disappeared and stayed disappeared.

Nolan went online.

It took some doing, but damned if Sean wasn't right. It appeared that many if not most high schools now put the yearbooks up on the internet. What's more, they were apparently going back and putting the old ones up, too. If Nolan wanted, he could probably hunt for his parents'.

As it happened, he'd seen their yearbooks. Those photos had cemented his awareness that he did not in any way resemble the man he had always called Dad. Once he'd known the truth, he'd felt dumb for not suspecting sooner.

Shaking off thoughts about his lying parents, he zeroed in on Fairfield High School, Oklahoma—the computer seemed determined to divert him to a high school with the same name in another state.

Allie had moved at the beginning of her senior year,

she'd said. Probably before photos were taken. He found
the year before she'd moved, although he could conceiv-
ably be a year off, depending on whether she was almost
twenty-nine or barely twenty-eight. The search by name
brought up one student with the last name of Wright—a
boy named James. He took a careful look, but the kid was
skinny, blond and had a big nose. Not Allie's brother—
and hadn't she said he was older than her, anyway? He'd
presumably already graduated the year she was a junior.

Grimly determined, Nolan scrolled through the freshmen. Despite his mood, he found it briefly entertaining,
since Sean was that age. The prettiest girls were trying
so hard to look sophisticated, the rest of the girls were
clearly wishing to be anywhere at all but in front of the
camera, and the boys might as well have been eight-year-
olds who'd grown strangely tall. Except for one—a guy
with serious shoulders who was probably already shav-
ing and could have been eighteen. Maybe he'd been held
back a year. Or not. Nolan had had a classmate like that.
He got all the girls until the rest of the boys starting catching up, maturity-wise, their junior and senior years. Nolan
smiled reminiscently. He'd been pretty damn happy when
he started needing to shave—and when he'd realized he
was as tall as Mitch Judson.

Sophomores were noticeably more relaxed. Even the
girls who weren't the prettiest were using makeup with
more confidence, relaxing into who they were. Allie's face
was not among them.

He was feeling some reluctance by the time he started
in on the juniors. Was he really so set on confirming that
she'd lied to him? And he already knew there was no Allie
Wright among the students pictured in this yearbook. He
was being stubborn, that's all, not wanting to admit she'd
really do that to him.

That he meant so little to her.

Halfway through, he was only glancing from face to face. He'd lost interest in reflecting on his own high school years, or how Sean would change so much over the next two years. He felt a little sick. Could he possibly have been so wrong about Allie?

His gaze stopped on some poor kid with the unenviable last name of Parfomchuk. Bet *he'd* spend his whole life having to spell his name.

But that wasn't what had stopped Nolan. Going back, his eye reluctantly passed over several faces—Opgaard, Oliver, Oakes, Numley, Neumiller…Nelson.

Stunned, he found himself looking at a very young and pretty Allie Wright—whose name, according to the yearbook, had been Laura Nelson.

He closed his eyes then opened them again. Yep. It was still undeniably her. Different, of course; at sixteen, she'd been astonishingly beautiful, and yet unlike most of the other girls she wasn't smiling. Her expression was…shy, maybe, but also grave.

He imagined her walking through the halls of the high school with that untouchable air. Pretty as a fairy princess, but he still bet she'd been labeled stuck-up. Unless the day this picture had been taken was a very bad one for young Laura Nelson.

And just who in the *hell* was Laura Nelson?

Or maybe the better question was, why, when Allie and her mother ran, had they been so scared they assumed new identities?

And what would Allie say if he asked her?

NOLAN BROODED ABOUT it for three straight days.

He called Allie Wednesday night and they talked for

nearly half an hour, but his questions weren't the kind he wanted to ask when he couldn't see her face.

Thursday he took lunch to her shop again. He would have sworn she was glad to see him—but he also saw the flicker of apprehension in her beautiful green-gold eyes. She didn't used to be nervous with him, but she was now, and he didn't like knowing that.

He kept reminding himself that she *hadn't* lied to him. There was a reason she and her mother didn't want to be found—domestic violence was rearing, real ugly, in his mind—but despite everything Allie had chosen to be honest with him. Nolan held on tight to that knowledge.

As they finished lunch Nolan nearly choked on the question, *Who is Laura Nelson?* Wadding up his sandwich wrapping, he was on the verge of blurting it out when three older women entered the shop.

Smiling, Allie rose and went to greet them. They'd apparently brought quilts for her to consider for her next mini-quilt show—he got that much out of what he heard— and it was clear that his private time with her was over. He couldn't decide whether he was frustrated or glad he'd been saved from possibly making a huge mistake.

He spent the next day trying to talk himself into letting it go. She had been truthful, insofar as she thought she could. Shouldn't he be satisfied to know that much?

But he wasn't, and Nolan knew himself well enough to be damn sure he wouldn't be able to live with this kind of ever-present itch. He was in love with a woman who was living a lie of some kind.

The parallels with the lies his parents had told were too blatant. Too powerful.

He had to know.

Ask?

Or get the answers some other way?

By Friday he'd decided. Allie might not forgive him if she found out…but maybe she'd never need to learn what he'd done.

He went online again, and searched the Tulsa Yellow Pages for private investigators.

ALLIE SO DID not want to be spending Sunday with her mother instead of Nolan, but he hadn't suggested they get together this weekend at all. So far he hadn't said anything about Monday, either.

With no good excuse, Allie had agreed to lunch and a movie. She and her mother had made stilted conversation on the drive to Mt. Vernon after agreeing on the Calico Cupboard for lunch. Allie was doing her damnedest to be pleasant and avoid any subjects of contention.

For one thing, she definitely didn't want to talk about Nolan.

She'd been feeling hollow for days now. He'd obviously cooled toward her. Either something was wrong, or he was getting bored. She didn't know which explanation she hated more.

She and her mother were seated at a small table next to a railing, overlooking an antiques store a half a level below in the old brick building. The minute the two of them had given their orders and the waitress left them alone, Mom ditched the smile and leaned forward.

"I'd hoped by this time you'd have come around to see-ing that I was right."

Allie stared at her in disbelief. "Because there's no chance you could be wrong?"

"All I'm doing is insisting we follow the instructions we were given. You know that, Allie. We made a com-mitment."

All her good intentions evaporated. "You and Dad made

a commitment." Oh, God—didn't that sound like a sulky teenager?

"What were our choices?" Her mother's voice had hardened. "I wasn't the only one in danger. A car bomb could have killed all of us. Or the Morettis might have decided to use my children as an example."

"I heard you and Dad arguing, you know. Back then."

Her mother looked wary. "What do you mean?"

"He didn't want you to testify. He said you'd already steered the police in the right direction—they could dig up evidence on their own."

"But what if they couldn't? What if a murderer got away with it, because I wasn't courageous enough to tell a jury what I heard?"

"Dad said something else." Allie had never meant to confront her mother about this, but an anger she didn't recognize had been driving her for weeks now. "He said the victim was another mob figure. 'Scum' was the word he used. He said it wasn't as if you'd overheard someone who had killed a child."

There was a tremor in her words now. "Mom, to ensure justice for a man who probably didn't deserve it, you damaged all of our lives. Shouldn't we have come first? Dad and Jason? Me?"

Her mother flinched when the shock wave of what Allie had said hit. Then she sat, very still, for a long time.

The waitress, smiling and chatty, brought the salads they'd ordered. Allie managed a distracted thanks. Mom didn't move a muscle.

Neither of them reached for their napkins or forks when they were alone again. Allie balled her shaking hands into fists on her lap beneath the tablecloth. They stared at each other.

"You believe I damaged your life."

Incredulous, Allie shook her head. "How can you even ask that?"

"You weren't exactly deprived," her mother said stiffly. "We gave you kids a good life."

"Yes, you did. But it wasn't the life we had. Do you have any idea how much I loved to dance? I was talented, Mom. I could have reached my dreams. You stole that from me when you decided it was more important to testify that day in court."

She saw the way her mother blanched and knew that she had hurt her. That hadn't been her intention when they started this, but a part of her had needed to say it, if only once. *See what you did to me.*

"You were thirteen. You might have lost interest or been injured or who knows what. Do you really think I should have violated my moral integrity because my teenage daughter had a favorite—" she waved a hand "—activity?"

Okay, that made Allie mad all over again. "You had to know how important it was to me. And what about Dad? He was so proud of Marr Industries. I remember how much he hoped Jason would want to go to work with him, be the fourth-generation Marr to be CEO. You stole that from both of them, too. Our grandparents lost us, and we lost them. We lost our *names.*"

The silence was thick and painful. "I had no idea," her mother whispered at last.

"What you did to us?"

"That this is what you've thought all along."

"Did you think I was starving myself for no reason?" Horrified, Allie realized she'd raised her voice enough that heads were turning. Thank heavens the nearest tables were empty. She closed her eyes for an instant, willing herself to a pretense, at least, at calm.

"I'm not unhappy, Mom. I love my business and I love

to quilt. But now I feel as if you're stealing my chance of marrying and creating my own family, too. And that's tearing me apart."

Her mother's face was pinched and almost unrecognizable. She seemed to have aged another ten years in the past ten minutes. "If he loves the woman you are right now, that's what matters. Can't you see that?"

Allie shook her head against her mother's pleading. "Let's not go there again. I told you, it's not Nolan, it's me. *Me*." She pointed her thumb at her chest. "I need to be loved for all of me. I need to be able to acknowledge all of me. But you know what? You've managed to turn the conversation around again so we're back to talking about why I am suddenly defiant. I think after all these years I deserve to know whether you really listened to Dad. I need to understand why you made the choice you did."

Mom's face crumpled before she composed herself again with a visible effort. "How could I have lived with myself if I hadn't done the right thing?"

"But Dad didn't think it was the right thing, did he? Did you ever listen to him?"

Her mother's chin shot up. "Of course I listened! Do you really think I'm that self-centered?"

Yes.

The silence hung as they stared at each other.

"Make me understand," Allie begged. "Haven't you ever had second thoughts? Regrets?"

"Of course I have!" Now her mother's voice shook. "When your father left me…and then to have Jason turn his back." Tears ran down her cheeks. Seeming unaware, she didn't lift a hand to catch them. "I never dreamed… my family fell apart because I asked all of you to support me in doing something hard. Was that really too much? It was the first time ever that *I* could do something important. My whole life…" She stopped as if she'd shocked herself.

"'Your whole life' what?" Allie whispered.

"I was never anything." Mom's face was ravaged. "My brother, of course *he* was going to college. After all, he was the boy. Why would I need a career when I'd be getting married and raising children?

"And then it was Mike. That damn company always came first. *Marr Industries.*" She said it with bitterness that corroded. "All I was supposed to do was support him. He didn't even like it when I got a job. Did you know that? He didn't understand that I wanted something that was *mine.* Of course, without an education the best I could do was assistant work. All I was doing was the same thing for someone else." She finally balled up her napkin and swabbed at her cheeks. "And then there was you." That came out muffled.

"Me?"

"You were so cute in your first recital. Do you remember your costume? Red-and-white checked, red tutu. You were four years old, and everybody watched you as if they'd seen a miracle. I wanted to give you everything you needed, I did, but sometimes…"

Allie's chest was so constricted, breathing had become hard. She had to say this, though. "Sometimes you resented me, too."

"Yes! Yes!" Through tear-swollen eyes, her mother glared. "I know that makes me a terrible person—you don't have to tell me. Maybe I should have been content to live my entire life doing nothing but supporting my husband and my children." Her face twisted again. The tears ran again, unheeded. "And I would have been, but then *I* was in a position to do something meaningful. Even the FBI agents were excited. They made me feel…important."

No longer focused on Allie, she seemed to see something far away and long ago.

Shaken by her mother's confession, Allie had no idea what to say. *I understand?* That's what she'd asked for, wasn't it? Enough honesty so that she would be able to understand? The awful thing was, she suspected she *had* understood already, subliminally.

That was why Mom had seemed so excited back then. Those FBI agents buzzed around her as if she was the most glorious, fragrant flower in the garden. The decision was *hers* to make, not her husband's, not her children's, not her frequently critical mother's.

When the U.S. Marshal decided to move them again, this last time, Allie realized that her mother had felt important again. She wouldn't be in danger if what she'd done hadn't counted.

Glorying in once again being the center of attention, she hadn't noticed how miserable her daughter was. She hadn't begun to understand why her son had chosen to stay behind.

"Thank you for telling me," Allie finally said, softly. A waitress approached, her concerned gaze on their untouched salads, but Allie gave her head a slight shake and the waitress stopped then retreated.

Mom had quit crying and mostly mopped her face, although she looked terrible. "In the end, it all went so wrong," she said, almost inaudibly.

"We can't know what would have happened if you'd said no," Allie was surprised to hear herself say. "Maybe you and Dad would have split up anyway. It doesn't sound like you were very happy in the marriage. And Jason might have sided with Dad no matter what."

"And you?" There was a great deal of pain in her mother's eyes. "You might be soaring."

"Or I could have been injured and had to give up dance," Allie said prosaically. "You were right. That was always a possibility."

"Can you ever forgive me?"

Can I? Allie wished she could say, *Of course,* and mean it. The honest answer was *I don't know.*

"You know I love you," she said instead.

Her mother's smile was crooked and more sad than pleased. "I know." She drew in a big breath and looked down at her salad. "I suppose we should eat this."

"Our salads look really good." Of course, Allie had no appetite at all right now, but she nonetheless picked up her fork and took a bite.

How did she now say, *Mom, the past is one thing, but I'm not sure I can forgive you if I lose Nolan because I can't tell him the whole story?*

And then it struck her: What if Mom had to admit that likely no one was looking for her anymore, not after all these years? That they weren't looking because *she wasn't that important?* If she was forced, finally, to let go of her belief in the choice she'd made. Think of the guilt she'd suffer. Would she be able to bear it?

Chest aching, Allie asked herself, *Can I do that to my mother?*

She didn't know.

They ate a few bites in near silence. The blotches gradually faded from Mom's face, although the lines seemed permanently carved deeper. Allie gradually realized how odd she felt. Maybe this was a case of being careful what you wish for. She hadn't wanted to know that her mother had resented her for being special in any way.

And yet she did understand how Mom had felt. Allie hadn't recognized that her grandparents were sexist enough to have devoted their praise and hopes and resources to their son while stinting their daughter. She had entirely misinterpreted those sharp voices she'd overheard coming from the kitchen. The fact that her granddaughter was interested in feminine arts like tatting had pleased Nanna, since her own daughter never had been. Maybe even Allie's dancing had seemed girlie enough to be acceptable.

What might Mom have done with her life, if she'd been encouraged to go to college and maybe even grad school? It was entirely possible that Mom was smarter than Dad. Had it especially rankled that Dad had inherited his position and the company that carried his name?

Maybe.

And do I blame Mom for that?

No.

Allie knew enough had been said today. Her mother had broken. She'd see herself as having lost her dignity. Allie couldn't bring herself to plead for more.

"You know, if we hustle we can still make that movie," she said, and Mom visibly wrapped herself in a semblance of her usual self-possession.

"Oh my," she said, glancing at her watch. "You're right. Why don't you see if you can catch the waitress's eye?"

Allie lifted her hand, glad she had an excuse not to have to continue to pretend enthusiasm to eat. "Here she comes now."

"My treat," her mother said, reaching for her purse.

"Thanks, Mom," she said, as soon as the waitress moved off with Mom's credit card. "We have enough leftovers to give us our dinners, too."

Her mother ruefully agreed. A moment later they both accepted take-out containers and scraped their mostly uneaten salads into them.

CHAPTER THIRTEEN

"Got to be honest," the P.I. said. "I've hit a roadblock. I can't answer your questions yet."

Nolan peeled off his goggles. He'd already set aside the ear protection. With his forearm, he swiped granite dust from his face, keeping the cell phone to his ear. "You can't track down any family?"

"Oh, yeah, I've done that. Haven't been able to talk to the brother yet, though. He's a sales manager for one of our bigger employers in these parts. My brother-in-law works there, too. Mannerville Furniture. You know them?"

"No," Nolan said tersely. "Should I?"

"The company manufactures fine wood furniture. Sells in fancy stores all over the country."

Nolan pinched the bridge of his nose. "And this is relevant how?"

Small silence. "Well, I guess it isn't. Only meant to say, this Jason Nelson is on the road most of the time. Hard to catch him home."

"And the father?"

"Him I talked to. Mark Nelson. First he said he didn't have a daughter and what was I talking about? When I took out a copy of the yearbook page and a printout of the emergency-contact page from the school records, he slammed the door in my face."

"Huh."

"He looked real shook-up," the investigator remarked

thoughtfully. "Not like someone who just didn't want to be bothered. More as if..." He trailed off.

"He was scared?" Nolan didn't even know where that came from.

"Yeah. That, or seriously ticked off. Hard to say."

"I assume you checked out newspaper archives? Arrest records? You didn't find anything suggesting domestic violence?"

"Nothing like that. There's no hint the divorce was anything but amicable. Mrs. Nelson never called the cops on her ex, that's for sure. Neither parent was ever investigated for child abuse."

Then what in hell *had* happened? Nolan asked himself in frustration. Could there have been an ugly incident when the family was out of state on vacation, say? He raked fingers through his hair, stirring a cloud of grit. No, of course not; Judy and Mark Nelson had been divorced two years before she and Allie took off. Ridiculous to think they'd have vacationed together.

"Aren't there other ways to investigate someone's background?" he asked, grasping at straws. "Where did the Nelsons live before they showed up in Fairfield? What's Nelson's working history? Did the school record show a work phone number for the mother?"

"Oh, I pursued all those avenues even though they were peripheral to what you asked me to find out," the man said. "I tried, anyway.

"Mrs. Nelson was a buyer at a department store that's gone out of business. I got the name and number of a former employer of Mr. Nelson's before they appeared in Oklahoma, only that number has been disconnected. The area code was Michigan, Detroit area. Did some searches for a Mark and Judy Nelson in Michigan back fourteen, fifteen years ago and came up with zip. No drivers' licenses on record, no traffic tickets, no indication they owned property." His tone was the equivalent of a shrug. "I can go back and knock on Nelson's door again, or try to find an acquaintance who knows something, but…"

"No." Whatever instinct had made him speak so quickly, Nolan was listening to it. Or, hell, maybe it was his bank balance talking. "No, let's call it quits for now."

"Your decision. What about the son?"

Nolan mulled that over. "Let's hold off for now. I'll let you know if I want you to talk to him, too." He pushed the button to end the call and tossed his phone back onto the counter. "Shit."

What had he stirred? It made him uneasy that Mark Nelson first denied he had a daughter at all then refused to talk about her. If Allie and her mother had changed their names to make good their escape from him, you'd think he'd have been intrigued by a P.I. coming around and asking questions. It might have occurred to him that this could be a chance for him to track them.

Why would he be angry? For that matter, why afraid? His wife and daughter had left town ten years ago. Too long for any crime he'd committed against them to be prosecuted now. Did they hold something over him? If they did, why had they run?

And where did Allie's brother fit in? Nolan heard a deep sadness in her voice when she talked about Jason. If the dad had hurt her, would the brother really have turned his back on her?

Too many questions, no answers. Nolan had a bad feeling he'd just wasted his money—and taken a chance of losing Allie once and for all besides.

Have I ever really had her, he asked himself bleakly, *when she hasn't even told me her real name?*

Now what?

Quit pushing, enjoy the relationship for what it was, hope that over time she'd trust him enough to tell him her story? A raw sound ripped its way out of him. Oh, yeah, there was a plan. Fall deeper in love with a woman who lied to him every time she opened her mouth?

It wasn't in him.

"Damn you, Allie Wright." *Laura Nelson?*

Right this minute, he wished he'd never met her.

ALLIE GLANCED AT the number displayed on her phone and groaned. She hadn't talked to her mother since they'd parted Sunday after the movie. She'd ignored a couple of calls because she still had no idea what to say.

This, she thought ruefully, was a perfect example of their differing styles. Or was it clashing? Mom wanted to confront problems head-on. Allie retreated into herself.

But I do love my mother. I know that much.

With a sigh, she picked up the phone.

"Hi, Mom."

"I was afraid you wouldn't answer."

"I was planning to call anyway." *Sure I was.*

"I'm glad." Her mother sounded a little hesitant. "I thought it would be good for us to spend some time together."

"Mom, I don't think I'm ready to talk about this again. Not yet."

"Talking is how we work out problems."

"How do we work out something that's over and done?" Bitterness made an abrupt appearance. "We can't have a redo, can we? Can you honestly say you'd do anything different if you had the chance?"

The pause was long enough she thought the call might have been dropped—or Mom had hung up on her. "You're not being fair," she said then. "You have the advantage of hindsight."

"But you still expect me to make any sacrifice you demand, don't you, Mom?" And there, Allie realized, was the crux. Her greatest anger wasn't felt for choices long past. It was for *now*.

"That's a hateful thing to say."

She needed her mother's blessings for telling Nolan everything, and she wouldn't be getting it. Mom still wanted to be the endangered heroine of their story, and giving Allie a happy ending would diminish that role.

"Why can't you respect my judgment?" she asked, her voice suddenly soft, hurt. "I have never loved a man before. I've never asked you for permission to tell someone the truth. I have kept your secrets for fifteen years. Do you really think I'm so foolish, I'd trust the wrong man?"

"You know it's not that!" her mother snapped. "I explained. So much could go wrong. Why take a chance when it's not necessary?"

Allie gently depressed the button that ended the call. She then turned her phone off.

She sat in her chair beside Sean's quilt, stretched in the quilt frame, but didn't reach for her thimble or needle. The deep blue and white blurred before her eyes.

She would be betraying her mother if she followed her heart.

Anger had transmuted into anguish that had her bending forward, hugging herself and breathing fast and hard.

It was a while before she had a moment of clarity. At least she still *had* her mother.

Both of them had been hurt by Allie's dad's defection and then by Jason's. Mom might only be desperate to know that at least one member of her family wouldn't desert her.

It was hard to believe in other people when the ones who were supposed to love you most abandoned you.

Who knew that better than Allie?

She never did work on Sean's quilt.

"WHAT'S THE DEAL with Allie?" Sean asked as he grabbed sour cream and steak sauce from the refrigerator.

Nolan set the platter with baked potatoes on the table. "What do you mean?"

"You didn't see her this weekend, did you?"

"I don't always tell you when I get together with her." Nolan checked the steaks he was broiling, decided they were done and grabbed a plate. He was glad to have his back to Sean. "Will you get me a beer?" he asked.

Silence. Reluctantly he turned to find his foster son hadn't gone back to the refrigerator. He was staring at Nolan.

"What?"

"You hardly ever drink."

"You know I like an occasional beer."

"You can tell me it's none of my business, you know."

Nolan groaned. "Can we sit down and eat?"

As ordered, Sean got their drinks and joined him at the table. They ate in silence for a good five minutes. Nolan finally broke.

"I've had a lot on my mind, that's all."

"It has something to do with her saying she lived one place and her mom a difference place, doesn't it?"

"Yes," Nolan admitted. "Like I told you early on, I've got a thing about lies."

"You think she lied."

The kid was a persistent little bugger, Nolan had to give him that. "It's more complicated than that," he said. "I think it was her mother who lied. But there's something going on that Allie doesn't want to tell me. I can't do a relationship where the trust isn't there."

Sean pondered that while inhaling baked potato heaped with sour cream. "Allie doesn't seem like someone who would lie. You know?"

Nolan grimaced. "I know."

"So maybe..."

"Maybe what?"

The boy's shoulders moved awkwardly. "I don't know. Maybe she has to keep quiet for someone else. Or what if she's scared or something?"

Scared, like her father was? "Scared of what?" The question was really for himself.

"Have you asked her?"

"No. I was hoping she'd come to me."

"Maybe she doesn't know *you've* guessed something is off," Sean suggested.

Nolan felt certain Allie was well aware of his doubts and questions. The tension had been there all along; even on their first date, she wasn't eager to talk about her history.

"You weren't all that high on me dating her," Nolan reminded the boy. "What's with the grilling?"

Some color touched his cheeks and he ducked his head. "She's cool. It was me, not her. She treats me like a person, not a kid. If she was my girlfriend, I wouldn't want to screw it up."

Nolan didn't want to screw it up, either. Was that what he was doing? In his obsession with honesty, had he blown it with the first and only woman he'd ever thought of the word *love* in connection with?

"I was your age when I found out my mother had been sleeping around," he heard himself say abruptly. "The man I'd called 'Dad' my whole life isn't my biological father."

Sean gaped. "No shit?"

"No shit," Nolan said grimly. "My brother, Jed, is his kid. My sister, Anna, isn't." He hesitated. "We think we have two different fathers."

"You don't know?"

"My mother won't talk about it."

"So you quit talking to her," Sean said slowly.

Nolan raised his eyebrows. "How do you know that?"

Sean looked at him as if he was stupid. "I hear you on the phone with your sister and brother, but never either of your parents." He flushed. "I mean, your mom and…"

"I still call him Dad." Nolan grimaced. "I got snotty for a while back then and called him by his name." A reluctant smile tipped his mouth. "He didn't like it. He persuaded me that he was, by God, my father in every way that mattered."

"So…" Puzzlement tugged the boy's eyebrows together. "Why are you so mad at him?"

"Because he knew. All those years, he knew. We all lived a lie."

After a minute Sean nodded and then applied himself to eating. Nolan looked down and realized his food was probably getting cold. He picked up his knife and fork, too.

"Allie might be different," Sean said at last, tentatively. "I mean, you don't know why she doesn't want to talk about…whatever."

"That's true," Nolan admitted heavily.

"I think you should talk to her."

"Yeah." Nolan smiled at him. "You're right. I should."

"So you will?"

"You don't give up, do you?"

The response was a wicked grin, one that would have girls' hearts fluttering. Maybe already did; Nolan remembered the teammate's twin sister who'd been asking questions about Sean. Good God, Nolan thought; there'd be girls beating down the door before he knew it.

"You going to answer?"

"Not sure it's really any of your business," Nolan told him, "but yes. I will talk to her. Give her a chance to talk to me. Okay?"

"Okay." Sean's gaze settled on Nolan's plate. "Are you going to finish the rest of your steak?"

Nolan had almost forgotten what it felt like to be hungry 24/7. "You can have it." He forked the steak and shifted it to Sean's plate. "The potato is all mine."

"That's cool." He'd earned another grin. "I saw the pie. We get that for dessert, right?"

"It's raspberry. And, yes, we do."

"Ice cream, too?"

"Can't eat pie without it."

"Awesome." Around the bite of steak he'd shoved in his mouth, Sean said, "I can dish it up."

"So you can cut the pie in fourths instead of sixths?"

"It'll get soggy if we don't eat it fast enough."

No denying it, fruit pies did get soggy as the days passed. He laughed. "You can dish it up."

Satisfied, Sean asked Nolan if he'd ever read *Lord of the Flies,* because he'd started it for English class but he'd already read the end because that's what he did. Nolan dredged up his memory of the rather disturbing book and they had a discussion about it that went deeper than he would have expected with a kid Sean's age. It almost succeeded in keeping Nolan's mind off what he'd decided he'd do right after dinner: call Allie.

Half an hour later, the kitchen clean, Sean bounded up the stairs to read a couple of chapters, he said. Nolan had noticed he was spending a lot more time online, too. On the whole, he thought it was a good sign suggesting Sean really was making friends. All those Facebook pages to check out.

With some reluctance, he picked up the phone and dialed Allie's number.

"Nolan," she said, her tone totally unreadable.

"Hey." He winced. Not the best lead-in. "Listen, I was wondering if I could come over tomorrow night. I'd like to talk to you."

The silence stretched long enough to make him nervous. "Is this a breaking-up kind of talk? 'Allie, I don't want to hurt your feelings, but I don't think this thing we have is going anywhere'? Because if so, I'd rather you said it right now and got it over with."

He scrubbed a hand over his face. He'd thought about saying something like that—and couldn't imagine now that he'd ever have been able to spit it out. Or that he'd ever have gotten over the regret if he'd been that stupid.

Yeah? What if I ask my questions and she says, "None of your business." What then?

Nolan didn't know. His heart ached.

"No," he said. "It's nothing like that. I really do want to talk to you."

"Do you want to come to dinner?" she asked carefully.

He hesitated. "Why don't I come over after? Is that okay?"

Silence pooled again, deep and dark. "All right," she said finally. "I'll see you when I see you. Good night," she added, and the dead air told him she hadn't waited for any good-nights from him.

Oh, crap. Now he was committed to laying it all on the line. He discovered that now *he* was the scared one.

ALLIE SURVEYED THE contents of her refrigerator and cupboards, but nothing appealed to her. She'd weighed herself that morning and knew she was in trouble. She'd be looking really scrawny soon, if she wasn't careful. But knowing Nolan would surely be here within the next hour, having no idea what he would have to say, she couldn't make herself eat.

She paid bills. Business had been good this fall, but that didn't mean she was able to draw a huge salary from the store. Looking at her public-utility bill, she got up and turned down the thermostat. Wow. Time to start wearing sweaters.

Her stomach was balled in a knot. She tried hard to focus entirely on her checkbook balance and whether she ought to completely pay off the VISA bill or let part of it ride until next month. She noted how many minutes she'd spent on her cell phone—lucky she and Nolan usually talked in the evening and not daytime—but her mind kept flickering to him.

The pain in her stomach grew. She saw that her hand, wielding the pen, had a fine tremor. Anxiety swelled until she could hardly breathe.

What was she going to do? She *knew* what he wanted, what he was going to ask of her. The idea of defying her mother to this extent terrified her…but so did the idea of seeing frustration close down Nolan's expression. He would walk out, she knew he would, and Allie didn't think she could bear it.

If that happened, the wound wouldn't only sever her relationship with Nolan. It would also be the killing blow to the love she felt for her mother, love that had been unquestioning until so recently.

Until Nolan.

At a sharp rap on the door, she jumped six inches. Why hadn't she heard his truck? His footsteps on the steps? *Oh, God, I'm not ready.*

No choice.

She looked at the table in front of her and was surprised to see that she was apparently done paying bills. A neat pile of envelopes ready to go sat on one side, the checkbook on another. Wonderful. She didn't remember putting stamps on the envelopes or even writing some of the checks, for that matter. It might be a good idea to check her math later, given that she didn't remember doing that part of keeping a checkbook, either.

She got as far as the door, closed her eyes and *willed* herself to some kind of composure. What if she was terrifying herself for nothing? What if he only wanted to apologize for going missing this week, and maybe suggest they do something special this weekend? What if…?

She opened the door.

He was the original stone man. That craggy face was completely impassive. Even his eyes were shadowed, less clear and penetrating than usual. No, Allie realized, he wasn't here to suggest they do something special this weekend.

"Allie," he said, nodding.

She stepped back. "Come in. Please."

His gaze did shift to the quilt. "You've made a lot of progress," he said quietly.

She let herself look fully at him. "I've had plenty of time to work."

That made a muscle in his jaw spasm.

"I had to do some thinking."

"I take it you've reached a conclusion?"

"Can we sit down?" he asked.

"Oh, um, sure." She turned her head. Here? Or at the table? "Can I get you a cup of coffee?"

He shook his head, crushing her last desperate hope that this visit was casual on some level. "I'm good."

She nodded and waved him to a chair. She turned hers from the quilting frame to face him. *I want to be numb,* she thought. *Please let me go numb so I can think.*

If wishes were horses...

She swallowed, looking into a face she realized now wasn't impassive. It was implacable. Hard as granite.

"Allie, I know you're hiding something. And maybe we haven't known each other long enough for me to have any right to demand answers. I keep telling myself I should be patient." He frowned, the first real expression he'd shown. "Funny thing is, usually I am. But you know how I feel about dishonesty. And why."

Unable to meet his eyes again, she gazed down at his hands. "I haven't exactly been dishonest."

"Haven't you?" His tone was as unbending as his face.

She opened her mouth to say no, then closed it. Her name was a lie. She was a creation, not a real person.

"I..." Her throat clogged. She didn't know what she'd intended to say anyway.

"Why, Allie?" Suddenly he sounded so gentle, she thought her heart might break. "What is it you're afraid to tell me?"

She lifted her head and saw that his eyes were kind, too. Despair washed over her, chased by something unexpected. Relief. He had made up her mind for her. If he'd been brusque, said "tell me or else," she might have chosen her mother. That's what this had come down to, hadn't it. Mom or Nolan.

I choose Nolan. The power of the emotional punch made her bow forward.

He half rose to his feet. "Are you all right?"

"Yes." She took a deep breath and straightened her back. "I'm fine. It's just that...I had to swear never to tell anyone." *Never, never, never.* Her nails bit into her palms. "I became Allie Wright when I was seventeen."

He stared at her.

"When I was born, my parents named me Chloe. I was Chloe Marr."

He made an odd, hoarse sound.

"When I was thirteen, my family went into the Witness Security Program. We had…we still have our own handler." She tried to smile. "A U.S. Marshal."

Nolan swore, leaning forward. His electric eyes never left her face. "Why? What happened?"

Allie took a moment to collect her thoughts. She felt as if, by saying her true name aloud, admitting to the Witness Security Program, she had peeled off a layer of skin. Every nerve in her body was now exposed. Allie was bared in a way she had never been before. She wasn't sure she could stand to be touched.

She told Nolan the story then, how her mother had stayed late at work one day to finish up a project and had overheard enough to realize the company was a front for a mob organization. Worse yet, a hit had just been ordered and carried out. The killer was reporting his success to his boss.

"Mom went to the FBI. If she was to testify in court, she had to disappear immediately. She would never be safe, they told her. My father didn't want her to testify. I overheard them arguing."

Her tone a dull monotone, Allie kept talking about her mother's determination to do the "right" thing, her father's anger. She even told him why her father had objected to the sacrifice all of them would be making when the victim of the crime had been a crime figure himself. She admitted to the bewilderment she and her brother had felt.

"His name was Jacob," she told him. "I was jealous

when they moved us because they chose the name Jason for him. It was close enough that it still sounded like *him*. They named me Laura. I hated it."

She talked about the three and a half horrible years in Oklahoma. The terror of the week when her mother had gone back to New York to appear in court, the fear her family felt that the Morettis would somehow get to her. Then she told him about Laura Nelson.

"I suppose I was always quiet, but I used to have friends. I was confident. But from the moment we left our house in the middle of the night, leaving almost everything we owned behind, I was paralyzed. I didn't make a single friend in Fairfield. I felt like I'd had my tongue cut out. People would ask me questions and I couldn't think of the answer fast enough because it wasn't *true*. I've never been a very good liar," she said apologetically.

He offered her a crooked smile. "I noticed."

"I suppose you think that's a good thing."

"Yes."

"My life would have been easier if I was a better liar. I might have adjusted."

"I am sorry for that," he said, voice low, deep and still gentle.

"That wasn't my only problem." She fanned her fingers and again focused on them rather than his face. "I was a dancer. I was in a special school. I'd already performed with the American Ballet Theatre. Because I was considered a dancer with unusual promise, I'd been featured in newspapers and on television. My face could be easily found with an internet search. When we went into Witness Security, I was told I could never dance again. Someone, somewhere, would recognize me."

He made another sound, gruff and grieving, and held out a hand. "Will you come over here, Allie?"

She shook her head. "Let me finish."

Nolan nodded. She still couldn't look directly at him.

"I realize now that my parents' marriage was probably already in trouble before all this happened. But Mom's decision ended it, although it dragged on for another year.

"Dad was the third generation to run his family's company. Of course it had to be sold. He had to find something different to do with his life. I think he felt so much resentment, whatever love he'd had left for Mom died.

"Jason...well, he's two years older than I am. He was really angry, giving up his friends and having no say in what happened to us. He blamed Mom. When Dad and she split up, he went to live with Dad." She swallowed. "He was the only person..." It was too much. She couldn't finish.

"The only person?"

"Who I could be myself with. Chloe."

"And he moved out."

"Yes." Heaven help her, this was hard. She felt naked in a way she'd never been. No, worse—raw. "Then we got word that someone might have found us or at least was getting close. It freaked the U.S. Marshals Service and they decided to move us and give us new identities again.

"They would have done the same for Dad and Jason, even though Mom and Dad weren't married anymore. In fact, I don't think they liked it when Dad said no, he was done. And then...and then Jason, too."

"Did you ever consider staying behind with your father, too? Finishing out your senior year where you were?"

She shook her head. "No. By then, Mom was all I had. And it wasn't as if I was happy there. I don't even know who Laura Nelson was. And I know it wasn't fair, but I felt as if Dad had already abandoned me." Jason, too. That might have been even more devastating.

"So you became Allie Wright."

"Yes. Of course, we were given an entirely new background we were supposed to memorize. I didn't do a very good job with that. I'd already decided when I was Laura that I just wouldn't answer when people asked questions."

"Then I started interrogating you."

She met his eyes for the first time in several minutes. Allie was surprised to find she was smiling, although it felt…not quite right. A distant part of her wondered what that smile looked like. "I kept getting muddled. I guess you noticed. Or I'd go blank and I could see you thinking, 'What's *that* about?'"

"Did you ever consider just telling me the truth? Or—" his tone was pained "—weren't you serious enough about me to think I was entitled?"

A part of her wanted to protect her mother, not admit to their painful conflict and her own realization that Mom's decisions all along had been about *her.* Not her husband, not her son, not her daughter.

"Mom was…scared," she said carefully. "I told her I wanted to tell you everything. That I *had* to. She said I couldn't. That we'd all committed to never looking back. She said I am Allie Wright and the past doesn't matter." She was very close to breaking down. "But it does. It does," Allie finished in a whisper.

"God." Nolan moved then, as if he couldn't wait another minute. He scooped her out of her chair and returned to his, sitting with her on his lap, wrapped securely in his powerful arms. "Oh, damn, Allie. I wish I'd known."

Her cheeks were wet when she pushed back enough to see his face. She had to ask. "Have I ruined everything?"

CHAPTER FOURTEEN

"RUINED EVERYTHING?" NOLAN cupped her face with one hand, wiping at the tears with his thumb. "Of course you haven't. I'm the one who should be asking you that. I've been such a jackass. Demanding everything from you, not letting myself see what stress you were under."

Her eyes shimmered, the dampness making them even more beautiful, like a pebble that came to life in the water. Droplets glittered on her dark lashes. For a long time, she searched his face as if she couldn't understand—or believe—a word he'd said. And then she crumpled. She grabbed his shirt in both hands to anchor herself, buried her face in the crook of his neck and sobbed.

Nolan's eyes stung, too. *He'd* done this to her. No, he thought on a burst of anger, not only him. The father and brother who had let her go as if she didn't matter, the mother who by most standards had made the noble choice but who, in doing so, had unalterably damaged her daughter's life.

He rocked Allie, his cheek pressed to the top of her head, and murmured nonsense meant to comfort. "It's all right. Oh, sweetheart. Thank you for telling me. God, I'm sorry. So sorry, Allie. Shh. Oh, damn it, honey."

He was sure she was going to make herself sick. But maybe, it occurred to him, she needed to surrender to all this hurt. Had she ever let herself cry like this? Somehow he doubted it.

He understood so much about Allie now. Her astonishing physical grace and poise, the seemingly unconscious care of every small movement down to the tilt of her head and any casual gesture of her hand. The creativity and absolute commitment she brought now to her quilting, learned as a young girl pursuing an entirely different passion. The shyness and caution that made her so guarded and even aloof. Her delight and surprise at moments of real intimacy.

The way she identified with Sean.

Her odd reaction when they talked about the possibility of changing the dog's name. That must have hit painfully close to home.

The crying slowed at last. By the time the final sob shook her slender body, Nolan was probably in as much distress as she was.

He wanted to take care of her, to save her from ever feeling this kind of pain. He hated everyone who had ever hurt her. He was furious at himself. And yet, the huge bubble of emotion in his chest was something altogether different. It was gratitude, because she had opened up to him even though doing so had been enormously difficult for her.

"I love you," he said hoarsely. "I love you."

She stirred at that. He loosened his arms so she could straighten and see his face. Her face, blotchy and swollen and wet, had never looked more beautiful to him.

"Do you mean that?"

"Of course I do. It's been killing me by inches, knowing you were hiding one hell of a lot. You've been tearing me in two."

Her face worked again. After a struggle she regained her composure. "I've been breaking into a thousand pieces. Oh, Nolan. I love you. I do. I was so afraid."

She loved him. The knowledge blazed inside him, torching every last doubt or fear. He bent forward until his forehead touched hers. "Thank you for telling me. Thank you."

Allie still hadn't released her grip on his shirt. From this angle, he could see her two fists clutching onto him. He liked knowing she wasn't willing to let go.

Her slight nod bumped against his head.

"Do you feel better now?" He squeezed her neck. "Or worse?"

"I...don't know," she admitted. "Somehow I have to put myself back together, and I have no idea how."

"I'll do anything I can to help. Anything."

On an inarticulate exclamation, she pressed her mouth to his. The kiss hurt for a minute, their lips jammed between their teeth. That bubble in his chest expanded until he couldn't breathe. He opened his mouth and coaxed her to do the same. The next instant, they were kissing deeply, passionately, utterly lost in each other.

"Love you," he growled, pulling his mouth away long enough to kiss her neck.

She took the opportunity to bite his earlobe. His body surged and he rose to his feet, adjusting Allie so that she wrapped her arms around his neck and her legs around his waist.

He wasn't sure he'd make it to the bedroom, but there was no sofa in the living room and not much floor space, either.

Somehow he made it around the quilt frame and stumbled down the short hall and through the door into her room. She didn't help matters, her mouth open and damp on his throat, her tongue slipping out to taste his skin.

Nolan collapsed with her onto the bed, his weight compressing her into the mattress. If she minded, it wasn't obvious. She moaned and lifted her hips to cradle him.

Their clothes disappeared. Fabric ripped at one point.

Getting a condom on was a miracle. Driving into her felt better than anything ever had in his life. The only way to silence the guttural sounds he was making was to kiss her again.

Her fingernails bit into his back. He'd lost all ability to take this slowly, to handle her gently, but she didn't seem to want that. She met every thrust with a ferocity that matched his urgency. He wasn't going to last, but he had to wait for her. He gripped her buttock and lifted her higher.

She cried his name and came in spasms that destroyed any last remnant of control he'd held on to. He pounded into her, blind, deaf, the pleasure barely short of pain. "Love you," he managed to get out. And when it ended, he collapsed.

If he was smothering her, it took her a couple of minutes to notice. At her first wriggle, Nolan managed to roll onto his side, taking her with him. To his regret, he slipped out of her body. If he could have stayed there for the rest of his life, he'd have been happy.

"Damn," he said in a thick voice. "I didn't hurt you, did I?"

"Hurt me?" Her lack of comprehension was obvious. A frown puckered her forehead while she thought about it. "No," she finally decided. "You couldn't."

"I could." He rubbed his bristly cheek on her head. "I'm so much bigger than you are."

A giggle was his answer. It fizzed, pure effervescence. "Bet I can jump higher than you can."

He'd gone to a ballet once. A woman he was dating in Chicago had bought tickets. He couldn't say he followed the plot, if there was one, and the experience wasn't one he'd had any interest in repeating, but the athleticism was mind-boggling. The lead ballerina had literally flown.

"I bet you can, too," he admitted. Light on his feet he wasn't. "Next time I'll let you dance on top of me."

She stroked his chest, her fingers curling in the dark hair. "That sounds like fun."

They were quiet for a few minutes. Nolan had never felt so sated, boneless, relaxed. The curve of her slight body against his was perfect. The only part of him inclined to move was his hand, which traced patterns on her back.

As his brain slowly revived, he became aware of how very thin she was. Damn it, he hadn't been able to feel her ribs the last time he'd held her like this, had he? Her delicate vertebrae were definitely more prominent.

"You're still losing weight."

She didn't move for a moment. He wasn't sure she was even breathing. At last she sighed. "I do that when I'm worried or unhappy."

"This time it's my fault."

"No. We couldn't have gone on with me lying to you. I told you. It was tearing me apart. Mom refused to understand at all." Allie went quiet. "That was the worst part," she said finally. "She was…pressuring me to stay quiet."

"Will you tell her?"

"That I opened my mouth and absolutely everything spilled out?"

"Yeah."

"Yes," Allie said softly. "She needs to know. Anyway, I'm not a good liar. Remember?"

"I remember." He nuzzled her hair. "Will she be upset?"

He didn't like the way she kept going quiet. He felt so good himself, he hated to think that all her worries were already building again inside her.

"Yes," she said. "I think she will be." She lifted her head to stare fiercely at him. "You have to promise me you won't tell anyone. Not even Sean. Especially not Sean. He's a teenager. Nobody can know. *Nobody.* Promise me."

"I promise." He couldn't imagine what he'd tell Sean, but not this. Allie's secrets, Nolan understood with some shock, had now become his. The man who insisted on complete honesty now knew things he'd never be able to tell another soul, even his sister. "I swear, Allie."

Her eyes burned into his, but finally she nodded and laid her head down again. The way she snuggled closer as she relaxed felt like trust to him. His arms closed more firmly around her. God, he loved her.

In the peaceful time that followed, he tried to decide how uncomfortable he was about keeping Allie's secret, but didn't find as much uneasiness as he might have expected. Her safety and happiness had become the most important thing in the world to him. He would never do anything to endanger her or her mother.

Thank God, he thought suddenly, he'd stopped the P.I. when he did. What if the guy had succeeded in tracing the Nelsons to New York? Somehow identified Allie Wright as the talented young dancer Chloe Marr? A chill passed through him. No wonder the investigator's visit had scared the crap out of Allie's father!

Did Nelson have some way to get word to Allie's mother that someone had come around asking questions? Nolan hoped not. Should he call the P.I. and emphasize that he should call it quits?

No. Better to pay the bill and let it go.

Guilt did a dip and roll in his gut. Did he have to tell Allie what he'd done?

He stared up at the ceiling. Yes. He'd demanded complete honesty from her, and he had to give it to her in turn. But…not yet. She'd had enough trauma for one day.

Tomorrow, he decided, ashamed of his relief. Or maybe

the day after. Right now, he'd keep holding her close and revel in the knowledge that she loved him.

ALLIE HAD AWAKENED the next morning smiling. She couldn't remember the last time she'd done that.

If only Nolan had been able to stay the night. Of course she'd understood; he had a teenage son and couldn't not go home.

She wanted to wake up with him every morning. Go to bed with him every night.

He hadn't said anything about the future. Given that he had Sean, Allie couldn't see him suggesting she move in with them. No, a man of his rock-solid integrity would ask her to marry him. Maybe he thought they needed more time first, though, and maybe he was right.

I love him. She hugged herself in delight.

What she didn't want to think about was the shadow that hung over her. She had to talk to her mother. Say, *Mom, I told him everything.* Soon.

Today. Better to get it over with.

Midmorning she called her mother's mobile number and suggested they have lunch together. When she offered to pop out to the Pea Patch or the bakery and pick up the food, Mom insisted that she had a full hour off, she'd be glad to bring the meal.

By the time she ended the call, Allie felt horribly guilty. Her mother had sounded so relieved. She thought everything was fine now, that their little tiff was past. She wasn't going to like what Allie had to say.

Mom had taken her break late to accommodate the quiet time in the quilt shop. She arrived in a bustle with bags in hand.

"The loveliest sandwiches on croissants," she announced, laying them out on the table in back. "Fruit salads and, for you, a ginger-molasses cookie. I can't afford the calories, but you can."

"Why don't we split it?" Allie suggested. "You're as slim as you were ten years ago. You can certainly get away with a decadent cookie now and again."

"'Now and again' has a way of creeping into 'every day,'" her mother said ominously.

Allie broke the cookie into two and set one on the napkin in front of her mother.

"Oh, I suppose this once..." She laughed, but gave her daughter a look. "You know me too well."

Aware that a customer could walk in at any time, Allie knew she had to get this over with. "Mom, I have something to tell you."

Her mother very carefully set down the croissant she had picked up. There was no sign of laughter on her face now. "What is it?"

Allie hadn't reached for her own sandwich. She squeezed her hands together on her lap. She couldn't think of any way to sidle into this. Blunt was best, she decided. Like peeling off a bandage with one yank. "I told Nolan everything."

"You...what?" Mom whispered.

"You heard me."

"Why would you do such a thing?" Horror aged her mother as much as the tears on Sunday had. "I *begged* you."

"You have to ask me why?" Allie's chin rose. "I've tried to make you understand. I've talked until I'm blue in the face, and you haven't listened. I love Nolan. I cannot make a life with a man who knows only the small surface part of me. I *trust* him."

"Oh, dear God." Mom was shaking. "What have you done?"

"I've made him fully part of our lives. That's what I've

done." She hesitated. "I made him promise he would never say a word about it to anyone, not even Sean."

"Easy to say, hard to do," her mother said bitterly. "Look at you. *You* couldn't follow through."

Acid burned in her throat. Allie pushed back her chair. "That's a lousy thing to say, Mom."

The bell over the shop door rang. Oh, great. Perfect timing. *I should have waited until this evening.* Allie recognized in that second that she'd chosen this time and venue in the hopes her mother's response would be moderated. The awareness that they could be interrupted and that they didn't have long to talk had seemed like a safety net.

She stood up, tearing her gaze from her mother's ravaged face. "Hello," she called. "I'm here in back."

There was no immediate answer. *Nolan. Oh, my God,* she thought. *It's Nolan.* Why hadn't it occurred to her that he might want to see her today?

He appeared, striding toward her between rows of colorful fabric bolts, his eyes smiling. She couldn't help contrasting his approach to that first time, when he'd been bemused and cautious, then clearly entranced by her Lady of the Lake quilt. White paper bags dangled from his hands.

"Nolan," she said. What was the old saying? Between the frying pan and the fire? No, not fair—it was Mom upsetting her today, not him.

He got a good look at her and his expression became warier. "Is something wrong?"

"No. Um…" She gestured. "Mom's here. She, uh, brought lunch, too."

He stopped short, suddenly looking blockish in a way he hadn't. "I'm sorry. I should have called."

"No, that's fine." What else could she say? "You know Mom. Why don't you join us?"

His eyes asked a question. Allie swallowed and nodded. *Yes, I told her.*

After a brief hesitation, he walked forward. "Cheryl. Good to see you again. I apologize for butting in here."

Her mother rose to her feet. "Well, it seems you've come at an appropriate time. Since we were just talking about you."

He set the bags down, seeming to sort through what he wanted to say. "Allie told me your history. What you did took a lot of courage."

"Thank you. I'm afraid Allie doesn't see it that way."

"I doubt that's true," he said quietly. "She talked about how close she's always been to you."

Allie didn't want to turn her gaze from his face—no, not handsome, but compelling and capable of such kindness. She made herself look at her mother, though, and saw deep hurt.

"I love my daughter. But I cannot say I'm happy that she felt she had to reveal a past to you that was meant to stay shrouded." Her eyes fixed on him with blazing intensity. "She says you promised never to tell anyone."

"I did, and I meant it."

"My life might depend on you keeping your word. You do understand that."

Allie stood by, watching the two people she loved most in the world stare at each other as if no one else existed. She hated her sense of helplessness.

"I do," Nolan said in his deep, slow way. "Of course I do." He looked at Allie and reached out a hand to her. The expression in his eyes let her know that she'd been wrong; he hadn't forgotten for a second that she was there.

She let his big hand engulf hers. The gentle squeeze he gave was as comforting as he meant it to be.

"Why don't we have lunch?" he suggested. "We've got

plenty of food, and if we don't eat now Allie will end up being interrupted."

"Well...I suppose..." Mom turned blindly back to the table. Allie doubted either of them had any appetite, but a pretense had to be made.

He took bowls of soup from one of his bags and said, "Feel free to help yourself, either of you." When no one made a move, he shrugged, pried the top off one of the bowls and picked up a spoon.

Allie's mother nibbled at her croissant. Allie did the same.

The silence grew uncomfortable. Nolan glanced from one to the other of them. Finally he looked at Allie's mom. "You must miss your son very much."

Her breath hitched. "Yes. We are able to exchange letters. He doesn't write often— Well, I don't suppose you write your parents often, either, do you?"

He laughed. "You've got me there."

"He sounds like he's doing well. He's a successful businessman. And I'm wondering if he might be serious about the woman he's been dating. Don't you think, Allie?"

Dumbfounded to realize that the worst was over—at least until Mom got her alone again—Allie thought back to her brother's most recent letters, few and short though they were. She had noticed a slightly different tone to his occasional mentions of his current girlfriend. "I kind of had that feeling, too," she agreed.

Mom told Nolan how handsome Jason had always been and mentioned that she'd told him all she wanted for Christmas from him was a new photo. "I do hate the thought of him someday having children and me never being able to see them." Her voice faltered.

Nolan nodded. His compassion had never been more apparent. Allie had seen the fury on his face when she talked about the pressure her mother had been applying on her. No trace of that was in his voice or expression now.

"That would be really hard," he said. "I don't have a great relationship with my parents, but I try to get home to Chicago at least once a year anyway. We're still family."

"Yes," Mom said softly. "Family." She had eaten only about half her croissant and not touched the fruit salad or cookie, but she made a point of glancing at her watch. "Oh, dear. I need to get back to work. Allie, perhaps we can talk another time."

"At least take the rest of your sandwich. And the cookie," Allie said, wrapping it in the napkin and holding it out. "You can eat it at your desk."

There was a glint of what might have been tears in Mom's eyes. She gave a shaky smile. "Thanks, sweetie. I love you."

Allie rushed around the table to hug her. "I love you, too. You know that, don't you?"

"Yes." Her arms finally loosened. She aimed an uncertain smile past Allie. "Goodbye, Nolan."

He had politely risen to his feet. "Cheryl."

"I'll walk you out," Allie offered, but her mother shook her head.

"Don't be silly. Enjoy your lunch while you can." She slung her purse over her shoulder and walked quickly away. Barely a moment later, the bell rang and the shop was completely silent.

"My timing sucks," Nolan said with a rueful half smile.

"No, actually your timing is brilliant." Allie felt like laughing and twirling. "It's done. I told her. She's bound to be reproachful later, but the shock will pass. And I think she does like you. Oh, Nolan." She took the couple of steps necessary to allow her to throw her arms around his neck and rise on tiptoe to kiss him. "You were so nice. You said all the right things." Her voice thickened. "Thank you."

"You're welcome. I didn't say anything that wasn't the truth."

"I'm so relieved." She did one small spin before collapsing into her chair. The dread that had weighted her down from the moment she called her mother that morning was gone. Or transformed, into this enormous relief and even ebullience.

A trace of amusement showed in Nolan's very blue eyes. "Saved by the bell, huh?"

"Yes! Mom was just getting really worked up when you got here." She chuckled. "And then we heard the bell."

"You needed me, I came." He grinned. "Didn't know you needed me, but still."

"My hero."

His grin died. "Yeah, about that."

Allie waited.

"You're okay today? Not…sorry?" he asked.

"No. I feel…" She frowned a little, doing an inward scan. *How am I really?* "I said I didn't know how I'd ever put myself back together. But I think I've already made a start. Just being able to tell someone, to acknowledge that I'm Chloe, too, that I was a dancer, and that I'm angry and confused. Lying has been hard…" She stopped. "I'd blocked out the anger for so long, you see. It was Chloe who was angry. Angry and bitter. But it's not safe for me to be Chloe, so I had to ignore that part of me. Laura was the confused one, but I'm not supposed to acknowledge her existence anymore, either." She laughed softly at herself. "You'll think I have a split personality. Um. Maybe I do."

"No, that's the whole point, isn't it?" Nolan captured her hand again. "You were being split apart by external forces. If you can say to yourself, and to me, 'The name I was called doesn't matter, I've always been myself, I am Chloe and I'm Laura and I'm Allie,' then you'll be all right."

"Yes." The backs of her eyes burned as she considered the magical notion. "Whole."

"You are whole." His smile transformed the rough angles of his face into something considerably sexier. "And you have some customers. Which means I'd better pack up and go."

She started, not even having heard the bell over the door. Women's voices carried from the front of the store, though.

Nolan leveled a stern glance at her. "But I'm going to leave some of this food. I want you to promise to eat. Grab a bite when you have a chance."

"I promise." Allie bounced to her feet and kissed him again. "Cross my heart."

Long after he'd left, she carried the memory of his smile with her.

And, yes, she eventually ate every single crumb of the food.

THE NEXT COUPLE of days were wondrous, fantastic. Allie was in love with a man who loved her. She had another talk with her mother, who still wasn't happy but seemed resigned.

"At least he's a nice man," she said grudgingly. "I always pictured you with a man not so…blue-collar, but I suppose I should be grateful he makes a decent living."

Allie had only laughed. "Yes, he does, but he's also a very talented artist. I suspect that, in the not-too-distant future, he'll concentrate entirely on sculpting. Someday you'll be able to brag that your son-in-law is Nolan Radek."

"He hasn't asked you to marry him yet, has he?"

"No, but he will."

"I do wish you'd waited," she fretted. "What if it doesn't happen, Allie? Then a man who isn't even part of our family knows a dangerous secret about us."

Allie felt a small flicker of anxiety, but ignored it. Nolan wasn't a man to say he loved her and then change his mind.

"I trust him no matter what," she said.

Her mother sighed. "We don't have any choice now, do we?" Fortunately, she didn't say it with any heat.

Friday night, Allie had dinner at Nolan's, where she also got soundly trounced by Sean at their second game of horse. Her shot was off, but mostly, he'd gotten better.

Triumphant, he dunked the ball in celebration. "Kicked your butt," he gloated.

Allie gave a very feminine snort. "You won't be very popular if you don't learn to be a better winner."

He grinned at her. "You mean, like saying you were awesome and it was just chance that I had the better day?"

She crossed her arms. "Like that."

If possible, his smile widened. "But we both know that's BS, don't we?"

"Snot." She flounced toward the porch, where Nolan waited at the top of the steps, one shoulder propped against a roof support. Amusement crinkled the skin at the corners of his eyes.

He looked past her. "You know, son, someday she's going to make you sorry. Very, very sorry."

"How's she going to do that?" Sean didn't sound impressed.

"She's a woman. She'll be creative."

"Bull." But faint uncertainty had infused his voice.

Nolan winked at Allie, who smiled back.

"Time will tell," he remarked, and escorted her into the house for a very passionate kiss that ended only when they heard the thunder of his foster son's enormous feet on the porch steps.

She teased Sean all through dinner and he teased her right back. His obvious acceptance of her made her feel giddy. Maybe he could love her, too. Maybe soon she'd have a real family again.

Nolan walked her to her car at the end of the evening for another passionate kiss. She'd noticed he hadn't turned on the porch light when they came out. He took advantage of the deeper night in the shadow of an old lilac to slide one hand up under her shirt and gently knead her breast while his hips rocked against hers.

"Damn," he muttered. "We could sneak out to the workshop."

She ached for him enough to give brief consideration to the idea. Finally she sighed. "Sean would see my car still sitting here. He's not dumb."

"No. Damn," Nolan said again. Reluctantly he removed his hand from her breast. "How about dinner tomorrow night? You and me. No Sean."

"I'll cook," Allie agreed. She kissed his jaw. "This was fun tonight."

"It was, wasn't it?" His smile was in his voice, even if it went unseen in the dark.

Once she was in her car, he bent down to kiss her one more time, lingeringly, before straightening and slamming the door. As she drove away, she saw him in the rearview mirror watching her go, an unmoving monolith lit only by a half-moon.

At home she got all the way upstairs before realizing she'd left her phone in her car all evening. She went back down to get it. Seeing that she had at least one new message, she dialed voice mail and learned that she had three.

"Allie, where are you?" The voice was so hysterical, it

took Allie a second to positively identify it as her mother's. "I got a call from the U.S. Marshal's office. Someone's looking for us and has gotten as far as Tulsa. Allie, I think they're going to move us again."

CHAPTER FIFTEEN

WHEN ALLIE RANG THE BELL, her mother flung open her front door and drew her in. She wore a robe over her nightgown, but didn't appear at all sleepy.

"Oh, thank goodness!" she exclaimed. "Why weren't you answering your phone? Do you know how scared I've been?"

"I left it in my car while I was having dinner at Nolan's." Who cared why she'd been out of touch for a few hours? "What do you mean, someone is looking for us? What makes them think that?"

"He said they already had some pings because someone was running searches for drivers' licenses, credit and all kinds of other things dating to the time we lived there. And then your dad called them to say a man had come to his door claiming to be a private investigator. He was asking questions about *you*."

"Me?" That made no sense. "Why would anyone be interested in me?"

"Maybe it was an excuse to draw him into conversation. Or maybe they had discovered he and Jason were still in the area and realized you must have disappeared with me."

"The computer searches—was that me, too?"

"No." Her mother paused. "I don't think so. You hadn't even gotten your driver's license yet, and you certainly wouldn't have had a credit record."

Not bothering to take driver's ed had been part of Allie's

general apathy during that period. She had finally taken the class as a senior at Lynnwood High and gotten her driver's license months after her eighteenth birthday.

"Wait," she said. "Why would we be moved? Is there any suggestion at all that our new identity has been uncovered? How could it be? Even Dad and Jason don't know our names now or where we are!"

"Nothing is impossible," Mom declared. Allie had sat down, perching tensely on the edge of the sofa, but Mom paced as though she was so wired she couldn't stop. "What if there's someone in the marshal's office who sells information? You read about things like that."

"Then moving us wouldn't help, would it?"

Allie was scared, too, but for a different reason from her mother. Had she jinxed her mother and herself by finally finding a real life?

"Allie." Her mother stopped in front of the sofa. "When did you tell Nolan about us?"

Allie's eyes widened. "Are you suggesting…?" She shot to her feet. "What do you think, he made some calls right away, offering us up for a price?"

"I know you don't want to think it's a possibility." Mom's voice had softened.

"It's not a possibility." She didn't remember ever being angrier. "Anyway, I only told him Wednesday night. There's no way all this could have happened so fast."

"Oh." Her mother's stiff stance briefly eased, and then she took flight again, resuming her frenetic pacing. "Of course not. I'm sorry, honey, but I had to ask."

Watching her, Allie had a truly awful thought. The timing *was* odd. Suggestive. Mom had never liked the idea of Allie's relationship with Nolan. She wouldn't have made this whole thing up, would she?

Allie gave her head a slight shake. No, of course not;

Mom didn't have the connections or skills to give them new identities. She couldn't make up that part.

She could have hired someone to pretend to be searching for them, though. *Look at her,* a voice seemed to whisper to Allie. *Is she* really *scared? Or is she excited, the way she was the other times?*

Feeling sick, Allie saw that her mother did have that same electrified air Allie remembered so well. If this scene were taking place onstage, every eye in the audience would be on her mom. *She's the star again.*

Allie actually had to swallow bile. "Mom, I'm going home. You're overreacting. We should wait and see what happens. What if Dad applied for a loan that triggered a routine background search?"

"Do you think he made up the investigator asking about you?"

"I don't know. No." She flung up her hands. "Mom, I'm twenty-eight years old. No one hunting for you would have any reason to assume that finding me would necessarily lead right to you. A lot of people my age live on the other side of the country from their parents. Did Dad ask any questions? Like, 'Why are you looking for my daughter'? What if whoever knocked at the door had the wrong guy? Did he mention me by name? And if so, what name did he use?"

"I don't know," her mother admitted. "I suppose I'm too alarmed to think this all through logically. But you seem to be in denial. And you know if they move us, they'll do it suddenly." She spoke sharply. "There won't be time to pack much or for goodbyes."

What she meant was that there won't be time to say goodbye to Nolan.

Allie's immediate, heartfelt reaction was *I can't.* But then, on a wave of cold, she realized the alternative: saying goodbye to her mother. Or discovering suddenly that Mom was gone.

"I'm leaving." She hurried to the front door. There, her hand on the knob, she turned to face her mother. "I can't leave Nolan, Mom. I can't."

Her mother stared at her in shock.

Allie went out, shut the door and raced for her car. She wanted to drive straight to Nolan's house, but knew she couldn't. Not at this time of night. Sean would want to know what was going on and no matter what he couldn't be told anything. Even a phone call at this time of night would probably wake him up. And that was assuming Nolan kept his phone anywhere he could hear it after he'd gone to bed.

No, tomorrow was soon enough.

This *had* to all be a mistake. She started the car, backed out of her mother's driveway into the empty street and was grateful not to have far to go home. She wasn't in any shape to drive.

"THEY'RE TALKING ABOUT moving us again." Allie stood in the middle of Nolan's workshop, looking as bad as she had the night she'd told him about the destruction of her family. She had called earlier; when he told her Sean had gone to one of his new friends' houses for the day, she'd come over so they could "talk."

That had alarmed him enough. He had suspected he wasn't going to like anything she had to say, but his sinking feeling had become a sense of doom when he saw her sprint from her car to the workshop through the rain without even bothering with a coat.

Her hair was wet and plastered to her head, her face blanched, the raindrops on her lashes reminding Nolan of tears. Her hands were knotted so tightly together in front of her, the knuckles were white.

He shook his head. "Say that again."

It didn't sound any better the second time. "Someone is looking for us," she said. "Whoever it was found Dad and was asking questions."

"Wait." *Oh, hell.* This wasn't how he'd wanted to tell her. At the same time, the relief was huge. Nobody from their past was looking for Allie or her mother. *He'd* been the one looking, stirring up something he didn't understand. "This is all my fault," he said.

"What?" Eyes huge and dark, she gaped at him.

"Allie, come here." He held out a hand.

With new wariness, she stared at his hand, then raised her gaze to his face without taking a step forward.

"Please."

She was trembling, he saw, when she nodded and then came to him. Once he had her small hand in his, he drew her forward.

"I did something stupid, Allie."

The green-gold was almost lost, as dilated as her eyes were. "You *told* someone?"

Oh, man. He'd give a lot not to have to admit what he'd done. But she'd understand. Surely she'd understand. And she'd be relieved, too, he wanted to believe. "You know how curious I was," he said gruffly.

She had gone so still, he wasn't sure she was breathing.

"You told me you'd gone to high school outside Tulsa. You even told me the name of the town." He was beginning to feel desperate. *Oh, hell,* he thought again. "Then when your mother had a different story, I called the high school in Fairfield. They had no record of an Allie or Allison Wright."

"Oh, my God."

"I was going to confront you."

"But instead you hired an investigator?" Her voice rose

with each word. Her hand writhed within his grasp, trying to free itself. He didn't want to let her go, but he did. She retreated a couple of steps.

"Not at that point. Sean said high school yearbooks are online. He's right."

"Online?" Allie looked and sounded as if he'd punched her in the belly.

"I'm afraid so. I looked through the one for the year I figured you'd have been a junior."

"Oh, no."

"Oh, yeah. I found you, Allie. But, surprise, surprise, you weren't Allie Wright at all. You were Laura Nelson."

"Then…when I told you, you already knew?"

"All I knew was that you and your mother had left Oklahoma and changed your names. You kept being resistant when I asked you about your background. I thought I could find out what had happened back then."

"So you hired a P.I."

He grimaced. "Yeah. That's what I did."

"How could you do that?" Her shock and hurt went deeper than he'd ever dreamed they would. "We were seeing each other, and you were having me *investigated?*"

In her words, it sounded even worse than it did the way he'd framed what had at the time seemed like a rational thing to do. Possibly paranoid, he would admit. It wasn't as if she didn't know he had one very hot button, which she had pushed.

"It was…actually during that week when I didn't see you."

Allie gave her head a small shake. "I can't believe this."

"I'm sorry." His throat felt raw. "It was a shitty thing to do. My only defense is that I have a big thing about being lied to. You know why."

"You never came to me and said, 'I know you're hiding something. If we're going to have a relationship, I need you to be up front with me.' Instead, you hired an *investigator?*" Her voice had risen again, in exactly the same way, ending up shrill and disbelieving.

"I'm sorry," he said again. "I was going to tell you what I'd done, Allie. I've been dragging my feet because I knew you'd be pissed or hurt or both. I don't blame you." His urgency grew as he watched her face. "Once I got the first report from the P.I., I knew I'd gone too far. I called him off."

"What if *his* questions caught someone else's attention? What if the very fact that he was poking around has put us at risk again?"

Guilt was a huge, indigestible lump in his belly. "What would make you think anyone else even noticed?"

"Did he run credit checks? Search for drivers' licenses? Property records?"

Nolan frowned. "I don't know. Drivers' licenses, maybe. Apparently your background story then had your family moving to Oklahoma from Michigan. The P.I. did try to find some evidence you'd actually lived there. He came up empty."

"Oh, dear God." She turned her back on him.

"I shouldn't have done it," he said. "But knowing I did is good news in a way, isn't it? It means you and your mother don't have to worry."

"I can't believe you did this." She sounded so shell-shocked, he began to get really afraid.

"What can I do to make you forgive me?"

She swung around and met his gaze, hers flat and chilling. "I don't know if I can. Or if I want to. Even if Mom and I don't have to move, I can't trust you, Nolan. I thought… I thought you'd never do anything…" Her voice broke. "I have to go home."

"Wait. Please." Goddamn it, he'd never begged for anything in his life.

"Do you have the name of the P.I. so I can pass it on?"

He told her the name. "Allie, there's no reason your mother should have to move."

"That man is an outsider. He knows too much. If the marshal has to ask him questions, that'll make him curious, won't it? What if *he* betrays us?"

"No. Damn it, Allie! He doesn't know your original names. He wouldn't know who to contact, and that's assuming he's the creep you're implying he is."

"I told Mom I could trust you." Her stunned gaze raked him.

"You can." Nolan took a step toward her and grabbed her hands. "I swear. I love you, Allie. I'll do anything."

"Sure you will. You proved that, didn't you?"

Bone-deep scared, he dropped her hands. "I would never hurt you on purpose. I was trying to answer my own questions. That's all."

"It doesn't really matter, does it?" She swung away and started for the door.

"Allie." He had this terrible fear that if she left now, he'd never see her again. "Even if your mother gets relocated for some reason, you don't have to go. I need you to stay." He barely hesitated. "To marry me."

She only shook her head and hurried out. Nolan caught the door and watched her dash through the rain, get in her car, start it and drive away without once turning her head toward him.

For the second time in his life, the bottom had dropped out of his world. This time, he'd done the damage himself, and he had no idea how he could atone.

TELLING HER MOTHER was one of the worst things Allie had ever had to do. She didn't know if Mom made it better or worse by accepting the news with surprising calm. She didn't once say, *I told you so.* Or, *This is why I didn't trust your judgment.*

"Oh, honey, I'm sorry" was what she did say, very softly. She put her arms around Allie and held her for a long time.

Allie couldn't make herself relax into the embrace. She didn't cry. She simply stood there, waiting until she judged an adequate length of time had passed before she gently separated herself. "You'll pass this on?"

"Of course I will. It does sound as if he stirred up a hornet's nest, though, doesn't it?"

"Maybe not. It might all have been the P.I."

Her mother looked at her with pity. "The problem is, now there's someone who can link Judy and Laura Nelson with Cheryl and Allie Wright in Washington State."

"Nolan may not have said anything about Cheryl and Allie Wright." She felt the tiniest twinge of hope. "I told you. He'd already discovered that I was Laura Nelson. He asked the investigator to try to find out about the Nelsons. Mostly he wanted to know why you and I took off and felt we had to change our names."

"Then why was he trying to discover where we'd lived before Fairfield?"

"I don't know," she admitted. "Maybe he was only being thorough."

"It doesn't matter anyway. The fact is, a man in West Fork, Washington, hired a P.I. to investigate the Nelsons in Oklahoma. Someone looking for us would come straight to West Fork, wouldn't they?"

Yes, Allie supposed if anyone in the Moretti family had ever traced the Marrs as far as Oklahoma *and* was still looking for them, that's exactly what they'd do. They would be very curious indeed why a stonemason in Washington State wanted questions answered about the Nelsons.

"You think we're still going to be moved, don't you? Even though we can explain what happened."

"That's my guess." Her mother really did look sorry. "Nolan couldn't have foreseen any of this. I'm sure he never meant to hurt you."

"That's what he said." There was a shift in the thin crust of anger that encased pain, as if a cataclysmic fracture was imminent. She couldn't afford that. "No matter what, I'm not sure I can get past the fact that he had me investigated."

"Between us, we did raise a lot of questions." Mom sounded rueful.

She'd decided to be sympathetic and understanding *now?* Because she actually did feel bad for Allie? Or because she could afford to be gracious knowing she'd won? Either way, Allie was suddenly mad in a whole new way.

"I'm going to work," she said.

Her mother frowned. "Why don't you wait until I've called the marshal?"

"You can tell me what he says. I promised Barbara I'd be there by noon."

I seem to be making a habit of walking out on people, Allie thought, as she did just that. It seemed that her instinctive reaction to powerful emotions was to flee. The insight gave her pause.

Had the fact that her family had spent so many years running imprinted itself on her, becoming as natural to her as breathing? Or was it that she was afraid of her own emotions when they grew too powerful?

Yes. Coping was beyond her. This time, she couldn't hide inside herself. *So I run away.*

Allie parked in one of the two spots behind her store and let herself in the back door. A quilter and excellent customer, Barbara was happy to work a few hours when Allie needed help. She didn't seem to need the money so much as she enjoyed an excuse to spend time in the quilt shop.

When Allie walked in, Barbara had finished ringing up a purchase and was adding two spools of thread to the fabric already in a bag while the customer wrote a check. Allie went immediately to help another woman who was wandering in apparent befuddlement with a bolt of fabric clutched in her arms.

"May I help you?" Allie asked.

"Please. I don't know what's wrong with me today, but I can't seem to make any decisions."

Allie pried out of her the fact that this was to be only her second quilt, intended to be twin-sized for her eight-year-old daughter's bed. She thought she'd use a pinwheel pattern. She'd intended to keep to perhaps three fabrics, but now she was wondering if a multitude of different fabrics used in the blades of the pinwheel wouldn't be more effective.

Allie showed her a couple of different options and led her to fabrics that would contrast rather than blend with the background she'd already chosen. Then she pointed out the bins of fat quarters. "If you'd really like to go for the scrap-quilt effect…"

The woman pounced and Allie was able to leave her happily browsing through dozens of packets of color-coordinated fabrics already cut into quarter-yard lengths.

She thanked Barbara and they chatted for a few minutes. Allie felt as if she was hovering outside of herself, watching. She was smiling, relaxed, completely natural, betraying no hint that anything at all was wrong. Inside, she churned with disturbing emotions.

A horrifying thought hit her. She wouldn't be able to open a new quilt shop if she and her mother were relocated. It would be like dancing, an obvious way to trace her. Stunned, she stood behind her counter and looked around the store, the place she felt most comfortable, most fulfilled, most *herself.*

She didn't know if she could survive the dual loss of this, her vocation, and Nolan and Sean, her future.

But the alternative was to abandon her mother, who had already been abandoned by her husband and son. *As I've been abandoned,* Allie thought wretchedly. And she would have sworn that she was being literally rended in two.

SOMEHOW ALLIE WASN'T surprised when she heard the deep growl of a truck engine that evening, followed by steady, heavy footsteps on the outside steps and then a knock on her door.

Allie gave very serious consideration to not answering. She didn't know yet what to say to him. She still felt so betrayed.

But she hadn't liked that morning's insight. It was bad enough knowing she was timid, inclined to retreat into herself. She didn't want to be a complete coward.

With a groan, she rose from where she sat curled on her easy chair and went to open the door.

Nolan did not look good. The bristles on his jaw and cheeks made her realize he must have shaved for a second time other evenings when he expected to see her. There were tired lines beside his eyes and deep furrows between his eyebrows. She didn't like seeing self-doubt and uncertainty in this man who had always projected solidity and confidence that she had believed would never fail.

After a moment she stepped back, wordlessly inviting him in.

She didn't quite want to say, *What are you doing here?* She searched for a better alternative.

"I didn't expect you."

"I had to see you."

"Why?"

"When you left today, I had this terrible feeling you were walking out of my life. That I'd never see you again."

"It's possible that will happen," she said carefully. She hesitated. "Would you like to sit down?"

"No." Desperation looked very different from the intensity Allie was used to seeing in his eyes. "I want— I don't know what, but sure as hell not to sit here politely conversing. Damn it, Allie!"

The rage and sense of betrayal rose with shocking suddenness, like a flash flood roaring down a narrow canyon. "I don't even know why I opened the door!" she cried.

"Yes, you do." His hands shot out and caught hers in a hard grip. "You said you love me."

"I do. No." She shook her head hard. "I don't know if I do anymore. Not after this."

He gave her a small shake. "All I did was try to understand you."

"You had me investigated."

"You were lying to me," he said flatly. "I knew it. You've admitted you were."

"So that makes it okay?"

"No." His tight grip eased. Regret altered the lines of his rough-hewn face. "I screwed up big-time. I let my fears get to me. Can't you understand that?"

She hurt too much to be understanding. "You've managed to do to me the one thing I most feared."

"God." He tugged her forward until her stiff body collided with his. "You asked me once if you'd ruined everything. Now I have to ask you. Did I?"

"Don't you see?" She tore herself away again. "It doesn't matter! If I have to go, I have to go. There's no future for us. What good would it do for me to say I forgive you?"

"Don't go." His voice was raw. "Stay with me, Allie. Marry me. Love me. If you take my name, it'll be yours for the rest of your life. I swear it."

"Don't do this to me," she whispered. "How can I let Mom go by herself? I'm all she has. She *needs* me."

He shook his head. "Allie, you're an adult. She's had you longer than most parents have their children. What if we'd met a year ago, gotten married, and then I'd wanted to move back to Chicago? Would you have refused to go because your mother is here?"

"It's not the same." She wished it was, wished it could be. "Don't you see? If that had happened, Mom and I could have talked regularly. We could have visited. If this happens, she'll lose me completely." She bit her lip so hard she tasted blood. "I'll lose her," Allie finished with quiet desperation.

His body jerked. He said nothing for a moment. "That's your answer?" he said finally. "If it comes down to it, you're telling me you choose her?"

"This is *your* fault," Allie cried passionately.

"Your mother has never done anything careless or stupid that hurt you?"

Allie felt as if her feet were stuck to the canyon floor as the deadly wall of water bore down on her. There was no hope of her riding it to safety.

Her throat was so tight she could barely speak. "She stole my life from me because *she* wanted to do something noble. She never even noticed what she'd done."

Staring at the past, she scarcely noticed his flinch.

"Is that why you're willing to pack up and go again, Allie?" The devastation and anger were on his side now, and she couldn't miss them. Nolan's eyes burned as he stared at her. "Because this life, the one with me, will never be good enough?" He slammed a fist against the back of her upholstered chair, rocking it.

"I'm wasting my time, aren't I? You want back what you had when you were thirteen, and I sure as hell wasn't part of it, was I?" A harsh sound escaped his throat. "Guess I got my answer. Hope you like your next life."

Aghast, Allie watched him stalk to the door. "No! It's not like that."

He didn't even slow down. The door quivered in its frame when he slammed it behind him.

CHAPTER SIXTEEN

NOLAN HAD MADE Sean's favorite dinner. He wasn't very hungry himself, but he watched as Sean slurped spaghetti into his mouth, shoveled in garlic bread and generally consumed enough food to have fed three or four normal people.

The kid managed to talk during a good deal of the meal, too, but Nolan refrained from issuing a lecture on not talking when your mouth was full. He was too grateful not to have to say much himself.

"Are you done with your torpedo thing?" Sean asked as he polished his plate with a last scrap of bread.

"No, I've been too busy with other work."

"You don't seem to be in a very good mood."

And he'd tried damned hard to hide his mood. Apparently he wasn't much of an actor.

"I guess not," he admitted. "Allie and I have hit a bad patch. I kind of think we're over."

"What?"

"You heard me." He pushed back his chair and started clearing the dirty dishes.

"But...did you do something?"

Punched by anguish, all he could do was lock his knees and stand there so he didn't stagger, hands full of dishes. "Yeah," he said hoarsely, when he could speak at all. "You could say that."

"What...?"

"I can't tell you, Sean. She's got some stuff going on I didn't understand. I screwed up. Sometimes saying you're sorry is good enough, sometimes it isn't. This is one of the times when it isn't."

"Wow." The teenager rose to his feet. "That's a bummer."

A bummer. In a different mood, he might have laughed. A bummer was missing an important shot in a game. Not being able to find a parking spot, so you ended up walking ten blocks in the rain. Hurting the woman he loved, losing her, that fell into an entirely different category.

So did finding out that what she called love was too shallow to qualify in his book.

Not fair, he told himself after escaping to the kitchen, as he scraped a good deal of his dinner into the garbage bin.

There was no doubt that she did love her mother. Maybe it wasn't reasonable for him to think he could compete given that he and she had only known each other for a couple of months.

And that he'd just broken her trust in him with a solid swing of his mallet. He'd seen fine chunks of stone shatter and fall apart in exactly the same way when he'd been careless.

"There's nothing you can do?" Sean asked behind him.

"I don't think so." He rinsed off a plate and put it on the rack in the dishwasher.

"You're *sure?*"

"Damn it, butt out!" he snarled.

It took all of about ten seconds for chagrin to kick in, but when he turned he found himself alone in the kitchen. He slapped his hand down on the countertop hard enough to sting, not nearly punishment enough.

You're sure?

No, he thought. No, he wasn't sure.

His head seemed to clear. For all his hurt, he couldn't see letting Allie go without trying something, anything, to keep her. To convince her that she could trust him.

"Shit," he said aloud, and reached for his phone to call his sister. Good excuse to put off apologizing to Sean.

HIGH ON ALL the excitement, Allie's mother phoned with regular updates.

The U.S. Marshal had spoken to Nolan, who didn't believe he'd ever told the P.I. where he lived. Most of their transactions had taken place online. The only solid clue would have been the area code for Nolan's mobile phone, which happened to be 206 for Seattle rather than 360 for the rural northwest part of the state.

Nolan was forwarding the report with specifics that the investigator had prepared for him. The marshal's office wanted to pin down everything the P.I. had done so as to determine whether there had been any other activity beyond what he had generated.

"They're pleased Nolan is being so cooperative," Mom reported.

In another phone call, she told Allie that so far, all indications were that the private investigator was ethical. With nearly the next breath, she added that she had partially packed, in case the move came suddenly. "I hope you've done the same," she said.

Allie went home that evening and looked around her small apartment. What would she take? Leave? She was dismayed to realize how little she actually owned. A few pieces of artwork, but none that were very expensive; furniture she liked, but which could easily be replaced; clothes, of course, but even there she didn't have a huge wardrobe. She didn't share the passion many women felt for shoes or jewelry or shopping in general. Some books, but she mostly used the library.

Her gaze reluctantly settled on the quilt frame. Would she be allowed to take one? She wouldn't be able to own a quilt shop, but there was no reason she couldn't continue to quilt and even sell her quilts.

In sudden panic she thought of the quilts hanging at the shop. She couldn't leave them behind. She couldn't! Tomorrow she'd bring them all home, in case. Of course, people would ask about the empty spaces on the wall, but she'd think of an explanation.

In the next second, Allie sagged into her chair. Why was she thinking about *things?* Every single thing she owned, even the quilts she'd lovingly hand-stitched, could be replaced. Things didn't matter—people did. Nolan did.

Mom did.

Oh, God, oh, God, what am I going to do? she asked herself for the thousandth time. She wondered what her father and brother would tell her to do, if she was able to talk to them. But in the end, she knew her choice wasn't the same as theirs had been. Neither had stayed behind because there had been a person he couldn't bear to leave.

What if her vacillating had killed what Nolan felt for her? Even knowing how angry she was, even after she had walked away from him, he'd come back to ask her again to marry him. But, remembering the expression on his face when he left the last time, Allie knew he wouldn't be back this time.

It was up to her now.

NOLAN STOOD IN the middle of his workshop and knew he wouldn't be safe using power tools today. Looking around, he asked himself how he'd feel if he had to leave this workshop and everything it meant to him behind.

Was that what dancing had been for Allie, young as she was? Had it been the only thing she could imagine doing with her life? Had she felt as if she were *meant* to tie on toe shoes, train and suffer until she could fly?

From the minute Nolan had handled his first chunk of raw stone, he'd been fascinated. *What if I was being forced to choose between this and a life with Allie?*

I wouldn't even hesitate, he realized with a strangely lightened heart. *I could be satisfied doing something else. Carpentry, maybe. I could carve in wood. I could be happy, if I had Allie and Sean.*

Would Allie have to give up quilting if she relocated with her mother? She'd lost so damn much already. He remembered her talking about how splintered she felt: Chloe, who was angry; Laura, bewildered and tongue-tied; Allie, who wasn't allowed to acknowledge her other selves.

She had sounded so bleak when she said, *Somehow I have to put myself back together, and I have no idea how.*

What if Allie Wright, too, became another self she had to deny? *He* was part of this life, which would cease to exist for her.

When she was given a new background, would she be able to remember it? Would she even try, or would she give up?

Nolan felt a painful cramping in his chest. Would she ever be able to put herself back together?

My fault. I caused this.

I need to find a way to fix it.

Anna hadn't been any help. Of course, he hadn't been able to tell her the whole story. He'd admitted to having Allie's background investigated and told his sister that Allie had found out.

"I can't imagine a woman forgiving that," Anna had

said flatly. "Has it ever occurred to you that you've carried this thing with Mom a little too far?"

"It doesn't bother you?"

"Sure it does, but not the same way." The silence suggested she was thinking. "I don't know why that is. I coped by deciding I wasn't going to be anything like her."

Nolan had had one of those lightbulb moments. "And I coped by deciding I wasn't going to be anything like Dad."

"Well, duh," his sister said.

Call him dim-witted, but he'd never framed it in those terms before. *I decided I would never tolerate lies. I would never gloss them over or enable someone else's lies. Above all else, I would never lie to the people I love.*

He'd known all that. He just hadn't recognized that he was more outraged by the choices the man he called Dad had made than the ones his mother had made. For Anna, the reverse had been true.

"I've been...blindly rebelling," he admitted to his sister. "The thing that kills me is, I *knew* Allie. I knew I could trust her, but I didn't let myself."

Like Sean, Anna had asked whether it was too late. He still didn't know the answer.

How do I fix this?

Nolan looked at the clock hanging on the workshop wall and watched the second hand sweep inexorably around. The clock was literally ticking, he thought. Allie and her mother could be moved anytime. Tomorrow. *Tonight.*

No, not that fast. He knew a careful investigation was being conducted. The marshal's office wasn't eager to have to produce entirely new identities yet again for two women who'd already been moved once more than the original plan had called for. Nolan hadn't asked questions and now wished he had.

Was the guy Allie's mother put in prison still there, or

had he served his term and walked out? If so, was anyone in law enforcement keeping an eye on him? Goddamn it, they'd know if he had died, wouldn't they? Or committed yet another crime and been put away again, maybe for a life sentence? Would anybody else in the crime family really give a damn after all these years about the secretary who testified in the trial?

Surely to hell the government wouldn't go to the expense of continuing to hide Cheryl Wright née Judy Nelson née... He didn't remember the first name she'd been born with, if he'd ever heard it. He shook off the irrelevancy. Nobody would waste the money unless there was at least a remote possibility that she could still be a target.

He hoped the decision would be made *not* to move Allie's mom—and Allie if she chose to go, too. But he had zero control over that decision.

I could try talking to Allie again. Getting on my knees and begging.

Had her father or brother begged her to stay behind last time? he got to wondering. Or had they shrugged and said, "Your choice"?

Nolan had a troubling thought. It was nice to think her father might have loved her enough to plead with her to stay with him rather than disappear with her mother. But ultimately, both parents had been selfish. No matter what choice Allie made, *she* was the one making the sacrifice. She'd lose her father...or she'd lose her mother.

This time, she'd lose the man she claimed to love...or she'd lose her mother. Once again, everyone in her life— everyone who claimed to love her—demanded she make the sacrifice.

Oh, hell and damnation, Nolan thought, appalled. There was a way *he* could offer to make the sacrifice so that she didn't have to. And maybe he'd been tiptoeing toward it without even noticing. Why else had he asked himself which he'd choose, the work he loved or Allie?

Now the dilemma lay in front of him, as impossible to miss as a meteor that had just crashed through his workshop roof and lay burning in front of him.

Nobody had ever offered to give up everything for Allie. Not her mother, who had made the original decision for her own reasons, despite the cost her daughter, son and husband would pay. Not Allie's father, who in divorcing his wife had left his daughter feeling abandoned even before he let her go forever. And certainly not her brother, who when the family divided chose Daddy's side, leaving his quiet, wounded sister behind.

This, Nolan thought with the same sense of shock, *is how I fix the disaster I created. This is how I make the words "I love you" have real meaning.*

He tipped his head back and groaned. He could cut the bonds that linked him to his family, although knowing he'd never hear Anna's voice again, knowing that she would always wonder what had happened to him, that would be hard.

But he could not abandon Sean, who had already lost everyone else he'd ever loved and trusted.

He couldn't present himself to Allie and offer to pack up and go with her without first talking to Sean.

Which meant breaking the promise he'd made her. He *had* to tell Sean what was going on, and ask how he felt about starting all over. Again.

THE HIGH SCHOOL basketball season launched that evening with a junior varsity home game. Nolan couldn't be anywhere else but in the stands.

He stood and clapped with the rest of the crowd on the home side of the court when the boys ran out onto the court. Students whistled and stamped on the bleachers, creating thunder and making them shake. Nolan hardly noticed. He was thinking how young those boys looked. Skinny legs, big feet, zits. Tank tops bared thin bodies. Sean was actually one of the better-put-together of the group. A couple of the boys blushed and cast shy glances at the crowd. Being the center of attention must be new to them.

Sean's head turned and he scanned the crowd. For a moment there was something achingly young and worried on his face. But when he spotted Nolan, he gave a huge grin. The relief and sheer pleasure in that grin did strange things to Nolan's heart.

He hadn't understood the impulse that made him take in the boy he had barely exchanged a few words with, but he supposed he'd thought he was doing something decent. What he hadn't known was how quickly he would come to love this boy, no different than if he was his own.

His mind did an unsettling, sideways shift. It occurred to him he'd never believed Dad really did love him the same way he loved Jed, who was his own. Maybe he'd been wrong, he thought now. Maybe being a blood relation wasn't actually that important.

I guess I should give him a call. Just to talk. Maybe it's even time—past time—I forgive him.

The one thing he'd never let himself think about entered his head. What if Dad had left Mom when he found out she'd had an affair, or later when he realized their oldest son wasn't his?

I wouldn't have had *a father, that's what.*

Would that really have been better? Because the truth was, his dad had been a damn good father. The best.

Once this is settled with Allie...I'll call him while I still can.

Feeling some sense of peace, Nolan tuned in when the referee blew the whistle and the game started, Sean playing forward.

Nolan might have been prejudiced—okay, *was* prejudiced—but he thought Sean was, hands down, the best player out there. He rebounded aggressively, shut down every opposing player he defended and, by the final buzzer, had scored an impressive eighteen points. Fouled once, he stepped up to the free-throw line and dropped in two shots, cool as could be.

I'll be asking him to give up this team, these new friends. Yeah, he'd be able to play basketball wherever they went—but maybe not this season. For a kid this age, starting all over mid-school year sucked. Sean would know, because he'd done it so recently.

Nolan didn't know what he'd do if Sean threw a fit and said, "No way am I going."

Crap.

What if the decision came down to an either-or? Nolan asked himself. Allie or Sean? The yawning pit in his belly gave him a good idea what she'd gone through when she was seventeen and faced the same dilemma. Maybe what she faced this time, too, if she really did love him.

Allie or Sean?

Suppressing a groan, Nolan had no trouble making that decision.

He was sticking to both of them. However much Sean bitched, this choice wasn't his to make.

That realization gave Nolan new sympathy for Allie's mother. Parents sometimes *did* have to drag their reluctant kids along, the way she'd done. Hell, it happened all the time, when one parent or the other got transferred on the job, say. Of course, her decision had been different in a big way, he reminded himself; her husband had had to give up his business, Allie the chance at a brilliant future as a ballerina. And, yeah, they'd all given up their names.

He'd be asking that of Sean, too.

It'll be tough, he told himself, but Sean will adjust. Kids did. The most important thing to a boy with Sean's background was finding out that his new dad wouldn't abandon him for any reason at all—and wouldn't abandon the woman he loved, either.

Settled in his mind, Nolan watched as the jubilant home team shook hands with their opponents and then headed for the locker room. Nolan joined the exodus from the bleachers.

Sean hadn't had much of an appetite earlier. "I guess I'm nervous," he'd admitted. Nolan had promised pizza on the way home.

When the boys disappeared into the locker room, Nolan called the pizza parlor and ordered an extra-large, everything-on-it one to go. This was a conversation they couldn't have in a restaurant.

In the parking lot, Nolan leaned against the fender of his truck and waited with the other parents. Sean emerged finally, showered and triumphant from the win. He and Nolan exchanged high fives.

"Man, I'm starved!" was the first thing out of his mouth.

"One step ahead of you. I called and ordered a pizza to be ready for pickup." Nolan hesitated. "There's something I want to talk to you about."

Predictably, Sean badgered him, but Nolan held his ground until they got home. He waited until he'd set plates, napkins and drinks on the table while Sean opened the box and devoured his first slice of pizza in a couple of gulps.

"This is about Allie," Nolan said, knowing the gravity of what he felt and was going to ask of the boy had to be obvious in his voice.

Sean didn't reach for another slice. "What about Allie?"

Nolan hesitated. "You can never repeat anything I tell you. Not to anyone. Not a best friend, not a girlfriend. Not ever. You can't hint at it on your Facebook page. This is… really important."

The boy stared at him. "You sound like…I don't know, like she works for the CIA or something."

"Do you promise?"

"Yeah. Sure." Seeing the look in Nolan's eyes, he added hastily, "I promise."

Nolan relaxed slightly. "Here it is, then." He talked, laying out the whole story. Mouth agape, Sean listened.

"Wow," he said finally, "you really stepped in it, didn't you?"

"No shit." Nolan grimaced at the bad pun. "Yeah. Having her investigated was the absolute worst thing I could have done."

"She's really just going to *leave* so she can stay with her mom? Is it because she's so mad at you?"

Nolan hesitated. "I think it's complicated. She's mad, she's hurt, sure. But also…her mother is the only continuity she's ever had in her life." He told Sean what he'd figured out, about how everyone Allie had ever loved expecting *her* to make any sacrifices that had to be made.

"I kind of get that," Sean said unexpectedly. "Grandma loved me, but even with her I could tell having me around wasn't really what she wanted. You know? I had to try to fit in depending on who I lived with." His shrug was awkward. "Until you, no one ever really put themselves out for me."

Choked up, Nolan had to clear his throat before he could speak. "You deserved better all along the way."

Sean shrugged, as if that was beside the point. "You're thinking you'll go with her, aren't you?"

Surprised at his perception, Nolan raised his eyebrows. "I guess I am," he said after a minute. "That's why I had to talk to you before I talk to Allie."

Sean ducked his head. "So I know."

"Because this affects you as much as it does me," Nolan said slowly. "I'd be asking you to start all over, too. Seems like school is going really well for you. You're making friends. Given that we're midseason, you might not be able to play basketball until next fall at a new school."

"You don't think they could find me a foster home in West Fork."

Nolan stared at him. "I mean *wherever* we go. It could be damn near anywhere. It doesn't sound like we'd have any say in that."

Looking stunned, the boy raised his head. "You mean…" His voice cracked. "You'd take me with you?"

"Oh, hell." Nolan rose to his feet and circled the table. "Of course I'd take you with me. I told you. You're my son now."

A single harsh sob broke from Sean's throat. His chair scraped back. His arms came hard around Nolan, as Nolan's did around him.

"You're my son," Nolan repeated.

It was a long time until Sean drew back, his face wet. Averting his face, he grabbed a handful of napkins and swiped at tears before blowing his nose.

Nolan discovered his cheeks were also wet, and he reached for a napkin, too. At last he went back to his seat. "Eat," he said, nodding at the pizza.

"Yeah." Sean scooted his chair forward again and reached for a slice. "So that's the deal? If Allie wants us, we go with her?"

"That's the deal."

"Would my caseworker let me go? Especially if we're leaving the state."

"I'm thinking the U.S. Marshals can make that happen if they want. You don't have family in the area. There's nothing holding you here." He studied Sean. "You're okay with this?"

"Me? Sure." The pizza hadn't made it to his mouth yet. "Moving to a new school sort of sucks, but I can do it again. Allie needs to know we're willing."

"We might even get new names," Nolan warned. "I'm not sure about that."

A gleam showed in Sean's eyes. "Can we pick them?"

"I don't think so."

"What if they call me something stupid?"

"It's more likely to be something boring. A name that won't stand out."

He mulled that over. "I guess I can pick a cool nickname if I don't like whatever they call me."

"Yeah." Nolan had never known pride could fill a man until his chest hurt. "You can do that."

CHAPTER SEVENTEEN

ALTHOUGH EXHAUSTED, Allie's body refused to succumb to sleep. She squeezed her eyes shut and tried every technique she knew for falling asleep.

A black velvet sky settling gently over her...deep, dark, like the shadows beside the old lilac bush where Nolan had kissed her. Damn it, no.

Okay, concentrate on happy moments. Cuddling a kitten. But instead, all she came up with was Cassie's long pink tongue wrapped around her hand.

Something fun, then. When had she last had fun? Waterskiing...knowing Nolan was waiting for her back at the dock, proud she'd been willing to try even though she was timid in the water.

And so it went. Every single blasted effort she made to relax herself seemed to involve Nolan, and her body got stiffer and stiffer until she felt as if only her heels and her shoulder blades were actually touching the mattress.

Groaning, she slapped the pillow down on her face. Oh, why not get up? She might as well read or quilt or something.

Except when she did get up, her eyes burned and felt gritty. Her chest was being squeezed by a tight band and her stomach was knotted even tighter.

Maybe I'm hungry.

She opened the refrigerator and stared inside. Some-

how a salad didn't sound very palatable in the middle of
the night.

Cupboard. Maybe soup…?

Finally she put water on to boil to make herself a cup
of herbal tea. Neither of the varieties she found promised
to aid sleep, but warm milk had always sounded disgusting to her.

Waiting for the teakettle to whistle, Allie stared blankly
at the refrigerator door, decorated only with a handful of
quilting-related magnets. Refrigerator doors, she thought,
were meant for displaying children's artwork.

The pressure in her chest became more intense, stealing her breath. For a moment she could have sworn some
colorful drawings *did* hang on the otherwise white surface. She heard a giggle and turned her head sharply, but
of course she was alone.

This might be my only chance. Do I even want *children,
if they aren't Nolan's?*

Allie wondered what their children would look like.
Would they take after him, solid and quiet and intuitive?
Or after her, small, slight, inclined to settle only in front
of her quilt frame? She would love to have children with
his bright blue eyes.

Nolan was so good with Sean. He'd be the best father
in the world, endlessly patient, gentle. She pictured him
swinging a little girl into the air and laughing up at her.

Oh, damn. She squeezed her dry eyes closed and dropped
her head onto her forearm, only to jump when the teakettle
whistled.

I love him.

Finding Nolan had been a miracle. The stone man, who
had the kindest heart she'd ever known and was incredibly sexy besides. She loved every minute she'd spent with

him. The past few days, once she'd admitted her secret to him and he had told her he loved her, had been the happiest of her life.

She tried to summon the memory of other joyous times—when she was accepted to American Ballet Theatre, or was cast in *Firebird,* but none compared. They were triumphs, but only steps along the way to a far-off goal. Loving Nolan was…finding where she belonged. Her dream of dance seemed very long ago.

She had been called to dance. But for all the joy dance had given her, all the passion and dedication and even pain she had been willing to give in return, she had lived without it. Ultimately, becoming a quilt maker had given her joy, too.

What she'd never done in her life was give her heart—until she had looked up at that almost-homely face and straight into Nolan's stunningly clear blue eyes, the expression in them equally arrested. *From that first moment,* she thought.

I don't want to be alone anymore. Who had said that, him or her?

We don't have to be.

She stood up and turned off the burner, moving the teakettle off it without bothering to pour water into the cup. Her tension and pain seemed to be floating away, leaving her feeling extraordinarily light. Maybe, she thought frivolously, absurdly, she could do that jeté now and stay airborne as long as she liked.

She made herself remember that he'd had her investigated, but couldn't muster any anger at all, because she did understand why he'd done it.

She really was a lousy liar, and Nolan had an especially deep-seated fear of lies. It wasn't hard to picture how incredulous he must have felt at the idea that in loving her he was replicating his parents' relationship. It was no surprise he'd had to get answers about her, one way or another.

Despite what he'd done, she believed with all her heart that she could trust him. When he made a commitment, Nolan would keep it. Even Sean was starting to have faith, Allie thought, although he hadn't been with Nolan all that long.

If I choose him, he'll be on my side forever and ever.

Between one heartbeat and the next, she made her decision. It was easier than she'd imagined it could be. She didn't understand why coming to it had taken her so long.

If only he'd forgive her. Allie couldn't believe that she'd ever been so foolish.

Middle of the night or not, she wanted to call him. Drive over to his house and pound on the door. But of course that was silly.

Mom, she thought, on a renewed stab of pain. *I have to talk to Mom.* It seemed only fair to clear the decks before she went to Nolan.

Come morning, heavy-eyed, she called her mother first. "We have to talk," she said simply. When her mother questioned her, she pretended to have a customer.

She couldn't reach Barbara, and made the decision to close the shop for an hour when her mother got here. She'd never done that before, but other shopkeepers here in town did it from time to time. Nobody would be able to see her and Mom sitting in back. She scribbled a quick note. *Family Emergency—Back at 11:00.*

When Mom walked in, Allie hung the note and locked the door, grateful not to have any customers at the moment.

"Let's go in back," she said, and her mother followed her down the central aisle.

They sat down and looked at each other.

"I won't be going with you," Allie said, and braced herself for the storm.

Instead, she saw dignity and pained acceptance. "I thought that's what you'd decide."

"You've been acting as if you assumed I would go."

"I've been hoping," her mother corrected. "Selfishly, I know." She gave a small, twisted smile. "Despite what he did, I think your Nolan is a good man. He can make you happy. You deserve that, Allie. And more. I suppose I've clung to you, but it's time for me to stop."

"Oh, Mom." Tears, hot and fierce, spilled from Allie's eyes. "I love you. I don't want to lose either of you. I don't."

Their hands connected, squeezed so tightly it was hard to tell where one began and the other ended.

"No. I know. I hope you don't have to."

Allie wasn't the only one crying. For once, the tears seemed to be freeing. For forty-five minutes, they sat and talked about good times and bad without any of the emotional tension that had been there for so long Allie wasn't sure when it had begun. It was as if, in a moment, they had both been able to let go of all the resentment, all the expectations, everything except the friendship and love.

At the end her mother looked at her. "If I'd known then what I know now, I would have made a different decision. I hope you know that." The movement her mouth made couldn't even be called a smile. "Admitting to myself how much I hurt all of you hasn't been easy. I've resolved to write Jason and tell him how sorry I am, too."

"Back then, you couldn't know what would happen," Allie said.

Mom shook her head. "I knew how miserable all of you were. I told myself… Well, it doesn't matter now, does it? I can't take any of it back."

"No." Allie in turn tried to smile. "Maybe you won't have to go anywhere, Mom. I want you to stay."

"I want to stay, too. Needless to say, I couldn't sleep last night. I kept thinking about you and what I was asking you to give up. I decided that I won't agree to a move unless there is real evidence someone is looking for me and may be close to finding me.

"I want to stay close to you. I want to hold my grandchildren. I like my job and my house and…darn it, I want to be president of the Friends of the Library!"

They both laughed, although Allie for one had a lump in her throat.

The next second, her mother was swiping at new tears. "Oh, damn. I'm crying a river. For goodness' sake. It's time I leave you to open the store again. You don't want to lose customers. We can talk again."

She'd mostly mopped up all the tears by the time they reached the front of the store. They hugged, whispered, "I love you," and her mother slipped out and hurried away.

Allie flipped the sign back to Open and crumpled up the handwritten note. She stood for a long time looking out the front window at the surprisingly busy downtown street of this small town. *Home,* she thought, but knew in the next second that it wasn't the *place* that mattered, any more than *things* mattered.

If she called Nolan, would he come? Remembering again the way he'd looked at her that night, she was afraid she knew the answer. *She* had to go to *him,* not the other way around.

As soon as she closed the shop, she would drive straight to his house and pray he was there and willing to listen to her.

NOLAN PARKED HIS truck at the curb in front of the beauty parlor a couple of doors down from Allie's store and wondered if this was a really bad idea. He sure as hell didn't want this discussion to be interrupted.

You've come this far, he told himself.

He grunted in something close to amusement. He had yet to display any patience at all where Allie was concerned. Why break a streak?

Finally he grabbed the warm bags from the passenger seat, got out, locked the truck and walked the forty feet or so to her door.

He was glad he'd worn his sheepskin coat. The pale gray sky and biting cold hinted at snow. It wasn't common at this elevation in November, but ski season did typically open Thanksgiving weekend in the Cascades.

Thanksgiving was less than a week away. Not that long ago he'd assumed he would be celebrating it with Allie and her mother as well as Sean. He'd thought about trying to talk his sister into flying out and joining them. He really wanted to see her, and he'd wanted her to meet Allie.

How quickly things changed.

Pausing outside her store, a part of him noted how effective her window display was, with a quilt draped artfully and surrounded by coordinating bolts of fabrics. Several quilting how-to and pattern books lay scattered as if left in an absentminded moment. *Enter*, the display whispered. *Look at the wonders within. You can do this, too, you know. Don't you want to find out if there's an artist inside you?* Irresistible.

You planning to stand out here for maybe an hour or two?

He muffled a groan and reached for the damn doorknob. It would be just his luck if there were half a dozen women in there, all of whom would turn and stare at him when he walked in.

The bell tinkled and silence enveloped him.

"Hello, I'll be with you in a moment," Allie called from out of sight, and he was thrown back to that first day.

He remembered his astonishment at the multitude of fabrics, the colors, patterns, the femininity of his surroundings. But determination had carried him forward, through the alien landscape, until he'd found...Allie.

Determination set his feet on the same path this time, although his goal had changed. He reached the back room, unlike that first time not even taking in the quilt stretched in the frame.

Allie lifted her head, shock widening her eyes. The black leather thimble she was using dropped to the quilt top and she pushed back her chair with a jerk and rose to her feet.

"Nolan?" Her voice squeaked.

He held up the bags, as if they were answer enough. His hungry eyes took her in. Her hair was up in that ballerina-do, exposing the pure line of her neck and throat. She wore one of her skirts that draped artfully, and a formfitting knit top with three-quarter sleeves. She was bright and beautiful, graceful and so precious to him he ached.

"I never thought," she whispered.

His mouth crooked up. "That I wouldn't take no as an answer even when you said it loud and clear?"

"Of course that's not what I meant."

He set down the bags of food. His fingers flexed. It took an effort of will to make them loosen.

"I told you I love you." That came out as rough as crude granite.

Allie took a step closer to him, her glorious eyes raised

to him. "Nolan, I was going to come and see you. To tell you…"

He ignored her. He had to get this out. "I'm here to say that if they decide to move you, Sean and I want to go, too. With you," he added, to be absolutely sure she understood. "We're okay with new names and the whole deal."

For the longest time she didn't move, not even to blink or breathe. Nolan tried not to twitch under that stunned stare.

"With me?"

"With you," he repeated. He cleared his throat. "If you'll have us."

She burst into tears.

OH, HELL. Was her reaction good news for him or bad? Either way, he took her into his arms, tucked her head under his chin and held her tight.

"It's okay." He squeezed his eyes shut and laid a cheek against her hair. "*God.* You don't have to cry. If you don't want us, just say so. I'll go away. I'm not going to become a stalker."

She grabbed handfuls of his shirt near his spine. He felt the tension in her fingers.

Okay, *she* was holding on, too. His hopes rose.

He murmured meaningless stuff until her shoulders quit shaking so hard and her body began to relax against his. Then he took a deep breath.

"I wasn't being fair," he said. "I was doing what everyone else always has, demanding you make a choice and assuming you'd choose me. I was an ass. But it's not going to be that way this time. All you have to do is tell me how much to pack and when we're going. We'll be ready."

Allie wiped her face on him. Tears and snot both, he

thought, his tenderness tinged with amusement. Be honest, tinged with fear, too. Because she might be working her way up to saying, *Thanks, but no thanks*. And then he'd have to keep his word, turn and walk out of here in the full knowledge he'd never in this lifetime set eyes on her again.

I don't know if I can do that.

I promised.

Apprehension made him feel big, clumsy, dumb. He had a flicker of seeing himself as the stone man he'd carved, beyond any feelings. Is that what would happen to him if Allie turned him away?

She let go of his shirt, one finger at a time. He wanted her to keep clutching tight. *If the answer is no, don't say it yet. Let me hope for a little longer.*

Stupid.

She struggled a little in his embrace, and he reluctantly loosened it so she could ease back enough to look up at him. The tears were smeared but still there on her cheeks. Damp tendrils of dark hair stuck to her forehead and temple. Her usually elegant nose was Rudolph-red. Her eyes were pink, puffy...and held an expression he could only interpret as awe. A smile trembled on her lips.

"I never even thought of asking if you'd go with me." The smile wobbled right out of existence. "I never dreamed anyone would. You would be giving up so much."

"Not as much as I'd be giving up if I let you go," he managed to say gruffly.

"And Sean is really, truly willing, too?"

"Yeah." He eyed her warily. "I broke my word to you. I had to tell him everything."

"That's okay. I trust him."

She kept searching his face, her expression so astonished and wondering. He knew that no matter whether she wanted him or not, the gift he'd offered meant more to her than even he'd imagined.

But, shit, he wished she'd say something. When she didn't, he couldn't take it another minute.

"So." He cleared his throat. "Is this a yes?"

"No," she said softly, "this is a thank-you."

He backed up a step, his muscles coiling painfully. "Because you're still mad at me? Or because you've realized you don't love me enough to commit to the long haul?"

"What?" Crinkles formed on her high, curved forehead. "No! What are you talking about?"

He unclenched his jaw. "Then what did you mean?"

"I meant thank you but I'm not going anywhere. I'm staying here." Her gaze was suddenly shy. "If *you* want *me*."

Shaking his head, Nolan tried to figure out what she was saying. "You mean, your mother has gotten word they won't be moving her?"

"No. She doesn't know. What I'm trying to tell you is that I was an idiot. I love you. I'm staying even if Mom is relocated. I was going to come to tell you as soon as I closed up shop. I need you to know how sorry I am for hurting you the way I did. I will never leave you."

He had to take a moment to let it sink in. She loved him. She wasn't leaving. She'd chosen him. The tsunami of emotions was almost painful. She loved him. She'd forgiven him. She…

Nolan let out a whoop, grabbed her and swung her in a circle. Laughing, Allie clutched his shoulders. Her nose was still pink, her face still blotchy, but with that smile, she was also lit with all the delicate beauty and promise of sunrise over the mountains. He slowed, came to a stop and let her slide down his body.

"God, I love you."

Her hands left his shoulders to cup his face. "I love you."

"I meant it, you know."

"That you love me?" She looked perplexed.

"That Sean and I are willing to go." Nolan needed her to understand this. "I'm more honored than I can say that you chose me, but I don't want you to suffer any more losses in your life.

"Some of what I said to you before was crap. Sure, most of us let go of our parents—but not all the way, like I was demanding of you. I understand why your mother is so important to you. Talk to her before you make up your mind, Allie. My offer is sincerely meant. Say the word and Sean and I will start packing."

She shook her head, but he saw a new shimmer in her eyes. "No. I love my store, and quilting, and being Allie Wright. Thanks to you, I can *be* Allie, with no regrets."

He looked into her eyes and saw that she meant it, heart and soul. The tangle inside him was still painful but also so sweet. Having everything you'd ever wanted handed to you was an astonishing experience.

"Does that mean you're not going to take my name?" Lightening the moment seemed like a good idea.

Allie's smile brightened. "Actually, I would love to take your name. I'm not all that attached to the name Wright, you know. You promised that I could keep Radek forever. I like that idea."

"Yeah." His arms contracted around her. "Forever sounds good to me."

"Me, too." She lifted her face for a kiss.

Kissing her was a damn good idea, too. He kept right on doing it long after hearing a stupid little bell ring somewhere.

One month later

"I HAVE THIS horrible feeling we've forgotten something important. Rushing is never a good idea." Mom paced almost to Nolan's dining room, then back across the kitchen. She frowned. "Flowers."

"Done, Mom." Knowing perfectly well why her mother was so nervous, so lacking in her usual confidence, Allie could be patient.

"Your dress is perfect."

Allie smiled at her. "So is yours."

"I can't believe tomorrow is your wedding day."

Allie could. She'd been ready from the moment she told Nolan that she was staying with him no matter what happened with Mom.

Their first thought was to get married immediately in a civil ceremony so Allie's mother could be there. But when it became apparent that she wouldn't be relocated, after all, they had decided to arrange a somewhat more traditional wedding.

The intervening month had seemed to drag on forever as far as Allie was concerned. Nolan had been even more impatient. Because of Sean, neither of them was comfortable with her moving into his house before they were a married couple, which meant not seeing each other nearly as often as they wanted.

And now here they were, less than a week before Christmas, and tomorrow was her wedding day.

But at the moment, it wasn't her wedding that had Allie and her mother both fidgety and hopeful.

They were waiting to hear the sound of Nolan's truck turning into the driveway.

Feet thundered down the stairs from the second floor.

Claws clattered on the hardwood floor, and Cassie galloped ahead of Sean into the kitchen, her tail and butt swinging with pleasure at finding two of her favorite people there. Allie's mother had become very fond of Cassie, and was even talking about adopting a dog herself.

"Something smaller," she had said. "You know how tiny my yard is. But I think I'd enjoy the company."

Allie had privately smiled and suspected Mom would come home from the shelter with a Great Dane mix or something equally inappropriate. Sort of like Lady the beagle, with her wandering gene. How many times had Mom thrown up her hands and exclaimed, "We should find her a home in the country!" just before sneaking a treat under the table.

"How come he isn't back yet?" Sean complained.

"He might have hit heavy traffic," Allie said. "Or the flight could have been delayed."

"I'm going to look stupid in a suit and tie."

Allie laughed, went to him and rose on tiptoe to kiss his cheek. "You're going to look handsome, and you know it."

His cheeks reddened. "At least no one I know will see me," he said gruffly.

"You know us. And now your aunt Anna and your grandparents."

Nolan's parents and sister had arrived the day before but had decided to sightsee and have dinner out this evening. Allie thought they were being polite, not wanting to intrude on this reunion. They planned to return before bedtime.

Jed's wife was pregnant again and vilely nauseated, and he'd felt too guilty to either drag her onto an airplane or leave her. Nolan had laughed and said, "That's an excuse I can accept." His parents were going home to Chicago for Christmas; Anna was staying to celebrate the holiday with Nolan and his new family.

Now Sean scowled. "They're not really my grandparents."

Allie smiled at him. "They will be." She and Nolan were going to officially adopt him after the first of the year. They had given him the choice of keeping his last name if he wanted, but he'd decided to become a Radek, too.

"Yeah." He shuffled his feet. "I guess so. It'll be weird."

"Who are you calling weird?" Allie's mom said in mock offense.

He looked at her in alarm. "I wasn't… I mean, I *know* you. They're, like, strangers."

"Grandma," she prompted him.

His blush deepened. But then, suddenly, he flashed her a wicked grin. "Grandma. Shouldn't you be sitting down? At your age and all?"

"Brat."

They both laughed. Allie watched their interplay with delight. Life couldn't always be this good, could it?

No. Jason might have changed his mind and not come. Maybe that's what had taken Nolan so long. He'd scoured the airport and had Jason paged and maybe finally discovered he had a voice mail message from him…

She heaved a sigh. Of course Nolan would have called to tell them. She knew that. But sooner or later, something lousy would happen. Sean would rebel and decide these new parents weren't so cool after all. Or she and Nolan would have a child with a birth defect or… Oh, who knew.

Yes, but I'll have him.

His steadiness would be her anchor, no matter what happened.

Sean cocked his head. "Hey, isn't that his truck?"

"Oh, dear God." Allie's mother pressed one hand to her breast and the other to her mouth.

Allie's pulse leaped and she listened hard. The deep rumble of Nolan's diesel engine was unmistakable. It always reminded her of his voice. "It's them," she said, excited and terrified all at the same time.

Dumb.

Sean and Cassie bounded enthusiastically for the front door. Allie and her mother stared at each other for a stricken moment before following more slowly.

"I can't believe this is happening," Mom murmured.

"Me, either."

Mom's "handler" had informed them that all the activity stirring the alarm could be traced directly to the P.I. Nolan hired. There wasn't the slightest indication of any other interest. Nor was there any indication that the Nelson identity had been penetrated. The U.S. Marshals Service didn't see why Jason couldn't resume cautious contact with his mother and sister, and Allie's dad with her. Jason had flown out to attend the wedding and stay for Christmas; Nolan and Allie had promised to visit her father sometime this spring.

Hearing her dad's and Jason's voices on the phone had seemed wondrous, but also…unreal, she realized now. She was having trouble believing she would be seeing her brother in person as soon as she stepped out onto the front porch.

Ahead of her, Mom hesitated for the longest moment before following Sean out the door. She had to be even more blown away, Allie realized. Mom had believed she'd never see her son again, and now here he was.

Taking a deep breath, Allie joined her mother. Sean was already loping down the porch steps to meet Nolan, who was climbing out of the pickup. The passenger side door opened, and a man got out. Allie stared, thinking, *Wait a minute—that's not Jason.*

But it was, she saw the minute he started walking toward them, at first slowly and then faster and faster until he'd broken into a jog. Allie's mother made a strange sound.

He'd been a boy the last time they saw him, only nineteen. He was thirty now, a man. His thin body had filled out.

Eyes filling with tears, Allie started down the steps. They met halfway. He squeezed her in a huge hug that lifted her off her feet.

"Chloe the dancing girl," he said roughly into her hair.

"Jacob. Oh, my God."

He gently lowered her, and she felt the moment he looked past her. "Mom," he said in a low, shaken voice. He set Allie aside and climbed the last two steps slowly, never looking away from his mother.

Allie had never seen anything like that expression on their mother's face. It was as if her every dream had come true. When Jason enveloped Mom in a hug, all Allie could see was his back, broader and stronger than she remembered it being.

Helplessly, she turned to Nolan, who was coming up the steps to her. He was smiling crookedly.

"Sorry we're late."

Unable to speak, she shook her head.

"You should see your face."

Maybe her expression wasn't that different from her mom's, she thought. When Nolan reached a hand to her, she took it.

"You know, if you hadn't had me investigated, none of this ever would have happened."

"You can't know that."

"I do. It was like…like shaking a bottle. All the bad stuff rose from the bottom."

He laughed, but not altogether happily. "I wish I could say that's what I meant to do, Allie. But we both know better."

She heard the sound of her mother weeping. When she looked, she saw that neither Jason nor Mom had moved. He held her, his head bent over hers. Allie's grip on Nolan's big hand tightened.

"I love you." The words trembled with her intensity.

"And I love you, Allie the dancing girl," he said, very deliberately, never looking away from her.

"Not the dancing girl anymore."

His smile was slow but sure, like Nolan himself. "Yeah, you are. Every step you take, every movement, is part of a dance. I figure, clumsy as I am, I got real lucky to be picked as your partner."

Although her eyes were stinging, she was smiling, too. "In dance, the male role is to lift the female dancer. He helps her fly. That's what you do for me, Nolan. And I always feel safe with you."

He climbed another step so he could wrap his arms around her. "Funny thing is, sometimes lately I think you've taken me flying with you." He kissed her with tenderness more than passion. "Are you happy, Allie?"

Her smile bloomed until she didn't think it could get any bigger.

Past Nolan, Sean waited at the foot of the stairs, his hand on Cassie's head. Both gazed anxiously upward. There was Nolan, his eyes so blue and intent on her. And when Allie turned, she saw that her brother had his arm around their mother and they'd turned. Mom was laughing through her tears. And Jason…the look in his eyes could have broken Allie's heart, if it wasn't also so amazing.

"I didn't know it was possible to be so happy," she told Nolan. She kissed his cheek and then called to Sean, "Come up here and meet my brother."

* * * * *

*If you enjoyed ANYTHING FOR HER,
look for the next book by Janice Kay Johnson.
WHERE IT MAY LEAD is available from
Harlequin Superromance May 2013.*

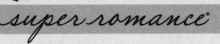
#1842 TALK OF THE TOWN • *In Shady Grove*
by Beth Andrews

Neil Pettit and Maddie Montesano share a history and a daughter. But that's it. Their relationship has been, well, *tense* for years. That wasn't a problem when Neil lived out of state. But now that he's in town, sparks are flying and everyone's talking about where they'll end up!

#1843 RIGHT FROM THE START by Jeanie London

A divorce mediator, Kenzie James has seen it all when it comes to commitment. And she can tell Will Russell is *not* a good bet. So why does she look forward to their encounters at work? Luckily she knows better than to fall for this single dad...or does she?

#1844 THE FIRST MOVE by Jennifer Lohmann

Seeing Renia Milek again is a clear sign to Miles Brislenn. Back in high school he might not have had the courage to approach her, but this chance meeting...? He's not letting it pass him by. The attraction is clearly mutual, until Renia's past threatens to come between them.

#1845 A BETTER FATHER by Kris Fletcher

Sam Catalano needs to prove he's a good father to his young son. And to do that he needs stability, which is why he's bought the summer camp he used to attend. But buying it puts him in conflict with Libby Kovak—his old flame and the rightful owner.

#1846 YOU ARE INVITED... • *A Valley Ridge Wedding*
by Holly Jacobs

The best man? Mattie Keith—maid of honor—thinks Finn Wallace is anything but. She's the legal guardian for his nieces and nephew, but he's suing for custody! They've vowed not to let their conflict spoil their friends' wedding, but when temperatures and attraction rise, promises may be broken....

#1847 THE SUMMER PLACE by Pamela Hearon

When it comes to fun and games, Rick Warren and Summer Delaney are definitely on opposite sides. Summer has a lot at stake in making this camp program work and proving she's right. Too bad the working rivalry is sparking a big attraction!

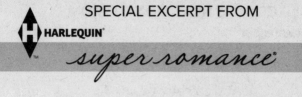

Talk of the Town
By Beth Andrews

Maddie Montesano shares a history with
Neil Pettit...and a daughter. Their relationship
has been rocky and it could get worse with
Neil back in Shady Grove...
Read on for an exciting excerpt!

Maddie Montesano swung her crowbar at the wall, focused on finishing this demolition. The back of her neck prickled with a warning of being watched...and let her know who stood there.

When it came to Neil Pettit, it was like some sort of homing device was imbedded inside of her. *There he is! The man of your adolescent dreams!*

It was annoying and as powerful as it had been when she'd been young and stupid with love for him.

Well, she'd gotten over Neil a long time ago.

Neil leaned against the doorjamb, his broad shoulders filling the space as he lazily slid his gaze from her head to the toes of her work boots.

HSREXPO313

There should be a law that when a woman saw her ex, she looked hot. Sexy hot…not sweaty, I've-been-working-and-am-a-total-mess hot.

"Hey, babe. Looking good." His greeting was the same as in high school when he'd wait by her locker. Oh, how her heart had raced with so many wonderful, conflicting emotions.

"It's the tool belt," she said, not bothering to keep the flatness from her voice.

He grinned at her tone, one of his slow, panty-melting smiles. It was more potent now than it'd been twelve years ago. "It's not the tool belt." He came closer until the toes of his sneakers bumped against her boots. "It's the whole package."

She rolled her eyes. "Please."

Golden stubble covered his cheeks and she noticed the dark circles under his eyes. He looked tired and that hint of vulnerability had her weakening. Not allowed.

"Something I can do for you, Neil?"

His expression changed. "Is Bree here? I'd like to see my daughter."

What are Neil's intentions?
Find out in TALK OF THE TOWN
by Beth Andrews, available April 2013
from Harlequin® Superromance®.
And be sure to look for the other
three books about the Montesano siblings
in Beth's IN SHADY GROVE series
available later in 2013.

REQUEST YOUR FREE BOOKS!
2 FREE NOVELS PLUS 2 FREE GIFTS!

HARLEQUIN

super romance

Exciting, emotional, unexpected!

HSRI3